Murder at the Commune

Other Books by Ron Cook

Charles Blue Paranormal Mysteries

Firebrand: #1

The Last Family of Wizards: #2

Time on Our Hands: #3

On Guard in the General's Chorus: Army & Korea Stories 1966-1968

Onward Through the Fog: Short Stories & Mystery Novelettes

A Young Upstart: Contour Drawings & Poetry 1977-1982

The Mountain Dulcimer

Murder at the Commune

Ron Cook

Murder at the Commune

First Edition | 2025

Ron Cook Studios Publishing
www.roncook-author.com

This story is a work of fiction. Any references to names and characters are the product of the author's imagination, and any resemblance to actual people, living or dead, is entirely coincidental.

Trade Paperback ISBN 979-8-9857889-6-9

Ebook ISBN 979-8-9857889-7-6

Printed in the United States of America

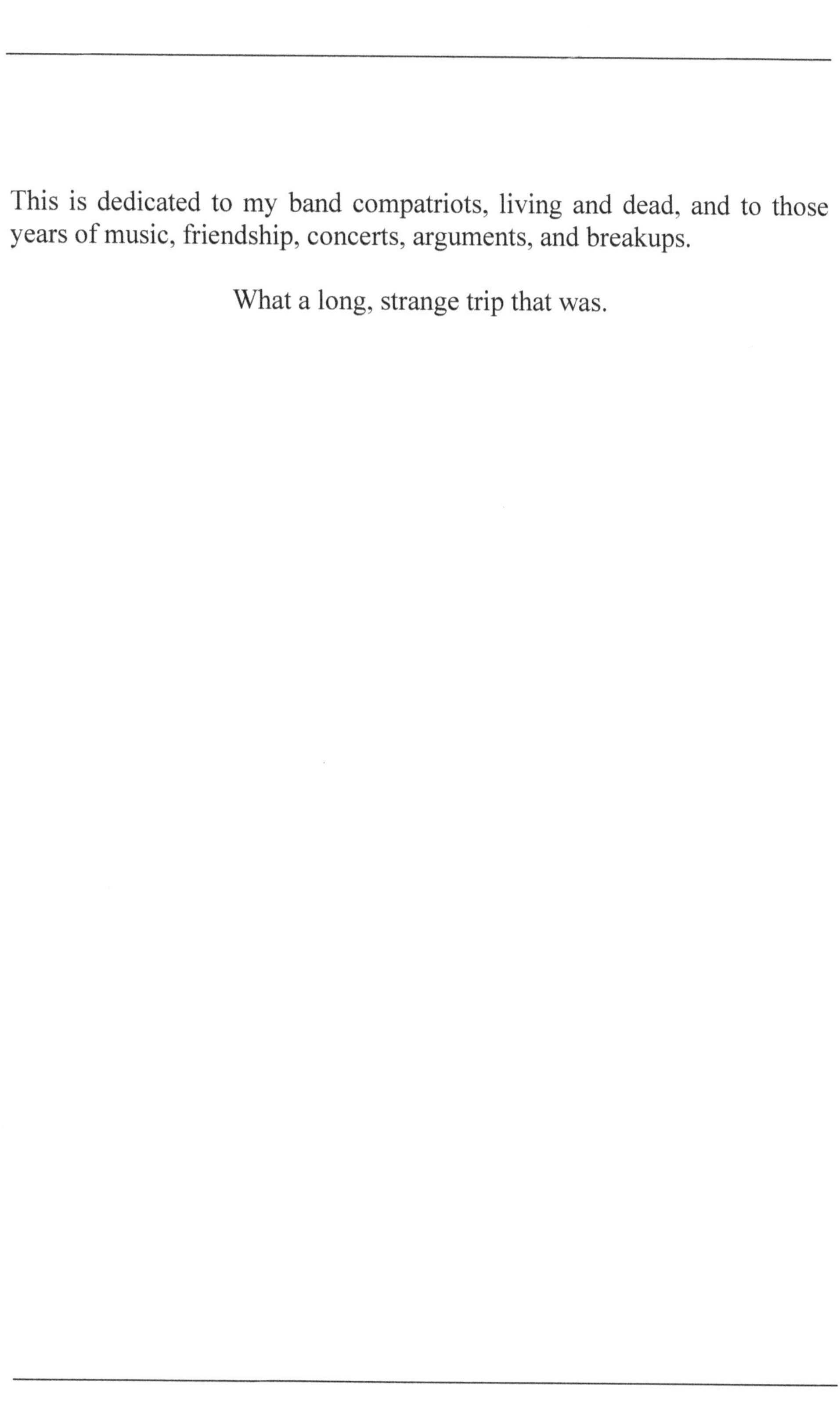

This is dedicated to my band compatriots, living and dead, and to those years of music, friendship, concerts, arguments, and breakups.

What a long, strange trip that was.

Part 1

Youngbloods

Chapter 1

1967
It Won't Be Long

Robbie

November started with a snowstorm, and I was freezing. Fuel for the inefficient space heaters hadn't been filled yet.

I was just a day away from ending my 13-month Korean tour of duty and was anxious to return to my central California home. I couldn't wait to get to where the weather was much warmer.

For my last year in the army, I lived and worked as an entertainer at RC1, Recreation Compound One. That base had everything for a soldier's rest and relaxation: a movie theater, an eight-lane bowling alley, a PX (post exchange) with a soda fountain, a gift shop, a woodshop, and a photo lab. There was also a smoke-filled servicemen's club, with a full bar, two pool tables, and four slot machines. The much larger service club had a big stage where USO entertainers, like Bob Hope and James Brown, entertained. The band I was in had also entertained there.

The entertainment corps had four traveling bands. There was a variety show, a jazz trio, simply called The Jazzmen, a four-piece blues-rock group called The Boogie Men, and a four-piece folk-rock group called The Wanderers.

I was the bass player for The Wanderers. The two guitar players, Martin "Marty" Thomas and Deke Kaye were from the same town in New Jersey and had been in a band together before both got drafted.

Marty and Deke's band had one album under their belts that did—well, okay, reaching 98 on the Billboard 100. However, just before they were supposed to go on tour, a letter of greetings from Uncle Sam came to both of them at the same time. It was fortuitous they ended up in the army entertainment corps together.

They had promised themselves when they got out to move to California to start a new band. They asked me to join them. I enjoyed the playing and singing we did in Korea and also enjoyed playing bass in a rock and roll band. So, I said, "Why not?"

Yes, it should be fun. Or so I thought.

I'm Robbie Jones. My folks and I lived on our small family ranch in the farming community of Gilroy in southern Santa Clara County. The always constant smell in the air? Garlic! Lots of garlic. Grown and cooked with.

My father had been a carpenter for fifteen years and, because I always had a horse and had been riding since my youth, he decided to stop pounding nails and start raising quarter horses as a business.

That didn't last long.

Unfortunately, the raising and sale of horses never became profitable. So, in 1964, a year before I was drafted, my father returned to being a carpenter to make ends meet. His commute to the San José area where he worked sometimes took over an hour, but that's where all the new tract homes were being built.

At the end of my senior year in high school, I purchased an inexpensive acoustic guitar and learned to play it quite well. I thought by performing folk music like Pete Seeger or Bob Dylan I could get a recording contract and make tons of money. I had no intention of going to college.

Well, performing solo turned out to be a lot of work. I auditioned and started playing weekends at a coffee house in San José. I was paid whatever patrons put in my tip jar. I barely made enough to buy a hamburger. However, a few months later, the coffeehouse stopped having live music, and I couldn't find any other local place to play. I played once more at a Lions Club dinner, but again, I was not paid. However, I did get dinner out of it.

Discouraged, I bit the bullet and signed up for classes at a new junior college in town. I still didn't want to be there, and for the next year I failed at every course I took except music and art.

Because my academics were so bad, I was ripe for the draft, and that is what happened. I was so glad my army days were going to be finally over.

It was going to be great to head back home, even if it would be temporary.

A month after arriving home, I left again and moved into a band commune in San José.

Chapter 2

With a Little Help from My Friends

Robbie

When Marty and Deke arrived in California, I invited them, at my mom's suggestion, to stay in a spare bedroom in our house. Within days we were driving around looking for a place for our new band to live and rehearse.

San Francisco was experiencing the afterglow of the Summer of Love and was the main location for some of our favorite popular bands. We hoped to be part of that scene and settle there. For two weeks we looked for a house big enough for a band but could find nothing affordable in the City to rent. We tried other locations from South San Francisco down to San José.

And in San José is where we found the perfect house.

The large Victorian at 55 Sixth Street, a half block from San José State College, had been rented to students for years. It was two stories, with four bedrooms upstairs, and two rooms off the foyer: the living room and parlor, both usable as additional bedrooms. One more small room, probably originally a maid's room, was in the back of the house off the kitchen. That could become another bedroom. The original dining room off the kitchen would become our living room. The good-sized kitchen had a dining table by one wall that could easily hold eight people. It also had an old Tappan range that looked like it had been in the house forever. The counters were wood and had many knife marks and gouges in them as if someone had been stabbing at them. The cabinets were also wood and painted in what one of the band members called baby-shit green. Their doors were pretty scratched up and would really need stripped, sanded, and repainted.

The full basement was perfect for rehearsing and for setting up a recording studio. The rent was reasonable for a fledgling band at $250 a month. Rent was cheap because the house had previously been rented by the SDS, Students for a Democratic Society, who had trashed the house. It needed a lot of work to make it livable again. The rental agent said she'd work with the owner to pay for materials if we'd do the work. We agreed, signed the lease, moved in, and immediately started working on it.

While fixing up the house, we also soundproofed the basement so we wouldn't disturb the neighbors while practicing anytime day or night. We also built a couple of walls in the basement for a recording studio, a woodshop, and a small artist studio where I would create our concert posters. Most of the wood we used for the walls came from 'midnight lumber supply'. Our sound man, Cliff, and Marty would drive off in my VW van in the middle of the night to pilfer wood from the many housing tracts being built around San José, some of the same tracts my father worked on.

A few of us who were handy with carpentry, led by me, as the nominal foreman, worked on the house repairs. The basement remodel progressed rapidly. Within three weeks, we were ready to begin rehearsing.

Marty and Deke had sprung on me after they first arrived that they had asked a couple more guys to be in the band. I didn't know them, but they knew them in New Jersey and New York before they were drafted. These two other guys were Terry Wenborn on organ, and Jimmy Porter on drums. Jimmy had played with Marty and Deke in their original band back in New Jersey. Terry had been playing piano at some club where Deke met him, and Deke asked him if he'd like to be in the band, and he agreed right away. Terry was a little shorter than me at five foot ten and had curly red hair he was growing out like an Afro. Jimmy was a few inches shorter than Terry and looked a little overweight, but it was all muscle. His nearly black hair was cut like a Beatle's mop top.

Jimmy and Terry were both married and brought along their wives, Carla and Dria. Carla was five foot four and a little stocky. However, she was very pretty in a well-endowed Rubenesque way. The bangs on her short auburn hair nearly covered her eyes. Dria was petite, an inch shorter than Carla, and thin. Her long brunette hair was tied back in a ponytail. She was cute but didn't seem to smile much.

Marty said he had a girlfriend who was supposed to move in with him when the work on the house was done, but Deke let slip that Marty was making that up.

Deke, however, had never had a girlfriend and in the army was always afraid to go to the village to visit any of the dozens of prostitutes that were always around the Army base. Deke constantly complained ad nauseum about still being a virgin.

My girlfriend, who I met in college and wanted to marry me after I got out of the army, didn't like the idea of living in a band commune.

6

She asked me why I wanted to become a communist. Stupid question I told her. We argued. We broke up.

Cliff was our sound man. He was a couple of years older than the rest of us and used his age as a reason for trying to run the commune. We called him The Dictator. He was nearly six feet tall and so thin he looked emaciated. That was probably because his main diet was Twinkies and Coke. His teeth showed his diet too. Not good. We were told that Terry knew Cliff in a Texas recording studio where Terry had worked as a session musician. He invited Cliff to come out with him and Dria to San José.

Within a month we finished work on our rehearsal space and studio and could start practicing.

The first songs our new band worked on were the cover songs we used to play in Korea, like *Tobacco Road*, *Sunshine of Your Love*, and *Born to be Wild*, popular songs of the time when we were in the army. Deke, with his high school choral background, worked hard to develop four-part harmonies to them. But the group had limitations. Terry couldn't carry a tune. Jimmy was a better drummer than singer. That left Marty, Deke, and me attempting to do four-part harmonies with three people. This was okay for old rocker tunes but was not the robust sound we needed for our planned new style of music.

Marty, Deke, and I had all been song writers before Korea. When I was a folk singer, I wrote a few protest songs and ballads. Marty and Deke had tried to compete with the popular British Invasion groups by writing songs in the same style, imitating the Beatles and the Dave Clark Five. With our songwriting backgrounds and eclectic musical interests, our newly written songs began to take on a new form containing jazz and classical elements: progressive rock.

But we were at an impasse with our vocal limitations.

We began to think we needed a lead singer. Marty suggested that we should have a charismatic one, like Roger Daltrey of *The Who*. The answer was closer than we thought.

The house next door to us was a similar Victorian. We were told it had an old-style letter press in the basement, where an independent newspaper, the San José Cinnabar was printed. After hearing about it, I wanted to find one to check out, but I never found any downtown. I figured it was probably only distributed on the college campus somewhere. In the first-floor front parlor were two telephones manned by a rotating staff of student volunteers. Two of them lived upstairs. One telephone was used for Drug Crisis Intervention, and the other was for Suicide Prevention.

Terry, our keyboardist, had a roving eye, even though he was married. He soon met the two students living next door and hung out with the young girls when we weren't practicing, usually while his wife, Dria, was helping Carla cook dinner for us.

The newspaper's typist, a gorgeous tall blond, was on Terry's 'hit' list, so to speak. She would have nothing to do with him, and he couldn't figure out why.

One evening, Terry got to talking to a guy in the house, who introduced himself as Dennis Dean. He told Terry he was the publisher of the newspaper and ran the Drug Crisis and Suicide Prevention businesses in the front room. When I met him later, he appeared much older than us with his short salt and pepper hair and full grey beard. A white stripe was in his beard by his cheek. It looked like a scar.

While Terry and Dennis talked, Terry overheard a beautiful voice singing to the radio in the next room as she typed. He asked Dennis, "Who is that?" He headed into the next room, Dennis followed, looked at her, sighed, and reluctantly introduced her to Terry, who immediately thought that it would be cool to have a beautiful, compliant woman to front the group. He walked over to the typist and asked her if she would be interested in auditioning for our band as the lead singer. She didn't even have to think about it. She said "Yes!" right away. That typist was Carol Legrand, and if she had noticed Terry licking his lips and the look in his eyes, she would have said "No!"

Dennis harumphed and went back to his office/bedroom and shut the door.

Terry arrived for rehearsal and confronted us with his suggestion. Marty and Deke were not keen on having a woman in the group. They kept saying a guy lead singer would work better. They kept saying, "you know, like Roger Daltrey of The Who". I kept trying to convince them that a woman would be a good fit, like Grace Slick in the Jefferson Airplane or Janis Joplin in Big Brother. They said they'd have to be convinced. Jimmy just shrugged.

Terry ran back next door and came back with Carol. When he took her downstairs to meet everyone, attitudes changed. The others were convinced by just seeing her. Carol, tall at almost six feet, with long blond hair tied back in a ponytail, was dressed in tight jeans and a fisherman's knit sweater that left a lot of room to imagine a great figure under it. She had a smile that melted our hearts. My heart anyway.

It was Marty, who really hated the idea of a woman lead singer, who smiled and said to let her go ahead and audition. He was obviously smitten.

Terry, our organist, had been classically trained on piano. He transcribed our few new original songs so we could copyright them. He handed a copy of my new song, *No Way to Remember* to her. She read through the words, quietly singing the music with no accompaniment. *Amazing,* I thought. *She's beautiful and can read music.*

I imagined she heard my thoughts. She smiled at me.

We all grabbed our instruments, and Marty told her he'd nod when it was time for her to come in. We began the song's intro and Marty nodded to Carol. She belted out the song with a voice that would have left Grace Slick and Janis Joplin in awe. It was also obvious she had a great stage presence. She moved to the music in a manner that I couldn't take my eyes off of. Also, she didn't even have to look back at the music. She had already memorized it.

"Wow!" I exclaimed. You got that perfect. How'd you know the words already?"

She walked over to me, got close and looked me in my eyes, or rather looked down into my eyes (*she was nearly two inches taller than me in her boots*) and smiled. *God! What a lovely smile*! I thought. She said, "Robbo, I have a photographic memory. I can read music, or anything, once, and it's embedded in my brain." She tapped her head.

She was close enough to me that when she spoke, I could smell her sweet breath and the scent of sandalwood.

Marty asked her if she'd like to try another song, one of his. Terry looked through his stack of music and pulled out a song called *After the Fall*. He handed it to Carol. She read it through, once again quietly singing along.

"Okay, guys," she said. "Let's go."

Marty started by playing a solo introduction that I felt always went too long before the rest of us came in. Yeah, Marty's ego was making itself shown again. Showing off his playing. I could see that Carol was getting a little antsy to start singing.

Finally, the rest of us came in and Marty nodded to her to begin singing. She did, but I could see her heart wasn't into the slow, ballad-like arrangement. She did okay, but her voice didn't have the volume or edge like the other song. My song.

Carol walked over in front of Marty but didn't get as close to him as she did to me. Marty was smiling at her. She was barely smiling back and had a questioning look on her face. "Marty, is it possible to up the tempo a little on that song? The tune is great…"

Oops. I could already hear that "but" coming up.

"…but…"

Yep.

"…but the words aren't ballad-like words. I feel the song needs to pick up to a more rock tempo. The nice intro like you started with, but shorter, then when the rest of the band comes in, I feel it's time to rock out."

Oops again. Marty's smile disappeared. I think he was gnashing his teeth. He looked mad. After a few seconds of quiet (*all of us were holding our breaths*), Marty (*and his ego*) said, "Well. Thank you. Carol. The audition is over. We'll let you know…"

Deke cut in. "I think we know already, Marty. Carol, we want you to join our band."

Terry, Jimmy, and I all nodded and said yes in agreement.

Marty turned away in disgust.

Terry then cut in. "Maybe you could even think of a good name for our band. So far, none of us have liked any of the ideas for a name."

God. Marty thought he had a great name for the band. He loudly sat his Stratocaster down on its stand then crossed his arms in front of him, staring at Terry.

"What the hell do you mean no good ideas for a band name? I gave us a great name…"

"Yeah, that nobody liked except you!" That was Jimmy. "Jeez. Valley Messenger Syndicate? People might think we are a Quicksilver Messenger Service tribute band."

Marty was so angry at that, he started sputtering, not able to put anything to words.

I knew Jimmy was right. Marty, I was sure, did too, but would never admit it.

Carol was leaning against the wall and began laughing. "Marty. Marty. Marty. Cool down lover. Your band name is okay, but too long. This band's name should be shorter and more unique. Something people will easily remember."

When Carol said *cool down lover*, Marty did cool down. Hearing her say lover, must have made him think she liked him. His eyes seemed to glaze over looking at her. Having known Marty for a year in Korea and another month here, I knew Marty tended to fantasize about how women thought of him. Deke had once told me about that and how Marty always got depressed when his 'imagined' girlfriends weren't real. He'll probably end up like that again, I thought.

The others seemed mesmerized by her. I was quiet and watched the interplay with interest. I could see she was smart and pretty sure she could come up with a good name.

Carol continued talking, looking straight at Marty. "Okay. From what I've heard so far, your original music has a new progressive rock style. A style that is, so far, unfamiliar to your prospective audience. That should change once you... we start performing, of course. So, any ideas?"

Usually, I was silent during band meetings, listening and watching to see how the different members acted or reacted. Our sound man, Cliff, had been behind the double-paned recording studio window putting the finishing touches on the four-track recorder and mixing board. He had the rehearsal mikes turned on and routed through his monitor speakers and had heard everything. He came out of the studio and confronted us.

"Jesus Christ, you fuckin' jerks." Cliff was a good studio engineer, but his acidic personality made him not a likable person. "This bit... woman has been here hardly a half hour, and you're letting her fucking talk to you like she's running things here?"

Marty and the other members were mumbling while Cliff was spouting obscenities. Carol was a little in shock. She hadn't met Cliff yet. I always thought Cliff felt anything he said was gospel.

I wasn't going to be quiet this time. I got mad. "Cliff! Shut! The! Fuck! Up!" Everyone quieted and stared at me. "This band is a democratic group, and we vote on who we want in the band or don't want in the band! Me? I want her in the band! You can't jump in as a dictator all the time trying to tell us what we should or should not do! If all you can do is bitch all the time, I don't care if you are a super sound engineer, I can't… I **won't** work with you!"

Marty started laughing and came over and put his arm around Cliff. "So, dictator, you got anything to counter that with?"

He shook his head. "Nope. If quiet Robbie speaks up, I can tell he's upset." Cliff released himself from Marty and came over and reached to shake my hand. I almost pulled away thinking he was going to hit me. "Sorry, Robbie. You guys are a fuckin' good band, and that tall bird there…" He pointed to Carol. "…she's got a damn fine voice. You're right Robbie. You convinced me. Marty, guys, you all would be idiots not to hire her."

Marty stopped laughing.

Chapter 3

So You Want to be a Rock 'n' Roll Star

Robbie

Two weeks after we had voted to call our band *Stonework* (Marty was the only nay), we worked up a good 50-minute set of originals and copy songs. Carol had quit her Cinnabar newspaper writing job next door, but instead of moving into our commune, she kept her room there. She always came to rehearsals on time and quickly learned all our songs. We felt we were finally ready to have a gig.

And Cliff, of all people, found that first gig for us. He told us there was going to be a series of Be-Ins, advertised as a San José Gathering of the Tribes, that was going to start up in a couple of weeks. It was to happen each Saturday at a new bandstand in a downtown park.

The first one was scheduled to be a benefit to help out a couple of the struggling "hippie" businesses in the area. No pay, but there was a promise to pass the hat so the three bands scheduled to play might get a few dollars out of it. Maybe we could earn enough to supplement our meager food stamp purchases with another loaf of white bread.

Saturday arrived and two different food booths had set up. One sold simple mild cheddar cheese quesadillas, the other faked donuts out of Poppin' Fresh dough packages, sprinkling them with sugar and cinnamon. Proceeds from sales were also to go to the businesses. Just before the music started, an ice cream truck drove up and parked on the street close to the food booths. All were sure to make money selling to the stoners in the audience.

Of the three bands scheduled, we were to play second. The first band, Raven, set up two huge speaker stacks. There was a large drum set with double bass drums and four tom toms. Jimmy watched it being set up, and I could see he was drooling. His own drum set was not even half that size.

Cliff agreed to set up and do the sound for all three groups. He was getting visibly upset since Raven insisted on having every amplifier and drum miked. He was also arguing, quite heatedly, with the guitarist. I noticed Cliff stormed off stage and didn't bother to connect all the microphone wires to his mixing board.

Raven was a trio of guitar, bass, and drums. They had a lead singer who was a Doors Jim Morrison clone prancing around in tight black leather pants and no shirt. With all the speakers, the band was loud, even without the microphones plugged in. They played only four songs but jammed each of them for fifteen minutes. The lead singer yelled into the microphone a few times, then stood aside and danced awkwardly through the jams. They were not very good. In fact, they were pretty bad, in my opinion, but by the time they finished, the audience had grown to several hundred, many of them stoned, who clapped and hooted loudly like they had just watched the real Doors play.

It took way too long for Raven to remove all their equipment. They kept stalling, talking, and toking. Cliff was again arguing with the guitarist. Nearly forty minutes later, we were finally set up. An angry Cliff installed vocal microphones for Carol, Marty, Deke, and me. We didn't need any mikes on the amps and drums like Raven had insisted for their set. Cliff had brought his tape recorder and had it set up to record our set.

Marty and Deke both had old Fender Twin Reverb amplifiers for their matching Fender Stratocasters. I had a short Ampeg bass cabinet that I played my Gibson EB-3 bass guitar through. Terry played his Farfisa organ through a small Fender Champ. Jimmy's drum set was, what he called, a jazz set. Small bass drum, snare, floor tom, hi-hat, and one tom tom and crash cymbal. A simple set, but Jimmy was a powerful drummer and made his drums sing.

We wanted to get the crowd moving, so we started with a standard rock and roll original I had written. We were just about done with the fifteen second intro when Carol trotted in from the back of the stage. Just her standing there made the audience come alive.

She was wearing tight red pants that showed off her long legs. Her pants were tucked into black cowboy boots with heels that added two inches to her six-foot frame. The pants were low on her hips so a little of her flat stomach was exposed. On her top was a short, tight, tie-dyed t-shirt. Her long blond hair was held in place with a black leather headband.

When she started singing, the audience really went wild. Her voice was perfect. Her stage presence was perfect. She took her microphone off the stand and was able to get right to the edge of the stage, lean over and shake hands with eager audience members while still singing.

For the more progressive songs, Carol would strut over and put her arms around either Marty, Deke, or me and share our mikes, putting her beautiful face next to ours. I noticed Marty played several wrong notes when she first put her face next to his. I don't think the audience noticed, but the rest of the band did. From then on, she shared my mike more than the other two.

Our final song was another heavy rocker that I had penned. That gave Carol one more chance to grab her mike and work the audience, which had now grown to over 500.

It was a warm afternoon and sweat rolled off Carol's face and chest. When she moved around and tossed her hair, her sweat flipped onto the crowd. The guys next to the stage kept trying to reach for her. Including Dennis, who I had just noticed. She knew to stay just out of reach. I could see she really knew how to work a crowd.

When we finished, the crowd went wild and demanded an encore. However, the MC, one of the local rock radio DJ's, said the next group had to come on since music couldn't be played in the park after six o'clock.

Because Raven took so long to set up and tear down, it was now after 4:30. The final band had to be set up by five to play their set.

The last band had been one of the most popular bands to have come out of San José, a garage rock band called The Syndicate. Their first single had done very well nationally, but they had become a one-hit wonder.

We hung around in back of the audience and listened to them for a while as they played their one big hit from 1965 early on. The audience ate it up. They played the rest of their set in a psychedelic style that sounded out of place for them, so we left halfway through their show.

After we returned to the commune and unloaded, we sat around the living room to talk about how we did.

Marty started since he always pictured himself as leader of the band. "Well, not too shabby for our first outing. We sounded pretty tight. What do you all think? Deke?"

"Yeah. Yeah. I agree. I agree. Tight. Tight."

Marty: "Jimmy?"

"Sure. It seemed like things went well. The audience sure seemed to like the music. Oh, and I have to say that Robbie's bass playing followed my drumming so well, I thought we were of the same mind. Good work Robbie."

"Uh… thanks, Jimmy. We did play well together."

Marty: "Terry?"

"Yeah?"

"Uh… what did you think about our gig?"

"Oh. Yeah. Okay."

I had to comment. "Terry, I think I know why you're not too happy about the gig."

"What?" Marty questioned with a little anger in his voice. "Guys, it was a great gig."

Carol spoke up. "I think I know what Robbie is implying. We couldn't hear the organ part. That Farfisa has such a unique sound that we only hear in rehearsals. It was lost at that gig. Terry, you need a better amp and speakers."

I agreed. "That little amp of yours doesn't have enough power for gigs."

Terry looked down at his feet. "That costs a lot of moolah to get a better amp and speakers. My wife may be pregnant…"

"What?" We all said at once.

"I can't spend money now. I have to save what little we have for the baby."

Carol spoke up again. "I can get you a better setup. I have the money. This band needs to hear you better at our gigs."

"You have money?" Marty asked loudly. "Why didn't you tell us! Even with food stamps, we barely have enough to eat in this commune!"

"I don't live in this commune." Carol said with an edge in her voice. "Besides, money isn't something I like to talk about. If you knew where that money came from…." She didn't finish her sentence and got up and walked out the front door.

"Damn!" Marty exclaimed. I told you we shouldn't have hired her! We should fire her."

Again, I wasn't going to be quiet. I was really mad at Marty. I got up and stood in front of him, poked him on the chest and yelled, "You asshole! You now know that Carol is an asset to our band. She proved it today! Her voice fits our music! She works a crowd like we would never be able to do! And, what the hell if she has money. Why complain about it! She doesn't live in our commune, so there's no reason for her to pay us money for us to eat better! It's not her responsibility! So, what if she wants to buy a new amp for Terry. You fire her, and I'll quit! And, while I'm ranting… Marty, your guitar playing was not your best! You made several mistakes. The audience might not have noticed, but I sure did."

The others chimed in, "We sure did!"

Cliff had just returned and was being uncharacteristically quiet. He finally spoke. "Robbie's right. Again. I noticed your screwups too. And I saw why. When Carol got close to you when she sang into your mike was when you fucked up your playing. Do you think about getting a hard on for her instead of paying attention to your guitar playing?"

We hadn't noticed that Carol had come back in. She looked upset.

"Look. I don't want to be the subject of any of your lustful cravings. Please, please don't! You are supposed to be goddam professionals. You need to know that I've always wanted to be a singer in a band ever since I was little. Today, I really enjoyed myself singing with you in front of an audience… even if it was for a bunch of stoned hippies. I saw that they really enjoyed it. And, Robbie, thank you for sticking up for me. I don't want to leave, and I don't want you to quit."

Chapter 4

People Are Strange

Robbie

Everyone in our commune except Marty was in a better mood the following day, especially after a breakfast of white bread toast with peanut butter. We didn't have any kind of coffee maker, so we had instant Sanka or weak Lipton tea. One bag for every two cups. *Oh, I missed the big hearty breakfasts my mom made at home.*

Most of us were night owls and usually slept until 10 am. Carla and Dria were just the opposite. They'd be in bed early and up by six in the morning, often cleaning up the mess several of the guys left around the house the evening before. They worked really hard to keep the place clean.

Our rehearsals were six days a week, every day except Sunday. Our plan was to practice from 1 to 5, take a two-hour break for dinner, then back to the rehearsal room from 7 to 10. Most dinners were sparse, usually spaghetti mixed with a can of tomato sauce. Once in a while we had meatballs, whenever Cliff shoplifted packaged ground beef from the supermarket.

Two weeks after our first gig was Deke's 22nd birthday. I stayed up later than usual the night before and drew a birthday card that looked like a psychedelic poster. I had everyone sign it, including the girls.

As all of us gathered in the rehearsal room on the day of his birthday, we had no idea how memorable it was going to be for him. When we gave him his card, he happily read the messages out loud to us, laughing at several of them. When he came to what Dria had written, he started to read it then went quiet. He looked at her and tried to say something but couldn't. His mouth hung open. She walked up to him, gently closing his mouth with her hand, and guided him into the recording studio. She left the door slightly open so we could still hear them talking. Cliff hadn't arrived.

"Holy shit! Dria, are you serious?"

"Very much so, Deke. You don't need to be a virgin anymore. I thought I'd give you a present to unwrap. Me."

"Uh… uh… are y… you sure?"

Drea leaned over and planted a warm, moist kiss on Deke's lips. She then wrapped her arms around him and pressed her body against his. It looked like the kiss and the close contact made Deke uncomfortable. His jeans were hurting his expanding manhood.

Dria chuckled. "Oh, I think you'll be more than ready to unwrap your present. Don't start without me."

She went back upstairs but wasn't smiling. Deke followed. He was smiling.

Marty was laughing. I thought he was in a better mood, but I was wrong. Within minutes, he was complaining about the delayed rehearsal.

I looked at Terry. "You okay with this?" I asked.

"Sure. I suggested it. I was tired of listening to Deke's droning on and on about being a virgin all the time. I told Dria she could have fun popping his cherry."

"Well, it's your call." Marty said. "Hope Deke doesn't take long. We need to rehearse."

Carol and I sat over to one side and talked quietly. We both thought Terry's telling Dria to go with Deke was a bad mistake. And was she pregnant like Terry said or not?

We also decided that if Deke was going to be upstairs for a while, the two of us could write a song together. It was nearing completion when Deke finally returned forty minutes later with a wide grin on his face.

"Jesus, Deke!" Marty exclaimed with an angry look on his face. He was tapping his foot. "About time you got your dick back in your pants! Now wipe that shit-eating grin off your face and put your guitar on. We're real late getting started."

Yeah, Marty was upset, and had been upset ever since Deke went upstairs with Dria. We tried to convince him a couple of times that we could rehearse without Deke, but he kept refusing, saying we needed everybody there. He was the only one who believed it.

Rehearsal the rest of the afternoon didn't go well. Deke played a new song he wrote, but Marty stopped him barely halfway through. I thought the song sounded great and would be a good addition to our repertoire. I told Deke that he had written a really good song. Carol agreed. So did Jimmy.

I was sure Marty was still upset with Deke. Even though it was Deke's birthday, Marty would rather be the center of attention. His ego said, "Oh, your song is… well, okay, but not for my… uh, not for the group right now. Let's put it on the back burner. We need to go over my new song I wrote yesterday."

Nope. Marty's new song was not at all as good as Deke's. It was also a kind of a sweet-sounding slow ballad about the death of a girlfriend. It was similar to the old English folk song, Barbara Allen. In fact, it sounded a lot like Barbara Allen.

Marty started the song with his acoustic guitar, an old Gibson J-50, and played and sang the first verse and chorus solo. Deke, not too enthusiastically, was to come in on a second guitar, also acoustic, quietly, after the first chorus. The organ was to come in, playing only two simple notes, very quietly, after the second chorus. After the third chorus, Jimmy and I were to come in. Our parts lasted barely a minute. We looked at each other and shook our heads no. There were no vocals or harmonies for Carol or the rest of us. It was Marty's song and only Marty's song. It also didn't have the type of progressive rock sound we were working toward. There were no jazz or classical elements, and no rock.

Jimmy was leaning on his snare drum with his arms crossed. "Marty, what the fuck are you doing? That song doesn't sound like us at all. If anything, it needs to get stronger as it goes. It needs harmonies. The way you're asking us to play makes this a real dull fucking folk song!"

Oops again. All afternoon Marty has been surly and bossy. Now Marty's face was turning red like he was holding his breath. He actually tossed his old acoustic aside, bouncing on the carpet we had put on the concrete rehearsal room floor. It bounced then crashed into the concrete wall. The head broke off.

All of us watched with our mouths open in shock. Marty knew he had done something stupid, but being Marty, once again he would never admit it. He stopped looking so angry, and calmly walked over and picked up his guitar, its broken head dangling from the strings. He calmly grabbed it by the neck and suddenly smashed the body into the concrete wall. The classic old Gibson blew apart into a dozen pieces.

"Well, mister Thomas," said Carol. "You've really shown your true colors. Mostly brown, shit head."

Whoa! That was a lot of vitriol from her. However, I had to agree with her. I think everyone else did too.

Marty didn't say a thing. He looked at her and at the rest of us. I could see his lips quivering and tears forming in his eyes. He ran to the back of the basement and up the stairs that led to the driveway in back. We heard a car start. It was the band's old VW van. *My* VW van. We heard it peel out and could hear the driveway gravel hitting the side of the house as he sped onto and down Sixth Street.

Cliff had come in right at the end of the psychodrama. "Jesus. Marty did that?" He was looking at the pieces of guitar scattered around the room. "What a fuckin' weirdo."

No one said anything for several seconds. Cliff broke the silence. "Well. Deke, can you play lead guitar? Yes? Cool. Anyone know someone who would make a decent rhythm guitarist?"

Silence. I was feeling like the band had barely started and was already breaking up. I think some of the others thought that too.

But not Carol.

"If Marty doesn't return, I know someone who could play rhythm. But let's wait and see if Marty cools down and comes back first."

Chapter 5

Changes

Carol

Close to dinner time, Marty hadn't returned. All of us, except for Cliff, were sitting around the living area talking about what to do if Marty decided not to come back. Carla and Dria were in the kitchen fixing dinner for them. I was hanging around but finally said, "Guys, I have to go home next door and get cleaned up and have some dinner myself. I'll be back this evening for rehearsal. There will be a rehearsal tonight, right?"

"We're not sure right now, Carol." Deke shrugged.

"Come on guys," I said. "If Marty doesn't come back, we can still rehearse without him. Deke, I'd still like us to practice your new song. It's really good."

Deke blushed and mumbled "Thanks."

"Besides," I continued. "I've heard you play lead. You're as good as Marty. Maybe better. You can do that. And… well, if we do happen to need a rhythm guitarist, I can play guitar quite well."

I patted an embarrassed Deke on his head, turned, and headed out the front door.

After dinner, I returned and came down the stairs to the basement and saw them cleaning up Marty's broken guitar shards. I brought my own large guitar case with me, sat it down and opened it. I heard Robbie and Deke let out gasps. I showed them my beautiful old Gibson J-160E, an acoustic electric identical to the one John Lennon played in the movie *Help*. I told them it was from 1954, and it did show its age. The top finish was crackled and showed wear.

Robbie asked where I got it.

"Family. It was my father's last guitar when he played old-time country and folk music many years ago. He never played it electric. Only acoustic. Even in the studio."

"Studio?" Robbie questioned. "Did your father make any records?"

"He did. He and his brother, my uncle, put out two albums for Mercury. Pretty standard folk music, but they sold quite well. My uncle played standup bass."

"What were they called?" Deke asked.

"The Legrand Brothers."

Deke sat down on the floor with a plop. "Holy shit, Carol. I have both those albums back home in Jersey. I liked them." Deke stood back up to take a better look at my guitar. "Plug it in. Plug it in. Use Marty's amp there. I want to hear its sound."

I tuned it up, plugged the cord into the amp, and turned it on. I set the volume low, around 3 on the dial, and strummed an E chord.

"Jesus H!" Deke exclaimed. "That sound will add a lot to our music. Let's try one."

"Deke," I said. "Let's play your new song?"

We got into it.

Terry, Jimmy, and Robbie made several mistakes since they hadn't played the song all the way through before because Marty had stopped us. However, I was able to pick up on the rhythm and tune right away. I was even able to sing harmony to Deke's vocals.

When we finished the song, we were all laughing and saying how cool it already sounded when Cliff came down the stairs into the rehearsal hall with a pair of San José policemen. We quieted down.

They looked the same size and almost like brothers. One had a thin mustache and the other was clean shaven. They were both fully equipped with their batons and guns hanging from their wide black belts.

The mustached cop opened a small notebook and spoke. "Which of you is Robert Jones?" Robbie raised his hand. "You're the registered owner of a 1962 VW van. Right?"

Oh, oh. I had a bad feeling. Robbie answered, "Uh… yes, I am. One of our band members drove off in it this afternoon."

"May I see your driver's license please." This was the clean-shaven cop speaking.

Robbie pulled his wallet out of his back pocket, took out his license and handed it to the cop. He looked at it, showed it to the other cop who wrote something in his notebook.

As he handed the driver's license back to Robbie, he dropped the bomb, so to speak. "Mister Jones, your car was found in a cherry orchard in the Berryessa district. It appeared that it jumped a curb and crashed into a tree then flipped. I'm afraid your car is totaled. We had it towed to our impound lot."

Robbie asked, "Was… was Marty hurt?"

"Mustache answered, "No one was found in the car or around the neighborhood. The driver must have gotten out and run away from the scene. It was a farmer who discovered the wreck and called us. Now, we need your cooperation. First, what was Marty's full name?"

Deke spoke up. "Thomas. Martin Thomas. Marty and I grew up together in Garfield, New Jersey. I can give you his parents' address there if you need it."

"Thank you, but not right now. Maybe later. If Marty shows up, we need to talk with him."

The clean-shaven cop walked over and looked at me. "Well. Miss Legrand. So, this is where you ended up. Too bad. You would have made a great cop."

"Uh… well… thanks Burt. Uh… hi Alan."

I noticed Robbie had a quizzical look on his face. He is probably wondering how I know them. I sheepishly shrugged, put my guitar back in its case, and leaned against the wall. I sighed.

Burt came up to Robbie. "Mister Jones, we'll contact you when you can come to the impound lot with your pink slip to show ownership."

"Uh, sure. Can my car be fixed?"

"You can check it out if you want to, but it's not a pretty sight. I doubt if you'll want to take possession. If you don't, we'll arrange for the towing company to be there too. You'll need to sign your pink slip over to them. They usually pay five dollars for the vehicle and scrap it. Sorry, that's their policy. Not ours. After that you'll have to go to the DMV within five days to report the transfer of ownership. Like I said, we'll contact you when you can come to the lot."

Both the cops started to leave, then Burt turned back to me, shook my hand, and said goodbye. He wished me well.

Robbie asked me, "Uh… Carol. You know those guys?"

I stopped smiling and sat down on the floor and leaned my back against the wall. I didn't want the band to know about my past, but knew I'd have to tell them. I sighed and began, "I've been reluctant to tell you about this. Anyway, here goes. I went to a police academy with both Burt and Alan. I was doing fine there and figured I could be one of the first female detectives in the force here in town. Burt, Alan, and a few others thought I would be too. Unfortunately, my father became ill with cancer, and I had to go home to take care of him. That's when he gave me this guitar and asked me to follow in his footsteps. I tried for a short while, playing the same folk songs that he did. However, folk music wasn't for me. Anyway, from the sale of our home in Mill Valley and from dad's investments… well, that's where my money came from if you need to know. I used some of it to buy the house next door."

"Really? You own that?" Deke asked. "Wow. So, that old grey-haired publisher next door is paying <u>you</u> rent?"

"Deke, that's between Dennis and me and really none of your business. Let me finish." I sighed again. "I missed finishing up cop school by a couple of weeks and never went back to complete it. After I bought the house next door, Dennis was already there and asked if I could do some writing for his newspaper. He was so nice to me, so I agreed, just to be doing something helpful."

Chapter 6

For What It's Worth

Robbie

Wow. She's had quite a life. I thought, then whispered to her, "Carol. I know it was hard for you to tell us about your past. I'm sure there's others of us here who probably want to keep their pasts secret." I then said out loud, "Carol, you're an excellent guitar player, you have a wonderful voice, and your stage presence is great. You really fit our style of music."

Jimmy and Terry voiced their agreement. "Right on!" "Cool!"

Deke was quiet and looked deep in thought. I said, "Deke?"

He snapped out of it and said "Huh? Oh, yeah. That's cool with me too."

A few days after the visit by the cops, the one named Burt called. He would pick me up and drive me to the impound lot.

When we got there, I wasn't prepared to see the mess my van was in. *Yes, my VW was totaled.*

The tow truck was already there, and the driver was talking to someone by the rear of his vehicle. Burt greeted them like he knew them. After a few minutes of talk, I was asked to go ahead and sign my pink slip over to the tow truck driver. He handed me a five-dollar bill to seal the deal. Then he hooked up my van and hoisted it onto his flatbed truck. Bummer. I was going to miss that old VW. I wondered if we'd have to rent a van if we got any gigs. Everyone else's cars were too small.

I didn't have to worry long. When Burt drove me from the impound lot and dropped me off in our driveway, I noticed an unfamiliar van parked behind the house. *Oh, no. Now what?* I walked back to examine it. It was a brand-new Dodge van with the dealer's temporary paper license plate taped to the back window.

I crept into the house to see the whole band sitting around smiling at me. "Whose van is that out back?" I said.

"Ours, Robbie." Deke said to me. "Carol here bought it for us. And guess what? We've got a gig!"

"Really? Where? Where?"

Carol smiled at me and answered. "San Francisco. The Fillmore."

"Holy cow! Really? How did we… Oh… I'm sorry, Carol. By the way, thank you very much for the van. That was quite a surprise."

"No problemo, Robbo. You were going to ask how we got the Fillmore gig? My cousin. He works for Bill Graham. We'll be the opening act on a Friday in two weeks."

"Who are we opening for?"

"Would you believe…" she chuckled. "…Quicksilver? They're headlining. The second band is a new horn group that's signed with Graham's new record label. They're called Cold Blood."

"That's so cool. So… we should figure out a good set list and start rehearsing."

The next two weeks of rehearsals went by quickly and still no word from Marty. Deke figured Marty had gone home to New Jersey. He told us Marty often got upset in their old band and would go home to sulk. But he always came back later.

On that Friday, we loaded up the new van, piled in, and drove up to the Fillmore West in the Carousel Ballroom. We pulled into an alley and unloaded, storing our equipment backstage where we were told to put it, then we were directed to a funky, and not very clean, dressing room. Band names were scrawled on the walls, some famous, most I'd never heard of. Jimmy found a crayon on the floor and wrote our name under the Kinks.

By 8pm we were set up and started playing to the standing room only crowd. Cliff ran our sound. By 9pm we finished our second encore. The band was tight, and Carol had worked the audience into a frenzy. We felt good.

After tearing down, we returned to the dressing room to find a tall stranger, an older man, in a dark navy-blue suit and tie. Apparently, he had been waiting for us. We stared at him with questioning looks. He handed Carol a card and spoke as soon as we came in. She looked at it and whistled.

"I'm Clive Davis. I caught your act from the sound booth. You're good. Your music has a different sound, and you… what's your name? Carol. You, Carol, are electric. Your stage persona and voice make your band very unique. I would be interested in putting you all in a studio and see what we could come up with for an album. Columbia is branching more and more into rock and roll. Your progressive sound might be a big seller for us… and you. I know you don't know me…"

Carol spoke up. "I know you very well Mister Davis. You knew my father and uncle, The Legrand Brothers."

"You're a Legrand? Great! They were a legend. I was just starting out in the industry when I met them. Ah. Memories." Clive drifted off in nostalgia for a few seconds. "Anyway, I would like to arrange for you to go into a studio. It may be down in San Mateo at Graham's Pacific Studio. Give me your number and I'll call you when it's arranged."

It was an exciting drive back to our commune in San José. We were all gabbing away during the entire journey. We felt this was going to be our big break.

Little did we know what the next day would bring.

Chapter 7

Strange Brew

Robbie

Having returned late from San Francisco, we decided to take the day off. We got paid $500 for our gig and, since Carol said she didn't want a share of it, we decided to use some to buy ourselves better food from the local Lucky Store than our food stamps could buy. It was only a block away from our commune. We'd save the remainder to pay our rent for the next month.

We gave Carla and Dria $50 to get something for the next few days. An hour later, they returned with a whole chicken, a pork roast, a bag of potatoes and several vegetables. They even brought back two six packs of beer and a decent bottle of red wine, items we could never use food stamps for.

As Jimmy and I were helping to put the food away, we heard a knock at the front door. Deke got up from the sofa and went over to open it. It was the same two cops as before. Coming up the steps behind them was Carol. She had seen them drive up from her room next door. She stepped by them into the house.

Burt said hello to Carol, then to us. "We're sorry to be here. This is one of those things we don't like to do. We have bad news." Burt looked uncomfortable. He paused and looked down at the floor.

His mustached partner, whose last name on his uniform said Spencer and who Carol called Alan, took up the story. "Martin Thomas was found dead yesterday in a shallow grave around a hundred feet from where your car..." Officer Spencer pointed at me. "...was found. The same farmer who found your car was disking his orchard and his tractor pulled up the... body."

Burt continued. "I'm sorry to say it appears there was foul play. We won't bother you right now, but we'll be back later today after the coroner gives us her report. We were able to get your car towed back to the impound lot before it got crushed. Forensics is checking it out. We'll be back later to interview you all about Mister Thomas. We must find out what happened to cause this tragedy."

Burt and his partner, Alan, returned two hours later. They had changed out of their blue uniforms and were in jeans and blue denim shirts with narrow red ties. Plain clothes detectives now. We were all sitting around in the living room waiting for dinner.

"Hmm. Something smells good." Burt said as he came in. Then he got official and said, "Okay, we'll try to get through this quickly so you can all have your dinner." He asked, "Is there a place we can interview each of you separately?"

I spoke up. "Downstairs in the studio. It's soundproofed and there's a table and a couple of chairs in it."

"That sounds perfect. Why don't you come down first. Lead on please."

I led them down the stairs and opened the door to the studio. The lights were on, and Cliff was sitting at the table soldering some wires to a small speaker. He looked up at us and angrily said, "Fuckin' come back later! Can't you see I'm fuckin' busy here?"

Alan walked behind Cliff and quickly pulled his chair back. Cliff jumped up, stared angrily at him, and clenched his fists.

Alan noticed and motioned with a raised hand, his palm facing Cliff. "Careful mister! We're police officers!" He tapped the badge on his belt. "We're commandeering this room for interviews! So, watch your mouth, and get out! We'll talk to you later!"

I could hear Cliff's rotting teeth gnashing in anger as he grabbed his bottle of cola and left. I heard him swearing as he headed up the stairs. Burt shook his head and closed the door.

"Let's get started." Alan pulled out a notebook and pencil. "Okay. First. What is your full name and your address?"

I told him and he wrote it down.

"And what was your association with Martin Thomas?"

"Marty and I, along with Deke, were in the army together in Korea. We played music all over that country, mainly playing for the soldiers. Marty and Deke told me they were in a band in New Jersey before they were drafted. They recorded an album that was popular."

"What about you before you got drafted?"

"I rode horses and played folk music at a coffee house here in San José. However, after a few months there, they stopped having live music, so I decided to register at a new junior college, Gavilan College. I was not doing well, so I got drafted."

"So, you and the others are veterans." Alan commented.

"Just me, Marty, and Deke."

Alan wrote that down.

Burt asked, "Okay. How long has this band been together?"

"Over five months now."

"And what about your other members? Did you know any of them before?"

"Just Marty and Deke."

"Let's see." Alan glanced at his notes. "Can you tell me anything about the others, now that you've lived here with them for five months?"

"Yeah? Well, okay. Jimmy is the drummer. He's good. He was in the band with Marty and Deke for a while. I don't know much about Terry. Deke told he met Terry in New York at some place Terry was playing. I have no idea when he moved to Texas, but he said he was a session musician in a studio in Austin. That was the same place Cliff worked as a recording engineer. That's the guy you shooed out. Carol, who you know, is our lead singer and lives next door. Terry met her and invited her over to audition with us. She's good."

Burt looked thoughtful. "Yeah. She was good at the police academy too."

I had a question for them. "Excuse me, what about Marty's… uh, body. Have Marty's parents been told about him yet?"

Burt answered with a sigh, "Yeah. They took it hard. He was their only child." He then said very quietly like he was talking to himself, "That's one part of this job I hate."

Alan heard and nodded in agreement. He finished writing a few more notes. "Okay. That's all we need from you for now. When you go upstairs, send down the one you call Deke."

Dinner was ready when I went back upstairs, and everyone was already sitting around the living room eating. When I told Deke that the police wanted to talk to him, he shoveled several bites of chicken and potatoes into his mouth, told everyone to leave his food alone, and went downstairs, chewing as he went. He was back in ten minutes.

Cliff went next, again swearing as he went down the stairs. He was down there twice as long as Deke and I were. When he came up, I could see he was fuming. His face was red with anger. He swore and told Jimmy it was his turn. Cliff loudly stomped through the kitchen and out the back door leaving the rest of us wondering what happened during his interview.

It was nearly an hour later when the last person went down the stairs to be interviewed. Carol.

She was downstairs for nearly a half hour. When she came upstairs, she was followed by the two officers. They were all laughing. She walked them to the front door and shook their hands. They left, and she came back into the living room.

"Well, guys. That was quite an ordeal. Oh, has Cliff returned yet? I want to talk to him."

Terry answered. "Nah. He probably walked over to the college grounds. Maybe he's at the Spartan Pub. He goes there to drink and cool down when he's angry, which he is quite often. He usually returns in a better mood after an hour or so."

Since we weren't rehearsing, I went into my room, put on the Beatles Rubber Soul album, plugged my headphones into my amplifier, and sat down in my old leather recliner I had picked up at a thrift store. After Rubber Soul, I put on a quieter album of classical music, which made me start to close my eyes. When the side ended it became quiet. I pulled my headphones off and turned off the stereo. I figured I might as well undress and got into bed. It was only 9:30. That was really early for me. I didn't want to go to sleep yet.

I was lying there under the covers in my birthday suit and was planning on reading for a while. I heard a knock at the door. Figuring it was one of the guys, I said, "Come on in."

The door opened, and it wasn't one of the guys.

"Carol? Uh… Hi. I thought you went home."

38

She came over and sat on the side of my bed. *She's so beautiful. Ouch!* My manhood was thinking for itself. I raised my knees to hide it.

"Sorry to bother you, Robbo. I was in the living room with the others waiting for Cliff to return. He still hasn't shown up. I was getting ready to leave but was thinking about our new song. I was wondering if... Ah, we can work on it later. I'll go."

"Don't go. I'm usually not in bed this early. How about meeting me downstairs in the studio and we can put in an hour or two. I'll bring my guitar down."

Carol got up then leaned over and gave me a kiss on my head and left. *Gee, that felt good.* She closed the door.

Five minutes later I was dressed and downstairs. The two of us spent the next two hours happily working on words and music. We made progress and promised to continue working on it the following day if and when we had the time.

I squatted down and put my guitar back into its case. When I stood up again, Carol surprised me with a beautiful smile as she wrapped her arms around me and planted a wonderful kiss on my lips. She left. *It's getting warm in here.*

I didn't know what to think. I must have stood there for a good five minutes savoring the kissing afterglow before finally going back upstairs and heading back to bed. I went to sleep smiling.

Chapter 8

Strange Days

Robbie

Carol came back to our commune around two the next afternoon looking clean and refreshed, her long blond hair held down with a brown leather headband. She smiled and winked at me. Time to rehearse.

When we went downstairs, Carol glanced at the empty recording studio through the window and asked, "Did Cliff ever come back last night?"

Deke answered as he was plugging his guitar into his amplifier, "Nah. I knocked on his bedroom door this morning to tell him breakfast was ready, and there was no answer. I looked in and his bed hadn't been slept in. We're kinda worried about him."

Terry chimed in. "Ah, don't worry. I knew Cliff in Texas when I was a session player there. I used to see him get furious at some of the bands… even big-name bands… that got so demanding that he refused to work with them. He'd storm out and be gone for a day or more leaving the recording duties to someone else. Yeah. He's done this before. I'm sure the police set him off on one of his tirades."

Hearing that from Terry eased our minds and we started rehearsing.

It was close to four in the afternoon, and we'd gone through a dozen of our best songs, thinking they would be a good selection for an album, if Clive Davis came through. However, it had been several days since our Fillmore gig, and we hadn't heard anything from him yet.

We were just getting ready to work on another new song I wrote when Dria came downstairs with the two policemen. *Crud*, I thought. *More interviews*?

Deke asked them if they were going to interview us again.

Burt spoke. "No, not right now."

Alan continued. "We found your friend, Cliff, and…" He hesitated. "I'm really sorry to tell you, he's… uh… well, he's dead too."

Several voices from our group were saying "No way." "Shit!" "No-o-o!" "Why. Why." I couldn't say anything. I was in shock. First Marty, now Cliff. *What's going on*?

Burt came over to Carol and asked her to follow him into the recording studio. They went in and he shut the door. We could see them talking through the window. Burt had his hands in his pockets, Carol had her arms folded in front of her. She didn't look happy.

When they came out, Burt tapped Alan on the shoulder, and they started to leave. Just before exiting, Burt turned around to us and gave the old police standby, "Sorry for your loss." Then he left.

Terry turned to Carol. "What was that all about? Why'd that guy single you out to talk to in the studio?"

Carol plopped down on one of the chairs in the rehearsal room and leaned over with her hands folded between her knees. She looked up at Terry and started to count on her fingers. "Three things. First, Cliff was bludgeoned and stabbed several times and hidden in some bushes on the college campus. Second, Cliff is not his real name. They told me his real name is Reinhold Clifton. They checked their police database and found that he has a record in New York. And third, they want me to help investigate the murders. They appear connected."

Deke yelled out, "Investigate? You? Really? For the pigs?"

Carol quickly jumped out of the chair, went over and poked Deke hard in his chest. "Listen, you asshole, I was only a week away from graduating from the police academy as a pig, as you so ineloquently call us. I was going to be a police detective like Burt and Alan when my father became ill. Burt and Alan know my qualifications. They know me well."

Deke rubbed his chest. "I'm sorry. I'm really sorry. But… but what about the band? Are you leaving us?"

Carol calmed down. "No. No. I'm not lying when I say I want to sing and perform with you guys. It's in my blood. Even when I was little, my father would play his guitar at home so I could sing for him. No, I'm not leaving. I'm hoping I can work with Burt and Alan to help solve these cases as soon as possible so we can concentrate on our music and promoting this band. We do need to tighten up for more gigs."

Chapter 9

Are You Experienced?

Carol

At nine the next morning I sat in a conference room at the police station with Burt, Alan, and two others who worked with them. Burt introduced them as Lucy Baldwin, forensic pathologist, and Rhys Grant, forensic scientist. Both looked middle aged. Lucy was a short slightly overweight woman with grey hair cut very short. She wore black slacks and a white Oxford dress shirt that fit a little too tightly on her big frame. Her white lab coat also seemed too small for her. Rhys even sitting, appeared tall and gangly. His grey hair was longer than Lucy's and looked like he never combed it. He wore grey corduroy jeans and a black turtleneck shirt with specks of dandruff on it. When he greeted me, he spoke with a British accent. Burt introduced me as a consulting detective.

I surprised Burt and Alan when I arrived. I had changed out of my usual hippie-style rock and roll clothes and now wore a charcoal-grey wool pants suit with a white turtleneck. My long hair was combed straight back and tied it in a ponytail with a black ribbon. I was wearing highly polished police-style black shoes I had worn back in my police academy days. Burt said to me before the meeting started, "Lookin' good detective."

Alan turned on a recorder and started the meeting. "This is our first informational meeting regarding the murders of Martin Thomas and Reinhold Clifton, aka Cliff. Both victims were members of a band commune at 55 South Sixth Street, and each left the house in fits of anger. Mister Thomas drove away in a VW bus belonging to one of the other band members. The car and his body were found by a farmer in his Berryessa District cherry orchard. Mister Clifton had walked out the back door and we were told he usually headed to the San José College campus. That's where his body was found the following day by a gardener."

Alan asked Lucy what she had learned from her autopsies.

"First, Martin Thomas's body had very little in his stomach, like he hadn't eaten for a day or so. Because of the temperature of the body and its condition, I figure his death occurred up to 6 hours before being found. Unfortunately, the farmer's tractor and disk mangled his body, first making it difficult to determine cause of death. However, I did finally find two wounds that were not consistent with the farmer's equipment. I located a stab wound on the body under all the tractor disk cuts and a mark on his skull showing that he was hit hard."

I was trying to look professional, but inside I was cringing listening to Marty, someone I had recently worked with, being referred to as "the body."

Lucy continued. "Now. Reinhold Clifton. The one thing that ties these two bodies together is the bludgeoning. They were hit on their heads in the same place. However, the number of knife wounds on the Clifton body makes this look like someone struck in anger, striking over and over again." Lucy acted out the knife striking by moving her right hand up and down several times. "Another item that we discovered with both bodies was that they were moved from somewhere else. We haven't been able to locate the first murder scene. Yet."

"Uh… thank you Miss Baldwin." Burt said. Then, "Detective Legrand, do you have any questions for Miss Baldwin?"

"Not right now. I need to get up to speed. Maybe later." I knew I had to distance myself from the band and the deceased before I could concentrate on the case.

Alan pointed to Rhys. "Can you tell us if you found out anything about the murders? Start with the Martin Thomas case. What did you find in the orchard?"

"Well, I wish I could have been there when they found the car. But, as you know, the officer who responded to the farmer's call thought it was just the car. No body was found at that time. If I were there then, my team could have seen the footprints from the car. But… when the body was found, every evidence of where and when it was placed had been destroyed by the farmer's tractor with all the disking it did. So, no. We could not find the path from where the car was to the body. However, we did bring the car back from the wrecking yard before it was crushed. We went through the interior and found two items of interest. First, there were a few drops of dark oil on the floor inside the side door. It was a type of oil used in cars or motorcycles. However, it was not the same grade of oil in the VW's engine. Second, we found blood in the back next to the boot."

"Boot?" Burt and Alan asked at the same time.

"Sorry. The back hatch door."

Miss Baldwin added, "We analyzed the blood, and it was a match for Martin Thomas. Yes, he was killed elsewhere and transported to the orchard in that VW."

"Okay. Thanks." Alan said. "Okay, Rhys, how about the second murder. Reinhold's murder at San José State?"

"That one is a little easier. We determined the body had been moved and were able to trace it to where the murder occurred. My team has both locations now cordoned off." Rhys sat back like he was done talking.

I spoke up. "Okay, Rhys. Where did it occur?"

"Oh. Sorry. I forgot to mention it. The murder occurred in the driveway of 55 South Sixth Street."

Chapter 10

You Won't See Me

Robbie

Carol returned to our commune to wait for Burt to show up to check on the forensics team's progress. Deke questioned her on why our driveway and garage in the back yard were cordoned off and why several people in white lab coats were running around the driveway and looking in the trash cans in back.

"Look," Carol said. "Don't blame me for that. It turns out that Cliff was killed in the driveway here and moved to the campus."

"Really?" Deke questioned. "Here?"

"I can't say more. I shouldn't have said that."

I could tell that Carol was upset after her meeting at the police station. Maybe they think we're all suspects. I thought I saw tears forming in her eyes. She turned away and rubbed her eyes.

I came up to her and whispered, "Carol. Maybe you shouldn't be here with us right now." I wanted to be as supportive as I could. "Can I walk you home?"

"Thank you, but no. Not right now. I'm waiting for Burt." Then she whispered back to me, "Robbie, we should be done in an hour or so. Come to my front door. I'm sure the forensics team will be done by then. I would like to talk to you. I'll let you in."

I was sitting at the kitchen table anxiously watching the clock on the stove tick away the hour when Carla and Dria came in to start dinner. I excused myself and went downstairs to the rehearsal room. I picked up my bass and sat on a chair to pluck its strings a while. I looked up at the studio window and sighed. *God. First Marty, then Cliff.* Then I thought, *are any of the rest of us on the list of some nutcase?*

Depressed, I couldn't play, sighed, and sat there a few minutes holding the guitar flat on my lap. I then put my bass back in its case and went upstairs and went into the kitchen. Looking through the back window at our parking area, I noticed that the forensics team had finally left.

Carla and Dria were behind me and it looked like something was wrong. I noticed they both had tears in her eyes.

"Are you okay, Dria?"

"I'm okay. I'm okay. Just tired. Never mind."

I let it go at that. For the several months we've all been in this commune, both Carla and Dria never took part in meetings or traveled with the group to attend our gigs. They barely talked to us. Sometimes I had the feeling they didn't want to be here. I knew Terry would say or do things that upset Dria. And I had the feeling she and Carla didn't feel like part of the commune. They probably felt like hired help, except they didn't get paid.

I left by the front door, looking carefully around to make sure none of the forensics team were hanging around and if any police cars were out front. The coast was clear.

I went next door and up the steps to the front door and it immediately opened. Carol was still dressed in her official police business suit. She looked around outside then motioned me in. She led me upstairs to her bedroom. It was a large room with a queen-sized bed close to one wall. There was a two-drawer side table on each side. The bed had a dark wood headboard with decorative pillows leaning against it, and a new-looking leather easy chair between the bed and a desk. A three-drawer dresser was on the back wall between the bathroom and closet doors. On top of the dresser was a small portable color television with tall rabbit ears sticking up from the back of it. It was on. Local news. Carol reached over and turned it off.

Carol hadn't said anything to me other than 'follow me' and 'have a seat'. I pulled the desk chair over by the easy chair that Carol sat down in.

She looked tired. She sighed and put her hand on my arm.

"Listen, Robbie, after all the times we've been rehearsing together, I feel you're the only one in the band I can talk to. You seem so much more responsible than our band mates. Deke acts like a spoiled child. Marty, the poor soul, had a terrible ego. Cliff was always angry and foul mouthed. I've noticed that both Jimmy and Terry don't pay much attention to their wives. Jimmie's not bad, but Terry can be downright mean to Dria. In fact, he's been fooling around with girls in the drug crisis group."

"Really? When does he have time to do that?"

"You've probably seen him quickly eat dinner, then tell Dria he's going out to walk it off. Right?"

"God. You're right. He's gone for an hour, then drifts back in for rehearsal at seven grinning like a Cheshire cat. Did you find this out from Carla and Dria?"

"No. They won't talk to me. I don't think they like me. I think they're jealous of me being with their husbands in the band all the time."

"I don't know. They barely talk to me either. However, something seems odd at our commune next door. When I was in the kitchen a few minutes ago, I think Carla and Dria had either been arguing or having a heated discussion about Jimmy and Terry. Both of them had been crying."

"Hmm. I wonder… You know, it's too bad those two girls keep to themselves all the time. I don't think they ever talk to anyone else, even their husbands. I pretty sure those two girls have been playing around too."

"Say what?"

"It's the detective part of me. We know Dria popped Deke's cherry, and I'm sure Carla was crying because she may have had an affair with Cliff."

"Cliff? Really? I had no idea."

"And there's one other thing about Dria."

"Oh, come on. Besides Deke, who did she have an affair with? Not Marty, I know. He would have bragged about it."

"No. Not Marty. Dria showed up here once."

"Really? Who did she see?"

"Terry."

"Terry? Her own husband? Why here and not in their room in our commune?"

"I think Dria had been wanting Terry to make love to her, but he suggested they do it through a three-way. Of course, Terry suggested it and set it up, the jerk. He had been seeing the cute little butchy blond who lives here down the hall and found out she was AC/DC. I also think another reason I think Dria doesn't like me is because when I came upstairs, I saw the two of them going into the blond's bedroom together. Dria noticed me. She looked scared and guilty."

"I do feel sorry for Dria. She never looks happy." I changed the subject. "I know you told the group you want to continue singing with us. Are you sure you really can? You do seem pretty serious about being a detective right now."

"Yes, dear Robbie. Like I've said, singing and playing is in my blood. I may have to take some time off to help the police find out who killed Marty and Cliff, but I fully intend to stay with the group. The music is great. The songs you write are well thought out and really cool. Even Deke's songs are good."

I stood up to get ready to leave. Carol also stood up and surprised me by putting her arms around me and giving me a hug and a kiss on the cheek.

She then said, "I'm glad we talked. But… uh, I trust you won't say anything, but there's one other thing."

"Something about the commune?"

"In a way, yes. Because Cliff was killed in your commune's driveway, everyone in your house is suspect."

"Really? Well, I kind of thought so. Me too?"

"That's what the powers that be think. I don't. Knowing you and the others, I can't believe any of you could have done it. Now, Robbo, I have to be up early to attend another meeting at the police station in the morning. I'm going to have to leave tonight's rehearsal early so I can get some sleep. Let me walk you out. I'll be over at our regular time after dinner."

At the front door Carol put her hands on both sides of my face and gave me a kiss. *Wow!* I felt sparks between us. I least I was sparking.

We said our goodbyes, and I walked the short distance next door to our band commune.

However, as I walked along the sidewalk and got ready to head up the steps to our front door, I noticed someone in an old dirty car across the street staring at me. When I stopped to look, the car started up and peeled out. I saw it turn without stopping onto Santa Clara Street and disappear. Could it have been the murderer checking out the house? I had better tell Carol.

Chapter 11

Heroes and Villains

Robbie

I figured I shouldn't go back next door, so I went into our band commune and picked up the wall phone in the foyer. Carol had given us her phone number in case something suddenly came up, like a gig. I dialed.

Carol picked up on the second ring.

"Carol. It's me. Robbie. Someone was across the street…"

Carol cut in. "I know. I saw the car when I kissed you goodnight. I was watching through my front door window. I tried to see the license plate, but it was missing. And I couldn't see if it was a man or a woman. They sped away too quickly."

"I don't like the idea someone's watching us."

"I don't either. When I go to that meeting in the morning, I'll mention it to Burt and Alan. I don't know if anything will come out of it. If not, I will keep a lookout. I've got a good street view from my front upstairs window. I'll be over soon. We should tell the rest of the band."

We hung up.

I could barely eat dinner. After all that had happened, I was nervous about someone watching the house. I didn't want to say anything until Carol got here. She should tell them.

Carol arrived right at seven. She had changed out of her police-style clothes and again looked like our lead singer. We went downstairs to rehearse.

Carol stood by the studio window and faced the group.

"Everyone, I have something very important to tell you."

Deke interrupted her. "Oh Shit. You're quitting, aren't you?"

Both Terry and Jimmy chimed in. "We knew it. That's it for the band. Shit!" They started to get up to walk out.

I groaned and thought. *Why do these guys jump to conclusions so quickly?*

Carol shouted at them. "Sit down and shut up! I'm not quitting! Let me finish what I need to tell you!"

They sheepishly sat back down, Jimmy on his stool behind his drums, Terry on a seat behind his organ. Deke leaned against the wall.

"You heard that those two officers who were here had been in the police academy with me. They've hired me as a consulting detective to help them research and hopefully solve who killed Marty and Cliff. I will be working with them, mostly in the mornings, I hope, so we'll still be able to rehearse in the afternoons and evenings. I hope. No, guys, I'm not quitting."

Deke and Jimmy apologized with a quick "Sorry". Terry said nothing and just shrugged.

"Now. I need to warn all of you. Robbie and I both saw someone in a car across the street watching this house. It was an older dark Chevy Bel Air with no license plates. If any of you see that car again, don't confront it. We don't know who it is or what their intentions are. Because of the murders, be observant, but be careful. We don't want anyone else to get hurt. Now, once in a while, at least until this is over, I might have to skip one or more rehearsals to work with the police. Please, guys, be careful. Especially you, Terry, when you journey next door for your little sex romps."

"Wha? Me? No. I…"

Deke spoke up. "Yeah, you. Everyone knows you play around. You're not that sneaky."

Terry shut up and turned around to face the wall.

I knew Carol said all she had to say, so I spoke up, "Okay, everyone. Like Carol said, we need to be cautious if we go outside. Now, we're here to rehearse! Carol and I have a new song we want to show you."

Rehearsal was strained that evening. Carol and I each tried to keep it upbeat but without success. Toward the end of the evening Deke finally got into working on harmonies, but that didn't last long. Terry and Jimmy had both been lackluster in their playing. Terry's mind was elsewhere and was missing notes, which was unusual since he was a classically trained pianist. Jimmy barely kept a beat, also unusual because he usually played well and hard. His rock idol was Keith Moon.

By 9:30, I'd had enough of their moping around and screwing up. Still trying to be upbeat, I said, "Okay, everyone. Let's call it a night. Tomorrow we can try to…" *I almost said try to play better.* …uh, we can take up where we left off."

Only Carol replied. "Yeah, guys. I look forward to it."

Deke, Jimmy, and Terry left in a hurry and headed upstairs. I went over and closed the door. Carol and I looked at each other. She spoke first.

"That was bad. Their hearts weren't into it at all. I'd swear Terry was looking daggers at me all evening. At least Deke came around somewhat at the end."

"Well, Deke loves to arrange vocals. He's good at it. Yeah, the other two made a lot of mistakes."

Carol picked up her guitar. "How about you and I practice our song for a little longer. Even though I have to get up early, I'm a little bummed and would like to stick around another half hour or so and play. Okay?"

I picked up my bass and turned the amp down. "I'd love to."

And we did play. I imagined what it could have been like for Carol's father and uncle. Guitar and standup bass. I hoped Carol was imagining the same thing. She was in the zone and played perfectly.

It wasn't just a half hour. An hour later, we both smiled at each other and sighed. We put down our guitars.

"Well, Robbo, I do really have to get some sleep. Walk me to the front door?"

"Of course."

Carol went first. I followed. When we reached the top and came into the living room, the guys along with Carla and Dria were sitting around the living room. It appeared that they had all been arguing about something. Carla and Dria got up and went into the kitchen. The guys just smiled. Strained smiles, I thought. I'll have to see what's up after Carol leaves.

I walked her to the front door. She turned to me and again grabbed my face to give me a kiss. She whispered to me, "Robbo, you made me feel so good playing with you tonight. You were able to get my mind off the case for a while. But you know I must get back at it again.

No. Don't open the door for me. Let me check first just in case someone is watching the house again."

Carol opened the front door enough to look out. The loud crack of a high-powered rifle broke the night's silence and shattered the beveled-glass window in the Victorian's front door, right next to Carol's head.

Chapter 12

What Goes On

Carol

I jerked back, grabbed Robbie, and we both fell away from the now fully open door. I heard a car screech away, and I jumped up and ran out the door to look down the street. The car had already turned up San Fernando Street by the college.

I came back in.

"Robbie. Robbie. Are you okay?"

When we dove out of the way and I pulled Robbie down, he had bumped his head on the floor and was rubbing his head. He also fell on some of the broken glass, and I noticed blood dripping from a small cut on his hand. All the others in the house came running in. Even the girls.

Deke yelled. "Is he dead?" Terry yelled. "We heard a shot!" Carla and Dria both yelled together, "Robbie! Robbie!"

"Easy. Easy." I said as calmly as I could. "Robbie just fell back and hit his head. His hand is cut from the glass. He's stunned, but awake. Can someone help him up and clean and bandage his hand? I'll call the police."

Terry's eyes opened wide and asked, "Uh… Carol, do we really need the police again?"

"Are you shitting me? Either Robbie or I could be dead right now. Someone shot at us with a high-powered rifle. Now, take care of Robbie. Everyone! Get away from this door!"

Less than twenty minutes later, the police arrived, a pair of regular uniformed policemen I didn't know. I invited them into the living room, which was now empty. Dria and the others had gone to their bedrooms. Carla had taken Robbie into the kitchen. I thought I heard her say something about Cliff.

I related to the officers what happened and made sure they knew I was working with Burt and Alan on the murder cases. One of the officers whistled. "I've been hearing that's quite a case there. So, what happened here? Think it's related to that case?"

"It could be. Someone yesterday had been in an old dark Chevy Bel Air watching this house. No license plates. I looked when it sped away. Couldn't see who was driving."

"Man? Woman? Could you tell that?"

"No. Like I said, I couldn't see the driver. Just saw a hooded figure."

I stood in the doorway of the kitchen talking to the cops while Carla was cleaning and bandaging Robbie's hand behind me. She didn't notice me there. I overheard her tearfully admitting to Robbie that she had done a bad thing. Her voice had a nervous edge to it. What I heard next made me almost say "What?"

She said, "I had sex with Cliff."

Robbie said what I was thinking, "What?"

Carla paused, sighed, and continued. "It… it was only once. You guys were rehearsing. I… I came out of my room in my robe to go take a shower. Cliff was in the hall. I don't know why he was upstairs, but he… he was just outside my door." She paused again. "He… he came on to me."

God, I thought, did Cliff rape her? I wanted to go console her, but the cops started talking to me again. I couldn't hear her anymore. I turned to look but Carla had left. I'll have to ask Robbie about it later.

He came back in and sat down on the sofa. I could see him wince as he rubbed his head. One of the policemen noticed the bandage on his hand and asked if he'd been shot.

Robbie answered, "Glass cut. I fell back and bumped my head."

"You need to go to the hospital?"

"No. I'm okay." Robbie turned to me. "Do I need to add anything?"

"No. Officers, this is Robbie Jones of this address. Burt and Alan know him and will probably want to interview him and the others in this house again. I have a meeting tomorrow morning at the police station with the team. They'll want to know about this shooting. Are we finished here for now?"

One of the officers answered. "Yeah. Good luck at your meeting. And good luck on finding the perp." The other officer, who I noticed looked bored, said "Yeah. Yeah. Good luck."

I saw the officers out. Robbie walked up behind me.

"Carol, you look really tired," he said to me. "Go home and get some sleep. Cliff left some plywood downstairs in his workshop that he was going to use to build speaker cabinets. I'll cut and tack a piece over the broken window."

"Robbie." I was tired. "I love that you're so responsible… and capable. I…" I wanted to say more, but instead, I looked away and walked out the front door.

Chapter 13

Come Together

Robbie

It was well after midnight, but I was still wired from all the events of the evening. I cleaned up all the remaining broken glass in the foyer, went downstairs to the workshop and cut some half inch plywood to a size to fit over the broken front door window. I drilled some holes close to the edge and screwed the plywood in place over the broken window.

After locking the door, I felt a little more secure. Now, overtired, I went to my room and fell into bed. I was asleep as soon as my head hit the pillow.

As tired as I was, I woke at seven in the morning and started thinking about last night. I couldn't go back to sleep, so I got up, went to the bathroom and took a long shower to warm up, and got dressed.

When I opened my door and walked through the short hall into the kitchen, Carla and Dria were already up and making coffee. With a little of the money we made at the Fillmore, the girls had picked up a coffee brewing filter cone a couple of days ago. They poured hot water over coffee grounds in the filter into a six-cup carafe. The coffee smelled good, even if it was from a can of MJB.

Carla came over and gave me a tight hug. Then Dria did the same thing, then asked me, "Are you okay, Robbie? We were so worried about you last night. We thought we lost you."

"Gee. Thank you, you two. That gunshot was a shock."

Dria asked. "Was it meant for you or… Carol?"

"I don't know. Maybe the shooter was aiming at whoever opened the door first. It could have been any of us opening that door. It just happened to be Carol. The bullet went right by her head."

I just had a thought.

"Hey! The police last night didn't even check to see where the bullet went. You want to help me find it?"

"Sure, but here, Robbie, have some coffee first." Carla poured me a mug. It was good. I sat down with them at the table for a few minutes sipping the hot coffee but was anxious to find where the bullet ended up. As the coffee cooled a little, I chugged the rest of it.

"Thanks Carla, Dria. I want to start looking for that bullet. Join in when you finish your coffee."

"We'll come with you now." Dria said. They both put down their mugs, got up, and followed me to the foyer.

I was trying to imagine the path and angle of the bullet. Where the car was when the gun was fired. Where the bullet came through the window. Where it must have gone after that.

"Okay, ladies. Look around for a hole. It will probably be above our heads, considering the angle from the street to the front door. Maybe along this wall. Maybe up…"

Dria nearly yelled. "I found it!"

Yes. She did find it. It was above our heads. The hole was in the molding above the door into the living room. I asked Carla if she could find me a long pencil. It took a few minutes for her to find one long enough that wasn't an overused stub.

I thanked her, reached up and inserted the pencil in the hole.

"See?" I said to the girls pointing at the pencil. "That shows the angle of the bullet. Let's leave that there to show the police. I'm sure they'll be here right after Carol's meeting this morning. I know they'll want to dig that out to find out what kind of gun was used." My heart was racing. "Whew. Let's go have some more coffee before the others wake up and drink it all."

It felt strange talking to Carla and Dria that morning. After some four months of barely talking to me at all, the night before, Carla came out and told me everything about her sad affair with Cliff and her problems with her husband, Jimmie. When Carla left to take a shower, Dria then did the same and opened up to me about her problems with Terry. Both of them told me how easy I was to talk to and to understand them. I felt kinda honored, but also a little uneasy. This had the potential to be fodder for breakups, marital, musical, and imagined.

Deke rose a little earlier than usual, a little after nine, and came into the kitchen to get some coffee. Dria looked at Deke, frowned, and left, saying she needed a shower too.

All Deke said was, "Is this all the coffee? There's barely a cup left. You drink it all Robbie?"

"Tell you what, Deke, you can make more if you want."

"How. I don't know how to use this damn thing."

"Christ, Deke. It's easy. Shit. I'll make it for you."

It was easy. Deke was just being lazy. He was one of those people who liked to be waited on. His mother probably did everything for him. Even in the Army, he was waited on. Served in the mess hall.

Clothes cleaned by house boys. Bed made by those same house boys. Even the dope he smoked was given to him by someone else. Yeah. Lazy.

By the time Terry and Jimmy got up, Carla and Dria had come back down and made some oatmeal for everyone's breakfast. They gave me a larger bowl than everyone else, which I enjoyed. It was good. Especially with the brown sugar and half and half they put in mine. The others got plain sugar and low-fat milk. Fortunately, none of them were observant enough to notice the difference. Carla gave me a knowing smile from across the kitchen. I smiled and nodded my thanks.

At two o'clock, the four of us went down to the basement to start rehearsals. Carol hadn't arrived yet.

I was just plugging my bass into my amp when Carol showed up with Burt and Alan in tow.

Carol spoke. "We're going to have to hold off on rehearsal right now."

Deke complained. Just like Marty used to do. "What? Jeez! We need to rehearse vocals for the new songs today!"

"Deke. Deke. We will. But later. That gunshot and attempted murder last night is more important. This was not a random drive by shooting. It was meant for whoever opened that door first. It just happened it was me…" She looked at me. "…and Robbie."

I put my bass back down. "Carol. Officers. Come upstairs with me. I have something to show you."

They followed me upstairs where I showed them the pencil sticking out of the door molding. Carol knew right away what it was.

"The bullet!" She exclaimed.

"Those nighttime men in blue that came here last night didn't bother to look for where the bullet ended up. They just took a statement and left. I found… rather, Dria found the hole up there. Carla got me a pencil to stick in it. See? The angle of the shot. I left that there for you or your team to see, and to dig out the bullet. See what kind of gun it was shot from."

Carol was smiling at me. A very pleasant smile. "You're good. You did right, Robbo… uh, Robbie. I'm glad you didn't try to remove it yourself."

"Yeah." Burt agreed. "That's true. Say, Alan. Give forensics a call. Get Rhys down here. His team should be here to get that bullet out. It might be embedded pretty deep. Also, bring those officers who came here last night into our office when they arrive for work. We need to have to have a little talk with them. They didn't follow protocol after a shooting like this. There was no report of this on our desks this morning."

Chapter 14

You Better Move On

Robbie

That afternoon, two men from the forensics team, along with Rhys, worked at removing the bullet. However, the force of the rifle shot drove the bullet halfway through the door's header, a hard piece of 75-year-old redwood, which made it difficult for them to reach the slug. They ended up cutting out a piece of the header the bullet was embedded in to take back to their lab. This would be a permanent reminder of our brush with death.

While his assistant worked, Rhys explained to me about how each gun produces different striations on a bullet, which I knew already from Perry Mason television shows I used to watch with my parents.

Before Rhys and his assistant left, Burt, Alan, and Carol had already gone back to the police station but returned an hour later. Alan had the police report from the two cops that came last night. They weren't happy about it.

They took me aside into the empty living room. Carol and I sat down on the sofa together. "We have problems." Carol said. "One of those cops wrote up a lot of crap about the shooting last night, implying it was a drug deal gone bad. The other cop's report wasn't much better. All he said was that it was a shooting by an unknown assailant. That's it. No mention of us being in the line of fire. I have a feeling those two uniforms are going to get censured. Big time."

I looked over at the two detectives. "I'm glad officers Burt and Alan seem on top of things."

"I am too. If they weren't, I wouldn't be working with them." She pointed her thumb at them. They grinned at her. She smiled back at them.

Deke came into the room. "So, when can we get back to rehearsing? I hate wasting time." Yeah, he was starting to sound more and more like Marty.

Carol answered. "Maybe tonight. Maybe not. Listen, Deke, someone seems out to get us. I'm working with the police to find out who. We all have to be real careful until this is over. Hey. By the way. Where's Jimmy and Terry? I haven't seen them since last night."

I answered this time. "I'm sure Terry is next door fooling around again. I don't know about Jimmy. The girls are hanging out in the kitchen where they usually are."

Carol was concerned. "Terry can't keep running back and forth between the two houses all the time. He's not being careful. He needs to stay here."

Carol and the detectives started to walk away. Deke said, "You police could handcuff him to his bed. I'm sure Dria would like that."

I could see Alan and Burt didn't like Deke's comment. They grunted their disgust and left. Carol stood up to follow them then turned to smile at me. A worried smile. "Robbo, I don't know yet, but I hope I can make it back this evening for rehearsal."

"Hey, Deke," I said before he headed back to his room. "How about you and I go downstairs and practice. Maybe jam a little. If Jimmy and Terry show up, we could jam on that jazzy instrumental you were fooling around with the other day. Who knows, we might come up with something new."

"Yeah. Why not. I need to play something. Geez, I was just thinking about Marty. You know he would always discourage me from being creative. He always wanted to take my ideas and say they were his own. Crud. I do miss the jerk though. We grew up together."

"Yeah. I miss him too. We've gone through a lot together, in Korea and now here. Ah, let's go downstairs."

Deke and I jammed on that jazzy instrumental for twenty minutes. I was amazed at how well he played jazz guitar, and I told him he played that style well. I thought it was much better than his rock playing. (*I didn't tell him that*.) I adjusted the volume and tone on my Gibson bass, so it sounded more like a standup bass. We played like a decent jazz duo.

We hadn't noticed that Jimmy came in and had been standing behind the door listening. "Wow. You guys sound great. Want to do it again with drums? I'll even use brushes."

Jimmy sat down at his drum set, did a little tuning adjustment to his snare drum, and we started playing Deke's jazz instrumental again. Now we sounded like a decent jazz trio. In fact, we sounded damn good.

When we finished, we were all quiet. Finally, I broke the silence. "Are you guys thinking what I'm thinking?"

Jimmy chimed in. "You mean if our main rock group doesn't pan out, we three could play jazz?"

Deke had other thoughts. "We've been successful with our main group. I mean, Clive Davis thought we were recording worthy… even if he hasn't gotten back to us yet. We gotta keep that going. The music is good. But… well, it won't hurt to have a splinter group, a jazz group that could play at venues other than rock clubs. I mean we could do gigs when it doesn't conflict with our main group."

Both Jimmy and I agreed. Then Jimmy snapped his fingers and said, "Oh. I forgot to tell you. Those people upstairs got that bullet out and left. They cut a large piece of the door's header out with the bullet in it. One of those guys, that British-sounding one, said the slice they took weakens that door header, especially with the weight of the second-floor stairway going over it. We need to fasten in some wood to strengthen it up."

I put my bass down and ran into the back of the basement to the woodshop and looked for some wood to use. Jimmy grabbed a tape measure and ran upstairs and stood on a chair to take measurements.

An hour later, the two of us bolted on the replacement and completed the project. Later we could patch the plaster and replace the top molding. But right now, we were tired. We plopped down together on the sofa. Deke, who hadn't helped us with the header, said he was also tired. *From what?* I asked myself. *Smoking dope?* He joined us.

We sat there talking about the shooting and the band. Deke and I were talking about collaborating on a song or two, which we'd never done before, when Carla and Dria came in and handed each of us a cup of coffee.

We thanked them, but they didn't leave. They kept standing there in front of us. I took a sip.

"Wow!" I exclaimed. "This coffee tastes great. Kinda chocolaty. It's not from that tin of MJB is it?"

Carla smiled. "No. Dria and I found an old coffee roasting place on Second Street downtown during one of our walks. Two old Italian men run it. We went back this morning and bought a bag of beans. Something they said was mocha."

Dria cut in. "Mocha java is what they said. They ground the beans for us."

Carla commented, "That place smelled great."

I thanked them but had to warn them. "Be really careful when you go walking. Remember, someone has been watching us and shot at us last night."

"We know." Dria said. "We were careful. No one seemed to be watching when we went out. I don't think anyone followed us either. Besides. We were armed."

"Say what?" Jimmy, Deke, and I said together. "Armed with what?" I asked.

"We both put kitchen knives in our purses," said Carla. "Just in case," replied Dria.

I didn't like the sound of that. I was sure Carol wouldn't either.

Deke wasn't concerned at all. He asked Dria, "Say. Is Terry around? We haven't seen him for hours. He should have been here for rehearsal, which we didn't really have because of all the police people running around. But he should've been here."

Dria looked down. Her smile disappeared and I noticed her eyes began to water up. "Terry's being Terry. He went out last night thinking I was asleep already. I saw him get up and leave. He didn't come back. I'm sure he's screwing some young broad's brains out!"

That last sentence came out in anger.

"Dria, Terry always made it here for rehearsals." I told her. "I'll call Carol and ask her to check to see if he's next door."

I got up and went into the foyer picked up the wall phone's receiver and dialed Carols home number. No answer. She must still be at the police station. I pulled Burt's business card out of my wallet and dialed his number at the police station. He picked up.

"This is Officer Peterson. Who am I speaking to?"

"Hi Officer. This is Robbie… Uh, Robert Jones."

"Oh yes. What can I do for you, Mister Jones?"

"Well, we… one of our band members is missing. Terry Wenborn. He didn't come back last night."

"That doesn't sound good. I know you're worried, especially with a murderer on the loose, but we can't put out a missing person notice until someone's gone for at least seventy-two hours."

"Officer Peterson. Is Carol Legrand there by any chance? She lives next door and might be able to check if Terry is fooling around with one of the student volunteers there."

"Student volunteers? For what?"

"Answering phones for Dennis at Drug Crises Intervention and Suicide Prevention. Dennis publishes the San José Cinnabar newspaper and runs both those businesses too."

"Hmm. Never heard of that paper. Well, Okay. I don't know if Carol is still here, but I'll check. Let me put you on hold for a minute."

The line went quiet except for a little static in the background. Less than a minute later, Burt was back.

"Yeah. Carol's still here. Here she is." Burt must have handed the phone to her.

"Carol. Robbie here. I need to ask a favor when you get home. Can you check to see if Terry is there, maybe playing around with one of the students?"

"Yes. I can do that. Burt told me you said he's been missing since last night. That's not typical. I know that. Terry has always been on time for rehearsals. I'll be heading home shortly. I'm almost done looking at the San José Mercury morgue files I had requested. I'll talk to you when I get there."

I thanked her, we said our goodbyes and hung up. I went back into the living room. Carla and Dria were together in an old easy chair across from the sofa. Dria looked up at me. She still had tears in her eyes.

"Dria. Carol will be home soon and will check to see if Terry is there. Hopefully, he'll return before that."

Dria said thanks, then both girls got up and went back into the kitchen.

Chapter 15

As Tears Go By

Robbie

After the girls left the living room, Jimmy, Deke, and I headed back down to the rehearsal room to jam a while.

For twenty minutes we started over and over but didn't get very far. Deke was frustrated. Jimmy and I weren't very inspired. We were all thinking about Terry and where he could be.

We sat around talking and worrying about the future of the group when Carol came in. She plopped down on one of the chairs. She looked concerned.

"No Terry. Dennis said he hasn't been next door at all. I asked each of the girls working the phones. When their shift started this morning, they replaced four who had been there all night. The bedrooms two of them live in and the kitchen they use as a break room were empty. Yeah. I'm worried. I'll try to get Burt or Alan to instigate a missing persons announcement right away instead of waiting for seventy-two hours to tick by. That might be way too late… if anything has happened to him.”

“Let’s hope not.” I sighed to Carol. “Has your research turned up anything on this person who’s attacking us?”

“How’d you know I was doing research?”

“Carol, you told me on the phone from the police station.”

“Oh. I did, didn’t I. I’m sorry, Robbo. I really shouldn’t have said that. I’m not supposed to discuss anything about the case… yet. Unfortunately, from the damn Mercury News blurbs on the murders, we’ve been getting calls from as far away as Sacramento from people saying they know who the murderer is. False leads. All of them. That’s my damn research.”

I said, “I’m sorry you have to do that, Carol.”

Jimmy said, “Yeah, I’m sorry too, Carol.”

Deke said with a little edge on his voice, “Yeah. Yeah. Sorry. When are you going to be able to rehearse again?”

“Deke, chill out. Take it easy. I wish I could get back to singing with you guys right away, but it looks like no deal until this perp is behind bars. Remember, guys, we might all be targets for whoever this is… as Robbie and I found out last night. Always be careful.”

I remembered what Dria told me.

“Uh… Carol. We just found out today that when Dria and Carla go to the store or for a walk, they carry kitchen knives in their purses for protection.”

“Oh. Not good. Knives won’t be much protection from a shooter, or someone who sneaks up behind and hits them on their heads. Try to get them to go to the store only when and where there’s a lot of people around. Well, guys. I’m sorry to say I really need to get back to the precinct. I’ve got more work to do. Robbo, can you come with me to your room a few minutes?”

“Sure, Carol.”

After we both entered, she shut the door. She kept her voice low, almost a whisper.

"Robbie. I didn't want to say this around the others, but we found out who that shooter is. It's someone we know. Remember that band that played before us at the first gig we did in the park? Uh, what was it called?"

"Raven. Pretty bad, weren't they? Someone from Raven? One of them killed Marty and Cliff?"

"No, he didn't kill anyone. We don't know yet if he tried to kill either you or me or at whoever opened the door. His shooting will be enough to put him away for a while… when we catch him."

"Carol. Who?"

"The guitarist. On stage he's known as Tommy Raven. His real name is Tommy Clifton."

"Clifton? Like Cliff's real name?"

"The same. Tommy was Cliff's brother, or rather half-brother."

"Brother!" I said a little too loud. Carol motioned to me to be quiet. I whispered, "Brother. That must be why Cliff was arguing with him at that be-in."

"I didn't notice that. They had words?"

"Yeah. Quite a few. They started arguing on stage before their gig, then went behind the stage and continued. They argued pretty heatedly again after Raven's set. I'm sure neither noticed that I was close enough to hear."

"Maybe Tommy did notice you. Maybe it was you he was shooting at."

"Crap. Just because I heard them arguing?"

"Did you hear what they were arguing about?"

"Only a few words. I did hear Cliff yell something about drugs. And something about money. Do you think Tommy killed Cliff over that?"

"People have been killed for less. Yeah, we're now looking into that possibility, but, personally, I doubt it. Cliff's death was too much like Marty's. Neither were shot. Robbo," Carol gently grabbed my hand. "Why don't you come with me to the station. You need to tell Burt what you just told me. Remember, the police in New York might have records on Cliff. There may be some here too. I haven't looked at them yet. Maybe they have records on his brother too. I'll drive you there. I know you're nervous about this, but it could help for this shooting case. Okay?"

"Okay, Carol. Yeah, I'm ready to go whenever you are."

At the police station, I repeated to Burt what I'd told Carol. While I was talking, Alan came in wheeling a hand cart with two file boxes. The labels on the outside said Cases: 1966-1 and 1966-2. He opened the tops. Inside they were full of tabbed manila folders. Some with a single paper inside, and some so full the folders were torn. On each tab was written a name and case number. Carol and Alan started looking through the boxes.

Burt finished writing down what I'd told him and put down his note pad. Alan handed him two full folders. I saw the names. Clifton, Reinhold and Clifton, Thomas. I was hoping he'd open them so I could see what their records were about, but Burt put them unopened in his desk drawer.

"Carol." Burt said. "Go ahead and take mister Jones, here, home. Then come on back and we'll go over those files. Mister Jones, thank you for letting us know what happened at that … uh, what's that type of concert called? Oh yeah. Be-in."

Our house was barely a mile from the police station, so we were back at the commune in less than five minutes. We barely talked until Carol came into the house with me. No one was in the living room, and the girls weren't in the kitchen. We could hear the muffled sound of music being played downstairs and figured Deke and Jimmy were practicing. I heard the organ. Maybe Terry had returned. Odd, though, it didn't sound like Terry's style of playing. Carol and I went into my room.

Carol came up to me and gave me a big hug. "Robbo. Thank you so much for helping out. I really want this over with so we can get back to playing… music and…" She planted a very loving kiss on my lips.

She gave me a sad half smile, patted my cheek and left. I sighed and thought about, *oh, so many things.*

I again heard the muffled sound of music and decided to head downstairs.

When I walked into the rehearsal room, it wasn't Terry playing the organ. There were Deke on guitar, Jimmy, with an angry look on his face, sitting behind his drum set but not playing, and a stranger sitting behind the organ. He obviously couldn't play it well and was just two-fingering the notes on the Farfisa.

"Uh, hi guys. Who's this?"

Deke answered. "Hey, Rob. This is an old friend of mine from back East. We went to high school and played music together there before I joined Marty's band. Meet Zeke Mayfield. He moved here recently. Lives south of here in Morgan Hill."

"Hi, Zeke. You guys played together?"

"Yeah," he replied without smiling. "We were known as Deke and Zeke. We played folk music."

Deke continued. "Yeah. We were kind of outcasts in high school, but once we released a single, that changed."

"Yeah. It sure did."

I asked, "Zeke. Did you play organ in high school?"

He seemed irritated like I was disturbing a serious rehearsal. "Mmm… no. Deke and I both played guitars."

"I had a Stella 12-string back then." Deke said. "It was like the one Mississippi John Hurt played."

"Whatever happened to that old 12-string?" Zeke asked.

"I stupidly leant it to Marty. You remember Marty? Yeah. I know. That jerk the late Marty. Well, he messed it up. Left it in his car on one of those hundred-degree plus days we had back East that year. It almost exploded in its case. Marty tried to fix it and made it worse. He gave it back to me in pieces and didn't even say he was sorry. Just dropped it off and left. The asshole."

"You didn't try to get it fixed?"

"Couldn't. Marty didn't bring back all the pieces. When I asked him about it a few days later, he insisted he gave them all to me. The asshole."

After several more minutes of listening to their complaining and reminiscing, I was getting annoyed that Deke and Jimmy were jamming with Zeke on the organ, Terry's organ, I thought *that's enough!*

"So. Deke. Jimmy. Any word about Terry yet?"

"No. Not yet." Deke replied. "Sure he's not hiding out next door with some college chick?"

"Jeez, Deke. You know Carol checked that out. Dennis said Terry hasn't been next door for nearly a week. Even though Dria knows of his infidelities, she does say she misses him. Carol's been able to get a missing person search started at the police station."

Deke looked at me kind of sideways. "Shouldn't the police have started looking for Terry right away?"

"Seventy-two hours. That's the 'legal' time…" I used air quotes, "…required before a search is initiated. Carol was able to get it started in less than forty-eight hours."

"So, when is she coming back for rehearsals?"

"Deke, is that all you can think of? Really. We can't have full rehearsals until the murderer is found out. Carol told you that. Also, we need Terry back on organ."

"Hell. Zeke can play organ."

"Shit Deke. I'm tired of trying to talk sense to you."

I didn't say anymore. I slammed the door shut as I left and stomped back upstairs and into my room. To chill out, I put the first Jimi Hendrix Experience album on, put my headphones on, and turned up the volume up to an ear-bleeding level. All I could think of while listening was why am I sticking around? The band is going through too many changes in too short of time. Maybe I'm only staying because of Carol. We get along and play well together. I don't care if she's maybe a year older than me. I don't care that she's taller than me. I really like her. I think she likes me. I wiped my eyes.

After listening to both sides, I put on Jimi Hendrix's second album, *Axis, Bold as Love*, and leaned back in my old recliner and closed my tear-filled eyes and started to think about the music our band played and got nostalgic about the few well-received gigs we had. We were good. *Shit. More tears*.

With Jimi's guitar screaming in my ears and my eyes still closed, I was shocked by someone touching my arm. I jumped. My heart jumped. I took my headphones off.

"Oh. Carol. I didn't hear you come in."

"I'm so sorry to have scared you. Hey, have you been crying?"

I wiped my eyes. "I'm sorry."

"Oh Robbo, you sweet thing. Don't be sorry. Please tell me what's wrong." Carol sat on the armrest and put her arm around me. It made me tear up more.

"Everything… it's all hit me all at once. Marty. Cliff. Terry missing. Our music. And… I… I can't talk any sense to Deke. He still wants to rehearse. He even brought in an old high school friend of his, and he was playing Terry's organ."

"You're kidding. Already? No shit?"

"No shit. And Deke seems to not care that Marty or Cliff are gone. Like I said. He just wants to rehearse." I was choking up again.

80

"Scoot over lover." I did and Carol sat down beside me draping one of her legs over mine. She put both arms around me. I laid my head on her shoulder. I broke down and cried… and cried.

Chapter 16

Nowhere Man

Carol

Robbie sighed and seemed to have pulled himself together. He raised his head. I still held on to him and didn't want to let go. *He's such a sensitive guy. They're so hard to find.*

I wiped some tears from my own eyes. "Dear Robbie. I really know how you feel. I've been on the verge of breaking down, too. I have to force myself to be strong during this whole damn investigation. I… I can't show any weakness to my old-school cops. I never did during training. I can't show weakness to the band either. Robbo, I don't worry about that around you. I can be myself. Not a detective."

I reached over and gave him such a long loving kiss that my toes curled.

"Robbo. Come with me. I have time off for dinner but have to go back to do more so-called research at the police station. So, let's go out and get something to eat. Besides, I don't think you want to eat here tonight. I heard Carla's fixing something called beef heart stew. Some Scandinavian dish I think. It sounds terrible. Let's go to the Crystal Creamery. I think it's safe to walk there.

The Crystal Creamery was an old-fashioned diner, across the street from the Lucky supermarket. It was only a short two block walk from the commune. The time was right. The streets were crowded with college students, so we felt pretty safe walking to the café. However, I kept an eye out along our route. I thought I saw Dennis not far behind us. I looked again, and he wasn't there.

The Creamery was moderately busy. It looked like half the customers were elderly. They'd probably been coming here for decades. The other half looked like students. Nearly all were drinking thick milkshakes out of tall glass goblets. The Creamery made their own ice cream in a building in the back of the main restaurant. Their milkshakes and sundaes were famous. At least locally.

An elderly waitress greeted us and dropped menus in front of us.

Having not eaten much since morning, I was hungry. I ordered a cheeseburger and fries and a vanilla milkshake. Robbie ordered a BLT club sandwich and milk.

Before our orders arrived, we made small talk. I asked Robbie if he'd written any new songs lately. He asked me about my father's albums. I asked him about where he grew up. Robbie asked me the same. No talk of murders, shootings, or missing people. Just learning more about each other. It felt so natural.

When the food came, conversation stopped. We were both famished and concentrated on eating.

This was one of those old-style diners where a cheeseburger was just ground meat and melted American cheese on a soft bun sitting on a thick dinner plate. On the side of the plate were the fixings: lettuce, tomato, and sliced dill pickle. Catsup, yellow mustard, and mayo were in plastic squeeze containers the waitress put on the table in front of us. This was not a fast-food burger joint. It was a fix-your-burger-to-your-own-liking kind of place… uh, restaurant. After fixing mine to my taste, I made short work of it. It was really good. The thick hand-made patty was not overcooked and still had a little moist pink in the middle. My milkshake was fantastic.

Robbie said the bacon in his BLT club sandwich was some of the best he'd ever tasted. Thick slices with a smoky flavor.

To go with the style of the old diner, you paid at an old cash register by the entrance. I paid. Robbie left a two-dollar tip on the table.

When we exited, I took Robbie's hand, and we walked hand in hand back to the house.

However, when we turned the corner, we quickly let go of each other. In front of the commune was a police car. We ran the rest of the way.

Burt and Alan were coming out of the house.

I asked them, "What are you guys doing here. We just had dinner. I was getting ready to head back to the station."

Burt spoke. He had a frown on his face and said in anger, "Mister Wenborn, Terry, was found a while ago at the sewage treatment plant in Alviso. He's…" Burt paused, sighed then continued. "He's dead."

"Her friend, Miss Porter, is in the kitchen consoling her." Burt said.

I felt tears forming and turned away from Burt and Alan. I rubbed my eyes, turned back and asked, "Where… where was he found?"

Before Alan answered, he took me aside. "Should we talk about this in front of him?" I could see his thumb pointing at Robbie, standing outside by Burt.

I got angry. "Look, Alan, Robbie's been part of this since the beginning! It turns out he was the shooting target the other night! Not me! And you know that now! Whatever you tell me, you can tell him! He's actually helped me in these investigations!"

"Okay. Okay. Don't blow a gasket. Sorry."

"Now. Where was he found?"

"You won't like this."

"Try me."

"He was dropped in a tank at the sewage treatment plant in Alviso. His body was found only because it lodged in a pipe. A maintenance worker located it, and we were called in. He's in the hospital morgue where he was cleaned up and awaiting pickup by Lucy's team. Burt and I saw the body taken out. It looks like he was hit and stabbed the same way as the other two murders."

"You're right. I don't like this." I sighed, put my hand on Robbie's shoulder and said, "Come on, Robbo. Let's go in and see how Dria is doing." Robbie again had tears in his eyes.

We walked up the steps and into the living room. Deke and his friend Zeke were sitting together on the sofa, half eaten plates of what must have been beef heart stew in their laps. Jimmy, frowning, was in the easy chair across from them. His plate was on the floor. It didn't look like he had touched it.

Deke and Zeke were talking like nothing had happened. Jimmy kept glancing at the kitchen with a worried look on his face.

I could hear Dria crying in the kitchen and Carla trying to soothe her. Robbie and I came in. Carla saw us and came over, leaving Dria in a chair and slumped over on the table, her head in her arms.

"I guess you want dinner. Let me get some plates."

"No. No. Carla. We've eaten already." Robbie said, waving his hands dismissively. "Put the plates away. Take care of poor Dria."

Dria looked up at Robbie then looked angry as she saw me next to him. She quietly said as she was trying to catch her breath. "Why… why the fuck are you in here?" Then she yelled at Robbie. "Why the fuck is she in here?"

Carla looked angry too. She was shaking her head in agreement.

"Hey! Goddam it!" Robbie yelled back, leaning his hands on the table and staring Dria straight in her face. Dria stopped wailing and look up at him in wonder. "You two have never accepted Carol in this group! Your jealousy is so unfounded! Why do you seem to think she's a threat to you! You think she's after your guys? That's so far from the truth and you should know it! Listen. She has done a great job as our singer. And now she's doing a great job working with the cops and trying to find out what the hell is going on around here. Dria, I'm really, really sad and sorry that Terry's gone, but you and Carla need to give her some slack!"

Dria laid her head down on her crossed arms on the table and burst into tears. Carla had her hand on Dria's back and started to say something but didn't. She looked at Robbie, then looked at me. Carla took a deep breath, let out a big sigh, then came over and gave Robbie a hug. She then reluctantly went over to me and gave me a hug around my waist. I almost backed away not knowing what she was going to do.

Dria finally looked up at me and said through sobs, "C...Carol. We...we're so s...sorry. W...we've always known that w...when quiet R...Robbie gets angry, everyone... listens. He...he's a wonderful guy." Dria stood up, walked up to me and, like Carla, wrapped her arms around my waist. "I'm sorry. I'm sorry. Please. If you are really working with the police, please, please find out who killed my Terry."

Robbie and I walked out of the commune and over to my house next door.

"Robbo, that was some rant you got into. I knew those two didn't care for me, but I was so intent on singing, I didn't think to talk to them. It is odd, though, that after how badly Terry treated Dria, she is so upset with his death."

"No telling. She might have really liked him or was just used to him. They were together for several years, so I heard."

"Maybe. Stick around. I have to take a quick shower and change my clothes before heading back to the precinct for a few more hours.

Ten minutes later, I returned wrapped in a towel. It barely covered me. I was a little embarrassed, but not that embarrassed. *I wanted to kiss him*. My towel nearly dropped away. *Oops. Stirrings.*

"Oh, Robbo. I wish this was over. I want to spend so much time with you. Lots of time."

"I know. Carol, I do too. I…" He hesitated.

I wanted to say how much I loved him, but this wasn't the time.

I glanced at my clock radio. "Damn. Look at the time. I'm sorry, but I've got to get dressed and go."

I took some clothes into the bathroom and came out dressed in a clean professional pants suit. I reached into a drawer and pulled out a shoulder holster and fastened it on, then put on my suit coat to cover it. I noticed Robbie looked concerned when he saw me put the gun in the holster. I told him not to worry.

We then walked back to the commune together. On the sidewalk I looked left and right and across the street. If anything happened, I hoped I would be able to protect Robbie. I walked him to the front door, gave him a quick kiss, leaving fresh lipstick on his lips. I turned and went down the stairs. Robbie was watching me as I got into my car and left. I hated leaving him. I felt like I wanted to spend more time not just with the band, but with him. I was missing him already.

Chapter 17

Break On Through

Robbie

It was nearly seven o'clock, and I felt like going down to the studio to fool around with the four-track recorder Cliff had set up. When I opened the studio door, no one else was there. *Quiet. Good.*

Even though Cliff was a pain in the ass most of the time, and had a police record, I still missed seeing him working in this studio. He was kind of an electronics genius. He had also recorded several of our rehearsals and our concerts. I was hoping to make copies for myself one of these days.

On a wide worktable next to the window that looked over the rehearsal space, sat a large professional audio mixing board. I had no idea how Cliff got it or where it came from. It was connected to a new four-track recorder and to a two-track that Cliff had used to make mixdowns and master tapes.

In my room was my old Harmony Sovereign Jumbo guitar that I wrote my songs with. I ran upstairs to get it and brought it back down. I closed the two doors to the studio.

I looked for the best microphone I could find in Cliff's stash. In the back of the studio was a metal cabinet. Actually, it was a section of three old school lockers Cliff had found somewhere. One of the locker's handles had a combination lock fastened to it. The other two were unlocked. I opened them and they were full of cables and microphones.

I was curious that one of them was locked.

Now, in my mind, instead of thinking of starting to record, I wanted to open that locked cabinet.

Yeah. Curious.

I headed to the back of the basement to the woodshop area. Another set of Cliff's acquisitions greeted me. No one had questioned where the new table saw, band saw, and drum sander came from. Nor did they question where all the hand tools that lined the wall came from. After all, this was Cliff's domain. However, thanks to my dad's tutelage, I knew my way around a wood shop.

I found what I came for. A metal hack saw.

I took it back into the studio and started sawing at the combination lock. It was hard, and my arm was getting tired and sore. It made a lot of noise, and I was glad the area was soundproofed.

Finally, I cut through. The lock fell off with a clank on the concrete floor. I opened the cabinet.

I expected something like pot, hard drugs, or, I don't know, pornography? Inside was a large grocery bag. I looked in.

Money. A lot of money in the bag. Hundred-dollar bills. Jeez. I closed the cabinet and slipped the cut lock back in place. For a second,

I thought I should take it. But only a second. I knew I had to call Carol. She can tell her police friends.

Before I could go upstairs to call Carol, I heard someone coming down the stairs. I didn't want whoever was coming to see what's in the locker here. I jumped over and sat down on the chair behind the mixing board.

The door to the studio opened. I glanced up.

"Oh. It's you, Zeke. What's up?

"Hi Bobby. Doing some recording?" Zeke's half smile and squinted eyes made him look almost sinister.

"Uh… that's Robbie, Zeke. And yes, I'm getting ready to record a new song. So, what are you doing down here?"

"Well, if you must know," he said with a sneer. "I'm meeting Deke. We're going to work on some songs."

I didn't like the sound of that. Was Deke trying to bring Zeke into the band, maybe to play Terry's organ parts without letting the rest of us know? *There's something about this guy that's creepy.*

And downstairs trotted Deke. He looked surprised to see me sitting in the studio.

"Robbie! What are you doing here? I thought you were still next door with that… with Carol."

"No. She went back to work at the police station. So, what are you doing here mister Deke?" I was annoyed that my private time was interrupted. I was also annoyed that Deke was going to practice with Zeke, a new guy we've never seen before. "Gonna jam?"

"Uh… yeah. We're gonna jam. Aren't we, Zeke."

"I thought we were…"

"Gonna jam. Aren't we Zeke!"

"Uh, yeah. Jam."

I looked at them with a questioning look on my face. "Is Jimmy coming down to… uh… jam too?"

Deke was looking very sheepish. "Jimmy… he's taken Carla out somewhere for a movie or something. Anniversary or something."

Yeah. Deke is going behind all our backs to bring in Zeke. I had an idea. "You guys go ahead and jam all you want. I'll just hang out here and fiddle with recording a new song I'm working on. Close the door for me, will you?"

I knew some of the microphones in the rehearsal room were still connected to the mixing board. I pretended I was setting up for my own recording. I put headphones on. I had my guitar in my lap and reached over to turn on one of the links to the rehearsal space where Deke and Zeke had gone. In my peripheral vision I could see both of them glancing my way. I didn't look back. I kept acting like I was setting up for myself. I even strummed my guitar then moved some sliders on the mixing board.

I could hear their conversation in my headphones. I stopped strumming and acted like I was making adjustments to the recorder. Actually, I turned it on. It was now recording Deke and Zeke, and I didn't like what I was hearing.

"Listen, Deke. You owe me. You screwed me over so much when you left back then. We were about to make it big with our own music. That asshole Marty convinced you to be a fucking rock and roller."

"That's not fair, Zeke. We weren't going to make it."

"Yes, we were! Goddamit! Guido said we were!"

"Jesus. Zeke. Guido was a fucking mafia goon. If we went with him, no telling how we'd have ended up. Probably in the bottom of the East River."

"That's not fucking true! Guido was family! My father's brother! My uncle!"

"Look. Keep all that quiet, would you?"

They both looked my way again. I was still pretending to be recording myself. Deke had picked up his acoustic guitar and strummed it a few times. They went back to arguing. The next thing I heard form Zeke really set off alarms.

"Shit, Deke. Guido, before he died said it was here in San José. We have to find where Cliff hid the money before Guido's San José friends break in to find it. They won't leave any witnesses."

Jeez. The money I just found? Why is Zeke mentioning that? Did he know Cliff? Was Cliff involved with the mafia? Is that why our friends are dying? Oops. I wasn't paying attention. They looked at me again. Strum that guitar, Rob. Strum that guitar. Look busy.

Deke put down his guitar. Both were heading toward the door. They didn't come in. They went upstairs. Whew. I could hear my heart beating in my headphones.

I put my guitar down and reached over and turned off the tape recorder. I rewound the tape and took it off and put it in the box it came in. *I'll give it to Carol when she gets home.*

I knew I had to do something about the padlock I cut. If anyone came in here, they'd notice it right away if they opened the other lockers for mikes or cords. Maybe…

I took the padlock off again and took the bag of money out and temporarily hid it behind the large four-track recorder. Then I picked up a pile of blank tapes Cliff had left off of the floor and put them in the locker. I put the cut padlock in my pocket planning to toss it in the trash can in the back.

Then, I had an idea.

Reaching behind the four-track recorder, I grabbed the bag, opened the door, and headed in the back of the basement to the woodshop. Deke never went there. He was for some reason afraid of the big power tools, or else too lazy to use them. I opened a cabinet under the table saw and slipped the bag in there under the sawdust.

Just outside the woodshop was the short stairway up to the back yard, to the parking area. I opened the door and went upstairs, looked around to see if anyone was out there, glanced up to the back windows and didn't see a soul. I quickly opened the garbage can lid and slipped the padlock in under a soggy bag of food waste.

I went back down figuring I'd stick around in the recording studio until Carol came home. I didn't dare go upstairs to call her. I'm sure Deke and Zeke are up in the living room, probably continuing the discussion they started down here.

However, when I opened the door to the studio, Deke was sitting in the chair behind the mixing board. He had a reel-to-reel tape box in his hand.

"Uh. Hey, Deke. What's up?" I asked, trying to hide my nervousness.

"Zeke left, so I thought I'd come down and do a little recording myself."

"He left? I thought he was staying here with you."

"Nah, he's rented a new apartment on San Fernando between Eighth and Ninth Streets and moved some of his stuff up here from Morgan Hill."

Deke put the tape on the four-track recorder.

"Were you done in here?"

"I was going to do a little more but go ahead. Before you record, let me make sure you're not using the tape I was recording on. I didn't get around to marking it."

"This isn't yours. I brought this tape down from my room. I've got a song on here I've been working on. I'm overdubbing my vocals."

I silently breathed a sigh of relief then reached behind Deke and grabbed the tape I knew was mine.

"Hand me that pen by you there Deke."

He did, and I wrote a fake song title on the back.

"Well, have fun, Deke. See ya."

I closed the door behind me and headed upstairs.

Great. No one is in the living room. Let's see. Yeah. No one's in the kitchen. I can call Carol.

I first went into my room and put the tape box under my mattress, then headed to the foyer and picked up the wall phone receiver. I dialed the police station and got some receptionist. I asked for Carol Legrand. She was not available. Must be out investigating somewhere. I asked for Officer Burt. Not available. Officer Alan. Not available. Crap. They must be all out together. I'll just have to wait for Carol to come home.

Chapter 18

No Way to Remember

Robbie

Jimmy and Carla returned from their anniversary outing around ten. He told me they had driven to a Campbell movie theater to see a Jack Lemmon comedy. It appeared that Jimmy was trying to pay more attention to Carla. I think with all that has happened, they're probably clinging to each other for love and support. Carol hadn't returned yet.

Just before Jimmy and Carla came back, Dria had come out of her room and made herself a grilled cheese sandwich for a late-night snack, white bread with a slice of American cheese. She spread a dab of margarine on the outside of the bread slices, so the toast browned nicely in the frying pan, then she cut the sandwich in quarters and gave Deke and me pieces. They were okay, but not Michelin star worthy.

Shortly after our snack Dria went back upstairs to her room and Deke went to his room in the back. As he left, I wondered about what I heard him and Zeke talking about earlier.

I went to my room and grabbed a book I had been reading, a horse racing mystery by Dick Francis, and brought it downstairs into the living room. I wanted to be there to be close to the phone if Carol called or if I could hear her car drive up.

I was barely two pages into my book when I did hear a car pull up in front that sounded like hers. I jumped up and ran to the front door, grabbed the doorknob, and swung the door wide open.

I heard a shot and immediately felt a sharp pain in my left shoulder. I yelped. The force of the bullet pushed me back against the newel post by the stairway. My head slammed against it. My feet slipped out from under me kicking the door shut. Everything went black.

I woke up in a hospital bed. My head ached and pounded. My shoulder itched. I reached up to scratch it and couldn't. A large bandage was in the way and my left arm was immobilized, fastened in a sling. My right arm had an IV sticking in it. The pain in my shoulder hit me all at once.

"Ohhh." I moaned.

"Robbie! You're awake! Thank the gods."

"Wh…where a… am I?"

"You're in O'Connor Hospital. Dria heard the shot and called 911. You were brought here in an ambulance."

Carol had been sitting in a chair next to the bed. It looked like she still had on the same pants suit she had put on earlier when I was in her room. There were dark circles under her eyes. She held my right hand.

"Robbie, I need to get the nurse to locate the doctor. We've been extremely worried. You've been out for over twenty-four hours."

"I… I don't know what hurts most." I was wincing, trying to close my eyes tight thinking that would ease the pain. No dice. "My… my head's splitting, and my sh… shoulder is throbbing. Wha… what happened to me?"

"You don't remember? I'll let the doctor explain. I'll be right back." Carol reached over and gave me a kiss on the forehead. Normally, I would enjoy it, but my head hurt so much I wanted to go back to sleep and wake later without the pain.

A few minutes later Carol returned following a nurse who looked old enough to be my mother. In fact, she looked a lot like my mother, at least through my squinting eyes. She had a syringe that she poked into a connection on the IV tube. Barely thirty seconds later, the pain became bearable. But it also made me woozy. I dozed off.

When I opened my eyes again a doctor was by my bed looking at a clipboard.

"Ah. Mister Jones. You're awake again. Good." He put the clipboard down. "I'm Doctor Diesner. I'm the surgeon who patched you up."

I painfully and quietly said, "Thanks."

"You're welcome. I removed a bullet in your shoulder, but it missed both your aorta and your lung lobe. You had some loss of blood, and we replaced it. Now, you had a bad hit on your head that required a few stitches. So, please follow my finger, but just with your eyes. Don't move your head."

I did. The doctor seemed satisfied.

"Can you describe your pain right now? Tell me by number. One to ten. One is light, five is medium, ten is bad."

"It's almost a ten right now. Why does my head keep throbbing?"

"You received a concussion when you fell. You cut your head, too. You have a few stitches up there. We were all glad you finally woke up."

"I know I got shot. Is that why my arm is fastened to this sling?"

"The bullet shattered your clavicle, just a few inches from your neck. To repair it I had to add some pins to hold it together. You won't be able to use that arm for at least a month, maybe longer."

"*Well, there goes my music career.*" I quietly told myself.

"Now that you're awake, there's some people waiting outside to see you."

I hoped it was Carol again. It was, but she was followed by Burt and Alan. Carol must have gone home to get cleaned up while I was asleep. She wore a different, but still official-looking and well pressed navy-blue pants suit with a light blue turtleneck and looked like she had finally gotten some sleep. *How long was I asleep?*

I could see this was an official visit. Carol stood back while Burt and Alan came up beside me. Burt started.

"We're really glad you finally woke up. This has been quite an ordeal for you."

"Uh… thanks."

"You feeling well enough to talk to us?"

"I'll… I'll try. Go ahead."

Alan pulled his notepad and pencil out and got ready to take notes. In fact, he was already writing something down.

Burt continued. "Now. First. The doctor was able to remove the bullet from you, and we took it to forensics. That was not the same bullet we dug out of your house. This was a different caliber and shot from a pistol, not a rifle. And the first shooter, that Raven guitarist, Tommy Clifton, is now in custody. We had found two unregistered rifles and quite a bit of ammunition in his room that we confiscated. This was a different shooter."

"Why so many guns out there?" I shook my head. Mistake. "Ow! Shit! That fucking hurt!"

Carol came over. "Burt. We shouldn't bother him anymore right now. He's hurting."

"One more thing. Mister Jones, did you see the car? Were you able to see it before… well, before you were knocked out?"

"I only remember hearing it drive up. I thought it was Carol coming home. That's why I opened the door. The car sounded the same. I didn't see it, though."

"Hmm. If it sounded the same, it might be the same type of car Carol has. Okay, Mister Jones, we won't bother you anymore for now. Get better soon, will you?"

Alan nodded yes. The two men left. Carol came over to me.

"So sorry. They insisted on coming. This case, well, these cases are keeping us all working hard and late. It's not going well. Oh, Robbo. Yes. Please, please get better. I was so worried I was going to lose you."

There were tears in her eyes. "I notified your parents. I'll call them again now that you're awake so they can visit. Robbie, I have to go. If you start hurting more, push that button for the nurse on duty for more pain juice."

She leaned over and gave me a light kiss on my forehead. This time it didn't hurt.

I was in the hospital ten days. My dressings were changed daily. The first day I screamed in pain. The second day I swore in pain. The third day I just squinted my eyes shut and said nothing. It was painful, but not as bad. I guess I was getting used to it. My parents visited me every day. Carol visited me daily. The cops visited me twice. No one from the commune came to visit.

When I was finally able to leave, Carol came to the room with a clean set of clothes packed in a small suitcase she brought and a blanket for my arm. I couldn't just walk out even though I had been up every day in the last week walking around the hospital. A nurse brought in a wheelchair that I had to get into. She wheeled me out to the front door. Carol had pulled up by the hospital's front door, and she opened the passenger door for me. I got out of the wheelchair and slipped into the car seat. My head wasn't aching anymore, but my shoulder still pained me. I couldn't use my left hand because of the immovable sling. At least I'm right-handed.

Even though the roads were smooth, the occasional bump jarred my sore shoulder. Occasionally I closed my eyes tightly waiting for the pain to pass. Carol kept asking, "Robbo. You okay?"

"Yes". I kept saying with a grimace. I lied. I felt like crap.

When we got back on Sixth Street, she pulled in the driveway of her house.

"Carol. Your driveway?"

"Robbo, if it's okay, I want you to stay here with me until you're strong enough to stay in your own place. I can go next door and get you clean clothes and your toiletries. I'm sure some of them want to see you too. When you're settled and rested a little more, I'll bring them over."

"Why? They didn't visit me in the hospital. I was disappointed. Especially during the last couple of days. No one came but my parents, you, and the cops."

"Robbo. They couldn't. There were police outside your room the whole time. No visitors other than your parents were allowed because of the situation. I know Carla, Dria, and Jimmy tried to see you but were turned away. Oh, and your parents are really nice. I like them. They were so worried about you."

I sighed and Carol helped me out of the car. She also helped me upstairs to her room.

"The sheets are clean, and you know where the bathroom is, right over there."

"Carol. I…"

"I can help you undress if you want. Then you can get in bed. If you're hungry, I'll bring up some takeout for us in a little while."

"Carol. Wait please. I need to tell you something. Something that happened just before I got shot. When you go to my room to get my stuff, you need to get a reel-to-reel tape I hid under my mattress and take it to the police station. You all need to listen to it. Also… I hope it's still there. I found a large bag of money in the locker in our recording studio. I hid it in the cabinet under the table saw in the workshop. That's about what's on the tape. It's Deke and Zeke talking about Cliff and the mafia. Whatever Cliff was up to, Zeke knew about it."

"Holy cow, Robbo. Yeah. I'll get the tape and take it in. Now. Let me take your clothes off for bed. I'll be gentle."

She was. She didn't remove everything. I still had on my boxer shorts and t-shirt partially cut out for my bad arm as I slipped under the covers. Carol put pillows behind me so I could sit up. She kissed me on the forehead and said she'd be right back.

By the time she returned, I was asleep.

Chapter 19

All You Need is Love

Robbie

Carol returned later with my suitcase, the tape, and the money bag I found in the locker. I woke up. Following her were Jimmy and Carla. Dria ran in a few minutes later.

Carla ran over and gave me a kiss on my forehead. "We were so worried about you. The police wouldn't let us see you in the hospital."

"Yeah. Jeez, Robbie." Jimmy said. "We were expecting the worst. The cop by your door wouldn't say how you were. No one would."

Dria did the same as Carla and kissed me on the forehead too.

Jimmy continued. "You might as well know, the band… our band is officially disbanded. Deke and his sour puss friend, Zeke, are always in the basement working on their own songs now. They wanted me to be their drummer. I said no. I don't like Zeke."

Carla agreed. "That guy treats Dria and me like servants. And Deke has changed too. He's acting like Marty was and trying to run things. He's also acting like Cliff, playing like he's the dictator of the commune now."

"Jeez!" I exclaimed. "I felt that Zeke guy was odd when I first met him." I wanted to say more about Deke and Zeke but held off. Carol and her officer friends first need to go over that tape.

Carol came over and put her hands on Carla's and Jimmy's shoulders. "Carla, Jimmy, I need to head back to the police station. Can you pick up some takeout from that Chinese restaurant on the other side of the college for Robbie? Don't walk there. I think driving the three blocks will be safer. Here. I'll give you some money. Get enough for the three of you, too. Dria, I'll leave Robbo in your capable hands."

Carla and Jimmy followed Carol downstairs. I heard Carol's car start up and drive away followed by the sound of Jimmy's old Datsun Bluebird pickup on the gravel driveway next door at the commune. Dria sat down on the side of the bed and held my good hand. I looked at her and could see tears beginning to drip from her eyes and run down her cheeks.

"Dria. Are you doing okay?"

"I miss Terry so much." She sniffed, sighed, looked at me, and then shrugged. "Yeah, Robbie, I know he played around all the time, and he was a little weird about wanting to see me with other girls, but he was my husband. You know I really wish we never left Texas. I liked it there. Cliff convinced Terry that coming here would be for the best. In fact, even though he complained the whole way here, it was him who demanded we all go. I don't even know why they were friends back there. Cliff's personality was as sour there as it was here. I didn't like him. I didn't like the hold he seemed to have on Terry."

"I'm so sorry, Dria. You know I really thought it was Terry who asked Cliff to come out here. With what you said, I guess it was the other way around. Anyway, I know Carol and the police are working hard to find out what happened."

"I kind of like Carol now. I didn't at first. Neither did Carla. We both thought her being in the band was a mistake. We were so jealous. Especially when all Terry could talk about over and over again was how pretty she was and what a good performer she is. He wanted **her.** Carla said Jimmy talked about her a lot too, but not like my Terry. Jimmy said he was impressed with her musicianship. I now know that she's a good person. And smart. I'm glad she's helping us. And, Robbie, I can tell she's falling in love with you."

I didn't know what to say to that. I just looked down and away kind of sheepishly.

Dria wiped her eyes and finally smiled. It was a Mona Lisa half smile, and I don't think she really focused it on me. Her mind seemed elsewhere. She then squeezed my hand. "You're in love with her too."

All I could say was "You can tell?"

Jimmy and Carla returned with two plastic bags full of Chinese takeout cartons. The mix of odors made my mouth water. I was hungry. Especially after a week of bland hospital food.

Jimmy brought up another chair for himself from downstairs and pulled over the desk chair for Carla. Dria sat on the side of the bed next to me.

Since I couldn't hold anything in my left hand, it was going to be hard to eat. Dria helped me. She held a container of chow Mein in front of me so I could use chopsticks with my right hand and eat. I'd take a few bites, then she would. We exchanged cartons and went through the motions again. It was a little hard for me. I should have asked for a fork.

Between the four of us, we ate it all. I just wished Carol had been here to enjoy it too.

Carla packed away the empty cartons in the bags they came in and Jimmy took it out to Carol's garbage can. He came back a few minutes later and said, "I passed that guy who lives downstairs… what's his name? Oh, yeah, Dennis. He was coming in as I was going out. He almost filled the garbage can with a lot of paper."

"He's another strange one," said Carla.

"Strange times," I said.

"Well, you old cripple." Jimmy joked. Carla poked him in fun. "We're going to head back next door and see what trouble those Dekezekers have gotten into. You get some rest. I can see your eyes are getting heavy… heavy… heavy." Jimmy raised his hands, wiggling his fingers in my face acting like he would put me into a trance. "Sleep… sleep." He started laughing. Carla and Dria joined in. "Hey, Robbie, we'll visit again tomorrow morning."

After they left, I glanced at the clock on the nightstand. It was after eight. I sat up in bed, swung my legs off the sides and walked slowly and carefully over to my suitcase. I opened the latch with a little difficulty, using my left leg as a counterweight to my usable right arm. I flipped open the top and pulled out my toothbrush and toothpaste and went into the bathroom. Damn. How do I put the toothpaste on with one hand. Okay. I stuck the handle of the toothbrush in my mouth, then put the toothpaste tube between my knees, unscrewed the cap setting it aside, then picking up the tube with my right hand, I squeezed a blob on the end of my toothbrush. Setting the tube down, I turned on the cold water, took the toothbrush handle out of my mouth, and began to brush my teeth. What a pain.

After rinsing my toothbrush, I set it in a glass next to Carol's. I smiled thinking this could be a regular thing. Keeping our toothbrushes together in the same glass.

At least being almost naked, using the facilities with one hand was no problem. I could see it could be a problem if I was dressed. I laughed to myself. Maybe I should become a nudist.

After washing my one hand (*one hand clapping*, I thought), I crawled back in bed. *Ow! That did hurt*! I gritted my teeth until the pain went away.

Yes, I was tired. I fell asleep right away.

I was awakened two hours later when I felt a warm body slip under the covers next to me.

"Oh, Robbo. I didn't want to wake you. We've both had a long, long day. Go back to sleep… lover." She reached over and gave me a lovingly soft moist kiss on my lips, her hand under the covers laying on my stomach. As much as I wanted more, I had turned a little toward her and my shoulder told me not to want any more. I winced. She removed her hand.

"Sleep Robbo." And she turned over and was soon asleep. I dropped back off to dreamland within minutes.

And dream I did.

God. What a dream. I was in a barracks in Korea with Marty and Deke. I walked out the barracks door and was then in the basement of the commune. Marty was breaking up the whole place. Guitars, my bass, drums. He was swinging an ax at everything. Then he had a knife and was chasing me around. Then disappeared. Now there was money lying all over the floor and everyone was yelling and picking it up. A gun was pointed at me. No one was holding it. It floated in the air. It went off.

Usually, I never remember what I dreamt about after waking up. But I woke up with a start just as the sun was rising.

"Robbie. Are you okay? Are you in pain?" Carol was facing me leaning on her elbow. She looked very concerned.

Thinking about the dream, I didn't think I hurt. But I did hurt.

"I'm sorry Carol. I'm sorry I woke you. It does hurt. I was having a really weird dream and it kind of scared me awake. Don't worry, I'll be okay."

106

I laid back down but knew I wouldn't be able to go to sleep again. Carol did drift off again. I looked at her and thought how lovely she looked even while sleeping. I said in a whisper, "I love you."

She moved and I thought I saw a smile on her face.

Chapter 20

I Want to Tell You

Robbie

I did fall asleep again, waking after Carol got out of bed. I looked at the clock. It was 9:00am.

I could hear her taking a shower. Last night I had noticed in her bathroom that it had an old clawfoot tub with a shower attachment rising from the old-style spigot. A circular shower rod was attached from the ceiling.

She came out a few minutes later with a towel wrapped around her. And, just like before, she came up to me and kissed me. This time her towel dropped off.

Drat. I wish I didn't hurt so much. But how could I look away. She was gorgeous.

Carol pulled her towel up around her again. "Oh Robbo. I wish I could stay here and take care of you all day…" She sighed. "But I have to go to work in an hour. Do you want to get up? You could really use a bath, but I know you can't get that cast and sling wet. Well. How about I give you a sponge bath like what you got in the hospital."

It was a sponge bath not like what I got in the hospital. Carol was still wrapped loosely in her towel. She helped me up and had me sit on a small teak bench. She then filled her bathroom sink with warm water, grabbed her natural bath sponge, soaked it, added a little soap, and began rubbing me all over. And I mean all over. We almost got distracted because I was getting a little aroused. As much as I was thinking about how I'd love to make love to her, I knew I had to abstain. I had to be strong. Anyway, sex would have been hell on my shoulder. Also, Carol had to be at work shortly. When she dried me off, we both sighed and she said, "You'd better get well quickly, lover."

She got dressed then helped me put on some clean clothes. She was able to put one of my flannel shirts on me and loosely fasten it with my cast and brace inside. It hurt, but she was incredibly gentle.

"Are you okay, Robbo?"

I had my eyes tightly closed. I opened them and looked up at her. "I… I will be. Can you bring me a glass of water for my pain pill before you leave?"

After I took my pill, I took a deep breath and asked her a question. "Did you get a chance to hear the tape?"

"Alan and I did, and it raised a lot of red flags. Burt and Alan have had run ins with local mafia types in town and would love to take them down, especially if they're involved in all of this. I'll be checking on this Zeke guy too. Any idea what his last name is?"

"I was told it was Mayfield. He and Deke were in high school together. Unfortunately, Deke now knows about the money that Cliff had. I wouldn't be surprised if they've been looking for it. Deke was never with Jimmy and the girls when they tried to see me in the hospital. And Deke hasn't made an effort to see me here either."

"That does sound strange, especially since Deke was trying to keep the band going after the deaths. At least until that Zeke showed up. Anyway, today, I'll be checking with the Austin police to see if they have anything on Terry. I'm going to try to find out more on Cliff too and see if there's anything linking the two of them together. Hey. That was pretty smart of you to catch their conversation on tape."

"Thanks. I was pretty nervous when I did it."

"Robbo, if you get stuck and Jimmy can't drive you to the doctor, call me. I'll take you. I should be at the station all day, so I could probably use a break this afternoon."

"Thank, Carol."

She gave me a long goodbye kiss that I hoped wouldn't end. She pulled away but kept one hand on my cheek.

"Oh, dear Robbo. I have to go. Dria should be here shortly with some breakfast for you. Keep resting up lover."

The days and nights for the next week were pretty much the same. Sometimes Dria brought me meals, sometimes Carla did. Jimmy usually came along with Carla. It was nice to have the company. Jimmy was able to take me to my first doctor's appointment where I painfully had my dressings changed. I would have a second doctor's appointment coming up in a few days to have my head stitches removed and to get my shoulder dressing changed again.

Nothing out of the ordinary happened for a couple of days. Then on the drive to my second appointment, I asked Jimmy, "What's been happening with the Deke 'n' Zeke team? I'm still surprised Deke hasn't visited me. After all, he and Marty and I went through a lot in Korea together. We... I thought we were friends."

"I don't know what those two have been up to. They say they're practicing, but they've also been tearing a few things apart. I think they're looking for something. I had to move my drums out of the basement. I was afraid they'd get dirty and messed up. I brought your bass up too and put it in your room this morning."

"Thanks, Jimmy. I appreciate that."

"But…"

"But?"

"But someone has been in your room. Your books and records were scattered on the floor, and your dresser drawers were open and in disarray. Even your bed was messed up. The mattress was moved. It's like someone was looking for something."

"Shit. It has to be that Zeke guy. After the doctor's through with me, can you drive me to the police station so I can tell Carol and those cop friends of hers?"

"Sure, if you're up to it."

"I have to be. This is important."

Carol hadn't told me about anything she has or has not found out about Cliff, Terry, or Zeke. She only told me that she and the police are still making inquiries. I got the feeling that means they're not making much progress.

Jimmy parked his old Datsun Bluebird pickup on the street and put a half dozen pennies in the parking meter. We got out and went into the police station.

At the front desk, I introduced myself and asked if Carol Legrand was available. He said he'd check. He pushed a button on his phone and asked whoever answered if Carol was there. Yes. "She'll be right down. Have a seat."

Jimmy and I sat down on a very uncomfortable straight-back wooden bench that faced the front desk.

We didn't have to wait long. I saw Carol come down the stairs behind the front desk. The desk sergeant pressed a button, and a partition gate buzzed. Carol opened it and walked up to us. We both stood up.

"Hello. What brings you to the police station? May I help you?" She was sounding official, then asked me quietly "Robbie, are you okay?"

"Yeah, I'm fine. Carol, we've got a problem at the commune. I'll let Jimmy tell you."

Jimmy related what he'd told me about the trashing of my room and the problems in the basement.

"Jeez, guys. Listen. Come on upstairs with me and we'll get an official statement. Robbo, are you okay to go upstairs?"

"Yeah, Carol. The damn wound itches like hell, but it's not hurting as much today. The doctor just said that I was healing well, and that I'm steady on my feet, so my head's okay."

The desk sergeant buzzed us in, and we followed Carol upstairs.

There were several desks in a large room, uniformed and plain clothes policemen and women manning electric typewriters. The noise from them and the loud talking was nearly deafening. Along one wall was a row of offices. Carol led us into the last one, a corner office with a window on each outside wall. No typewriter, but a lot of papers and notepads. Two phones were on her metal and Formica topped desk. Alongside her desk were three banker's boxes of case files.

She sat down behind her desk, and we sat down on the two chairs opposite her desk. She picked up her phone and pressed a button. She asked for Burt and Alan to come in. They walked in barely a minute later sliding in a couple of chairs to sit on. Burt had a note pad. Alan had a small tape recorder.

"Robbie, Jimmy, wait for Alan to turn the tape recorder on. Okay. First, state your names for the record."

We did.

"Now, go ahead and repeat what you told me."

Jimmy and I both told the story again. Jimmy was a little nervous in a room full of cops and when he stammered a little, I took over.

Alan turned off the recorder. "Thank you, Mr. Jones, Mr. Porter."

Burt patted Jimmy on the shoulder and chuckled. "You can relax now Mr. Porter." Then he said to both of us, "Alan and I will be over to check out Jones's room and the basement. We're pretty sure what is being looked for."

"Yeah. The money I found, I'm sure."

"Probably." Alan said. "You were smart to hide it so Carol could bring it in."

Carol said, "You'll have to come down here again to sign your statement once the recording has been transcribed. Probably tomorrow." Then to Burt and Alan, "Thanks guys. I'll walk them downstairs."

She not only walked us downstairs, but she led us out the door and to Jimmy's pickup. She gave me a kiss. "You sure you're okay, Robbo?" I said I was. "If you're up to it, can you go into the commune with Jimmy? Burt and Alan will be there very shortly. Robbo, could you check to see if anything is missing in your room. Okay?"

"I'll be fine, Carol. And I'll be careful."

It was a short drive back to the commune. Jimmy pulled into the driveway and parked behind the house. We both walked up the back steps, through the sunroom addition and into the kitchen. Carla and Dria sat at the table drinking tea. They jumped up when we came in. Carla hugged Jimmy. Dria hugged me, almost a little too hard.

We explained to them what was going on.

Carla had something to add. "Deke and that asshole Zeke had a huge argument a while ago in Deke's room. They were so loud, I'm sure the neighbors could hear it. Also, Zeke's still treating us like we're his personal maids. He's also tried to come on to both of us."

I could see anger building up on Jimmy's face. He's pretty strong from all his drumming and could be volatile when angered. I hope the cops get here quickly, or there might be another murder.

Saved by the bell. Or rather, door knocking. We heard someone say, "It's the police."

Jimmy and I both went to the front door and opened it. I invited Burt and Alan in and led them into my room.

I'd only heard from Jimmy what happened here, but I was not prepared for the extent. And the broken records. And, looking around, I saw my stereo was broken, as were my tape recorders. It was a lot of the stuff I purchased in Korea and brought back. Destroyed. The damage had to be intentional.

I angrily swore and kept swearing as I went from end to end, side to side in my room. Finally, hyperventilating, and exhausted, I sat on the edge of my bed and almost fell. The mattress had been pushed halfway off the bed, and the edge folded down where I sat. I caught myself, but it did hurt that time. Jimmy put my tipped over recliner upright, and I plopped down in it with a grunt.

Alan pulled out a small camera and took some photos.

Burt shook his head and tsk tsked. He was taking notes. "Such a mess. Mister Jones, is anything missing?"

"No. No. Just fucking destroyed," I angrily said. "Jeez. Look there. Someone even broke my recordings. My audio tapes. The reels are broken. The tape is unwound and crumpled. That's years of my work down the drain. Shit!"

I sat there fuming while Alan took more photos and Burt took more notes.

Finally, Alan asked me, "Are you up for going downstairs?"

"Yeah. I don't want to stay in here any longer. I don't want to be in this house any longer. Jimmy?"

Jimmy looked angrier than me.

"Jimmy. Let's go downstairs."

Jimmy and I led the officers down to the basement. Jimmy opened the door.

Music.

Deke and Zeke were practicing. Zeke was on the Farisa organ again, and Deke had his Strat on. They stopped when we all came in.

Zeke looked up. "What the fuck! Who the fuck are all these jerks? Can't you see we're fuckin' rehearsing here!" *Gee. He sounded like Cliff.*

That was enough to set Jimmy off. He stormed over to Zeke and actually lifted him off his chair and pushed him up against the wall and began pounding his face. Zeke was screaming for help.

Well, help came. Burt and Alan came over, not too quickly I might add, and separated Jimmy from Zeke, whose nose looked bent and bleeding. I was sure it was broken.

Jimmy was struggling to get loose from Alan's grip and was still trying to reach Zeke. Zeke plopped back down behind the organ dripping tears and blood all over the keys.

Deke was still holding his guitar and had a shocked look on his face.

Burt came over and stood in front of Deke. "You got a car? Yeah? Take your friend there to urgent care down Santa Clara Street at the medical center. Don't just sit there! Put that guitar down and go!"

Deke came over and put his arm around Zeke. He got up and they left, Zeke crying and dripping blood from his nose the whole way.

"Well, mister Porter. You're a strong one, aren't you."

"Uh…I have to be in order to play drums for hours on end." He said sheepishly. "Uh… sorry I blew up. I don't like that guy. I'm sure he's the one who messed up Robbie's room."

"We don't know that for sure. We're going to call in forensics to check for fingerprints. Now. Let's look around. Mister Jones, show us where you found that money."

I took them into the recording studio. I was surprised to see it had also been turned over. The three lockers were open, and the cords and microphones were on the floor. The Teac 4-track was tipped over as was the Revox 2-track. They didn't look broken. The mixing board was in worse shape. It had been pulled away from the wall and the back pulled off. It looked like wires were pulled out. At least the few tapes of the band were still intact, tapes when everyone was alive, and Cliff was recording rehearsals.

I wasn't mad now. I was sad. Then I got to thinking, Carol owns the house next door. Maybe we can move the still working parts of this recording studio over to her basement. I'll ask her. When I heal up a little better, I'll go through my room and see what I can salvage and bring that over too. I really want to get out of this house. I know Jimmy, Carla, and Dria would like to leave too.

"How about showing us the rest of this basement." Burt said, not as a question, but as a statement. In other words, get a move on.

Jimmy and I showed them the wood shop. Someone had moved things around, and the workbench drawers were all open, but nothing had been damaged.

It was a different story in my small art studio. The wall of samplings of several concert posters I made had been pulled off the walls and torn. My watercolors, colored pencils, pens and ink were all over the floor. One India Ink bottle was broken, a black pool drying on the floor. Alan took more photos.

Burt asked, "Are there any more rooms down here?"

"No, that's it."

"What about upstairs. You think there are any other rooms to check? What about the room that mister Clifton…"

"You mean Cliff?" I said.

"…that mister Clifton lived in."

"I'll show you. I don't think anyone's been in there since Cliff died. I don't think. Follow me."

We all went back upstairs, and I tried to open Cliff's door, but it was locked.

"Stand aside, mister Jones."

Alan raised his foot and kicked out. The door banged open, taking a large chunk of door frame with it.

"Hey! This door was padlocked from the inside!" Alan noted.

"Someone's been in here. Turned over like your room was, Jones." Burt commented. "But how? The windows are not open. There's no other door."

Cliff's sofa bed was open, and the mattress was on the floor. Cliff's worktable was tipped over, wires, small speakers, and soldering equipment were all scattered around the room.

"Okay, Alan, go out to our car and radio in for forensics to hurry down here. Jones, don't touch anything."

"I'm not. Are you through with me for now? My shoulder's hurting again. I need to go back next door and take one of my pain pills."

"Yeah, Jones, go ahead." Burt said. "You don't want to get in the way of the forensics team."

I was about to head out and glanced at the side window. "Uh… officer, that window isn't latched."

"Ah. I didn't notice that. I'm sure forensics would have seen it. Thanks. Go take care of your pain."

I headed out the front door just as Alan came back in. He asked where I was going, and I repeated what I told Burt. He told me to take it easy and get some rest.

While waiting for the pain pill to start working, I sat in Carol's easy chair reading one of the books she brought over from my room before it was destroyed. It was kind of hard holding it on my lap and turning pages with one hand. I nearly dropped the book several times.

I heard a van and car pull up in the commune's driveway, and the loud yelling back and forth of the forensics team. I was curious if they found any fingerprints other than mine or Carol's. Ah, if it was Zeke, he probably wore gloves.

Then I heard Carol's voice. She must have followed the forensics team. I was sure she was at the house talking to Burt and Alan.

Since I was having a hard time holding and reading a hard-bound book, I set it aside and got up to turn on Carol's small color television. I flipped through the channels and settled on a mid-day news program on channel eleven, a local San José station.

There were newscasts on Nixon, Apollo 11, a small airplane's accidental landing on the roof of a shopping mall, a stock report, and baseball scores. If there was any news on the band deaths, I either missed it or it's old news now.

I got up and changed the channels to the UHF band and to channel 36, a local independent station that showed old sitcoms. I came in the middle of an old *I Love Lucy* episode.

Nah. I turned the TV off.

Carol came in just as I sat back down and picked up the book again.

"Hi, lover. Burt said you were hurting and came back here. Are you okay?"

"Doing better. The pill's finally taking effect. Been trying to read, but not having much luck at it."

"You can watch TV if you want."

"I did for a bit. Watched the news. Nothing at all about the… murders."

"We're keeping the news reporters at bay for a while. At least until we get some results."

"Are you? Are you getting any results yet?"

"Some. We did find a connection between Cliff and Terry that went back a year before Cliff's Austin, Texas, recording studio. They knew each other in New York."

"Really? How'd you find that out?"

"I only found that by accident. I was tasked to call Terry's father with the bad news. He took it hard. Also, when I mentioned Dria to him, he didn't know her or that Terry was married. Then he started reminiscing. He told me he lives in Queens by himself, and that Terry's mother passed away ten years ago. Anyway, he told me Terry had been playing piano at a private club in Brooklyn several years ago. He couldn't remember the name of the club but knew it was on Atlantic Avenue. I called a Brooklyn precinct to see if they knew of it. They did. It was known as the Sanctuary, a private members-only club owned by a local mafia."

"Did you find out who owned it?"

"Oh yeah. A local crime boss named Bernardo Clifton."

"Christ! Clifton? Related to Cliff? Reinhold Clifton?"

"Yep. Bernardo was Cliff and Tommy's father. Different mothers. I'm sure Cliff was around at that club too. It had to be where Terry met him."

"So those two had some kind of mafia connection. But… what about Marty? I've known him for a year and a half. Deke too. Was Marty connected too?"

"That we haven't figured out yet. Say, listen, lover. I have to head back next door to check on the progress and then go back to work. God. I miss singing and playing. Robbo, when this is over and you're all healed, let's do some music together. Maybe Jimmy will want to keep playing too."

"I'd love that. Yeah, Jimmy has turned out to be a much better friend than Deke or Marty. I hope Jimmy and Carla stick around."

"Are they thinking of moving away?"

"They, and Dria, were talking about it. I just think they want to leave that house. Bad memories."

"I feel bad for them. But… Robbo, I do have to leave. Can I get you anything before I go? No? Well, there's sodas and bottled water in that little fridge over there and also some cheese if you get hungry."

"You're too good to me."

"Robbo…" Carol reached over and gave me one of her wonderful kisses. "Because… I… I love you."

I felt tears forming in my eyes. That's the first time she said that to me. I reached out with my good hand and put my hand on her face. "I… I feel like I've always loved you."

A tear trickled down her cheek on to my hand.

"My lover, I hate to leave you again. I so hate it."

She pulled away and reluctantly left the room.

Chapter 21

Come Together

Robbie

Jimmy, Carla, and Dria came by at six with some dinner. I had been in the easy chair watching the evening news and got up to turn the TV off. I never liked eating dinner and watching television at the same time as my parents always did when I was little, which they still do.

They brought takeout again, but this time it was burgers and fries from the Burger Barn, another favorite inexpensive college eatery. They also picked up an assortment of sodas from a convenience store close to the Burger Barn. I picked one of the Royal Crown Cola bottles. Jimmy and Carla took the grape Nehi sodas. Dria had water. I stayed in the easy chair, the rest sat on the floor in front of me. The burger was a little overcooked but tasted okay.

We sat around talking and not saying anything about what has been happening. We needed the break. I really liked having these three around.

But I was curious about something and had to ask Jimmy, "What have Deke and Zeke been up to lately? Are they still playing together as a duo?"

"They've been upstairs in Deke's room practicing," he replied. "Folk music. Can you believe it? They're playing acoustic guitars and singing harmonies to old-time folk songs. Maybe one or two originals. Funny, though. I was just heading out the front door when Zeke was coming up the front steps. When he saw me, he backed away and went up the driveway instead. I think he came in the back door and up the back stairway. His nose had a big bandage on it. His eyes were black too."

"Well, maybe he'll be a little nicer to the girls now. Or totally leave them alone."

They spent about an hour with me, then prepared to leave. Jimmy gently shook my hand, both girls gave me a light hug and pecks on the cheek, picked up their purses, and left to go back next door.

By ten I was able to undress myself and get into bed. I was tired and immediately dozed off, only to be awakened when Carol slipped in beside me. I didn't even hear her come in.

"I'm so sorry to wake you. You looked so peaceful."

I yawned. "That's okay. Love, you sound tired."

"I am. These long days wear me out. I'm not used to that."

"I wish I were able to get around and do enough to wear myself out."

"Let me help."

What she did made me forget about my wounds. For being our first time, she was extremely slow and gentle with me.

With both of us sexually sated, we quickly fell asleep.

Eight hours later, when I awoke, Carol had already risen, taken a shower, and dressed for work. She noticed I was awake.

"Good morning my wonderful lover. How are you this fine morning?"

Carol was in a good mood.

"Ah, gee. I feel pretty good. Usually when I wake up my shoulder hurts. Not today. Carol, you have healing powers." I chuckled.

"Here's another power I have."

She gave me a kiss and slid her hand under the covers and held me. I immediately responded.

"See? Now you'll be thinking of me all day, right?"

"How can I not."

She gave me another kiss.

"I love you so much. I'll try to come home earlier tonight."

"I love you too. Please don't work too hard, but don't worry if you need to work late. I'll be okay."

The next three days were pretty much repeats. Meals with Jimmy, Carla, and Dria, making love after Carol got home, and sleeping.

That changed the next day.

Chapter 22

It's Not Easy

Robbie

I was getting cabin fever and wanted to get out of the house. I thought I'd go back to the commune and see what I could salvage in my room.

When I walked in, I got depressed again seeing the damage. Now, a lot of the stuff had dark fingerprint dust all over it. I'd heard from Carol that no fingerprints other than mine were in there. Same in Cliff's room and in the basement. Nothing unusual. Yeah. Whoever made these messes had to have worn gloves.

With my one good hand I started picking through my records still scattered on the floor. The broken ones I tossed in my waste basket. I saved the record covers hoping to replace them someday, at least the ones I really liked.

I did find some records that weren't broken and some that had a few scratches on them. I'd hold on to those. If the scratches were too embedded and would make the records skip, I'd toss them. Of course, I'd have to get a new stereo and record player first. Mine was in pieces. Someone even unscrewed the cover on my old stereo receiver and pulled wires out. I have no idea why anybody would do that. Just like the mixing board in the studio. Cliff could have fixed both of these if he was still around. Instead, I strained to pick it up with one hand and take it out the back door where I set it down to open the garbage can lid then tossed it in. I did the same with the broken record player. My good arm was getting tired by the time I emptied my waste basket full of broken records in the trash. The big, galvanized garbage can was filling up.

If I had two hands, I could have finished cleaning my room in an hour. Instead, three hours later I had put the clothes that had been taken out of my closet and tossed around on the floor into my laundry hamper. My old leather flight jacket, I took out back and shook the dust out of it. Another hard thing to do with one hand. I hung it back in my closet.

I pushed my mattress back in place on my bed after taking off the blanket and sheets. They needed cleaning too.

The commune didn't have a clothes washer. The girls had been taking theirs and some of the band's clothes to a laundromat a few blocks away on San Fernando Street. Certain times of the day students filled the laundromat and commandeered all the washers and dryers. Carla and Dria got there early in the morning long before the student rush. I could ask them to do my laundry, and I would pay them.

Someone who seemed to never have his clothes washed was Deke. There were times when we practiced that I could smell the mildewy scent of sweaty well-worn clothes. Also, I think he took a shower maybe once a week, if that. One time the girls got fed up with it and snuck all the clothes he piled up in his closet floor and took them to the laundromat. Deke seemed annoyed that they did it.

The room looked better, but fingerprint dust was still sprinkled around on the windowsills and floor. I was too tired to clean it up.

When I left my bedroom, I headed to the basement to see if any of the tapes Cliff made of our band were salvageable. They were the only record of the songs our original group played.

As I went in, I looked through the studio window into the rehearsal space and saw both Deke and Zeke in there rehearsing again. They both had on acoustic guitars. No electrics. Deke was playing a jumbo Epiphone 12-string that I was sure had belonged to Marty. *Why hadn't he sent it back to Marty's parents.*

Zeke was playing a very expensive Martin dreadnought. With all the abalone and mother of pearl inlay, it must have been a D-45. *How the hell could he afford such a guitar?*

They stopped playing when they saw me. I came out of the studio and went into the rehearsal room.

"Hi guys." I thought I'd act really friendly. "How's the rehearsals going?"

Zeke looked at me askance. He looked angry, like I was the one who pounded him. Deke answered.

"Hi Robbie. Going fine. How's your arm?"

"It's my shoulder. It's healing slowly, but it is healing."

"Have they found out yet who shot you?"

"Not yet, but I understand they have some leads. Carol can't say too much about it yet."

Zeke finally said something. "So, what are you doing here in the studio?"

Why does he want to know?

I directed my answer to Deke. "I wanted to see if any of those damaged tapes could be salvaged. You know, Deke, those are the only record of our old band's songs. I think the Revox might still work, so

I was going to try to rewind what I can. Probably not today, though. Too hard with one hand."

I could see Zeke was getting antsy. "Come on Deke. Let's get back to rehearsing. See you! Don't let the door hit you on the butt when you leave!"

Zeke was definitely running this show. His 'see you' comment was said with emphasis. I was being shooed out.

To be told what to do by someone I did not like made me just stand there. *I'll leave on my own accord.*

"Well, Deke. Have a nice rehearsal. Say, Zeke. That's quite a nice guitar you have there."

He just stared at me and said nothing.

"Have a nice day… guys." I half smiled at Zeke, gave a sort of friendly wave, then left.

I went back next door to Carol's room to find her coming out of the bathroom. She greeted me.

"Lover. When I came home on break and you weren't here, I was worried. Are you okay?"

"I'm fine." I smiled at her. She came over and gave me a kiss. "I had cabin fever, so I went next door to start cleaning up my room. I was trying to salvage what I could. Filled up my laundry hamper too."

"I can bring it over here if you want. There's a laundry room downstairs behind the kitchen. There's a nice washer and dryer there."

"Thank you. That would be great. I was going to ask Carla and Dria to help me by taking my stuff to the laundromat. Say, I just thought of something."

"What's that lover?"

"I didn't see Jimmy or the girls in the house. Well, maybe they were upstairs in their rooms."

"What about Deke? Did you see him?"

"Oh yeah. I did. He and that sourpuss Zeke were practicing old folk music. Zeke is running the show there now. Oh, and also his guitar is a very expensive brand-new Martin. The last time I saw one like that in a music store, it cost over $3000."

"Did Deke have a new guitar too?"

"No. In fact he was playing Marty's old beat-up Epiphone 12-string."

"Hmm. Interesting."

"What? What?"

"We finally found out something about Zeke. I can't say much right now, but I can say his last name is not Mayfield. I'll tell you about it when I find out more. Anyway, lover, I need to get back to work."

Carol put her hands on my face and planted a long, long kiss on my lips. I felt her tongue slip into my mouth. She reluctantly pulled away.

"Oh, Robbo. My dear Robbo. I'll try to get home earlier tonight. God, how I want this to be over."

"You and me both."

She reluctantly removed her hands from my face, turned and left.

128

Chapter 23

Paint It Black

Robbie

Jimmy and Carla came over soon after Carol left. Jimmy was carrying a large pizza container.

"Feel like some pizza Robbie?"

I was really hungry. I had been just about to get some cheese out of Carol's little fridge. Pizza was a much better idea.

"Oh yeah. I haven't had pizza in ages."

Carla said, "We didn't bring any drinks. I could get some water for you."

"Nah. Look in that little fridge. There're some sodas in there, or there's a couple of cans of beer too if you want. Yeah, hand me one of those Coors. How about you?"

Jimmy said, "I'd like one, but do you think you should have alcohol while you're taking pain pills?"

"Drat. You're right. I don't need that kind of buzz. Hand me an orange soda."

Carla said she'd have an orange soda too.

The three of us sat on the floor and dug in. The large pizza had everything on it. Sausage. Pepperoni. Olives. Onion. Green peppers. I asked if there were anchovies in it, but Jimmy said he couldn't stand them. There were three different cheeses and a very flavorful and garlicy sauce. *Yum!*

I had to ask. "Where's Dria?"

Carla answered. "She's not feeling well, so she's in her room. She's depressed and thinking about Terry. She wants to arrange a funeral for him. I'll help her if she'll let me so we can all go. Also, I don't think she's eaten anything today either. I'm going to take her a piece of pizza when we go back next door and try to cheer her up."

"I hope so," I said.

Jimmy said, "I'm sure she'll be okay. Like they say, time heals all wounds. Or is that wounds all heels? Speaking of which, how's the wounds?" Jimmy asked, pointing at my shoulder.

"Still healing but taking too much time. By the way, can you take me to my doctor again tomorrow morning at eleven?"

"You already asked me, but sure. Glad to."

We ate, drank, and talked for another forty-five minutes. Two pieces of pizza and the soda filled me up. There were two pieces remaining in the box when they left. I told them I hoped Dria would eat it and feel better.

Having drunk the soda, I had to head to the bathroom. While in there, I decided I should brush my teeth, so Carol wouldn't be offended by my pizza, onion, and garlic breath.

I sat back in the easy chair and tried to read for a while. I wasn't in the mood. So, I got my spiral notebook and jotted some notes for songs. I hadn't finished any new songs for a while. I was also thinking that when I was healed, Carol and I could start a new group. I also wondered if Jimmy would play with us. I hoped so.

I must have been writing for an hour when my eyes got heavy, and I drifted off. I fell asleep in the chair. Or so I thought.

Carol did come home early. It was fortunate she did. When she came into the room and began coughing, she knew right away something was wrong. She threw open both her windows, opened her door wide, and turned off the gas to her small gas heater, a heater she never used because the pilot light didn't work. Someone had turned it on.

Carol ran over to me. I was still out, and she felt my neck to make sure my pulse was still throbbing. It was. She gave me mouth to mouth resuscitation. I awoke right away and thought she was just kissing me.

"Robbie! Robbie! What happened? Are you okay?"

I coughed. "I just fell asleep, love. I'm okay."

"Robbie. The gas was turned on. Someone was in here and turned it on. Crap! I've always meant to take that heater out. It has never worked right."

"I didn't smell gas when I dozed off earlier. I… I do smell it now."

"How long ago did you fall asleep? Do you know?"

"I'm not sure. Let's see. Jimmy and Carla left here around seven. I tried reading, maybe only ten minutes, then for maybe a half hour I was trying to write some poetry for songs. I got drowsy. Maybe because of my pain pills. I put down my notebook, right there, and… Crap. It's not there. Did I drop it?"

"No. It's not on the floor. It's not on the other side of the bed or under it. Why would someone sneak in and attempt to kill you and take your notebook? It doesn't add up."

"It doesn't. Jeez. I had a lot of material in that notebook. It had all the songs I wrote in Korea and here with the band. I even had some journal writing in there. My notes on happenings in both houses."

"Maybe… maybe it's your journal notes someone is after. Deke? Zeke?"

"I can't see Deke doing anything like this. He sometimes talks like he's a tough guy, but he's pretty much a lazy coward. He was like that in Korea, and he's been like that here. Marty used to call him a wimp behind his back. And now Zeke is being real bossy to him. You think he snuck in here? Some kind of revenge thing? He sure didn't like me being in the basement while the two of them practiced."

"I'm going to have to call Burt. Get him and Alan here to check this out. Ah. Forensics too. See if there are fingerprints on the heater key… other than mine. Yeah, lover, I'm afraid we'll have to postpone tonight's… bedtime… at least for a while. Here. Let me give you a little more mouth to mouth."

Oh, so nice. So warm. So… Damn. She got up and went to the phone and dialed Burt's number.

It took only fifteen minutes for Burt and Alan to arrive, with Rhys, the forensic scientist tagging along behind them. Carol showed him the heater and he opened his case and went right to work.

Before Carol and the cops started talking, Burt came over to me and actually shook my hand.

"How are you doing, Mr. Jones?"

"I'm doing okay. You know, you can call me Rob if you want."

"Okay, Rob. I'm glad you're okay. This is the second close call for you." He shook my hand again and went over to Carol and Alan, who had started discussing what happened. Alan, this time, was taking notes.

It only took Rhys a few minutes to dust for fingerprints on the heater key and the doorknob. He got a couple of impressions and took some photos.

As Rhys packed up, he said, "I was able to get a couple of latent finger and thumb prints. Keep your fingers crossed that I'll find prints other than yours, Miss Legrand."

"I hope so." She turned back to Burt and Alan. "I'm going to see about getting rid of that old heater tomorrow. That's got to be over fifty years old."

"Yeah. You should have a new one installed. There are newer heaters that are extremely safe these days."

"I'll call a heating and air conditioning company and see about switching it out. For now, I just want to call to get this gas line capped off."

Carol accompanied Burt and Alan out and came back a few minutes later. It was nearly midnight. The gas was completely cleared out, so Carol closed the windows. It was a chilly late summer night. Fall was waiting in the wings. She pulled an extra blanket out of her dresser's bottom drawer and put it on the bed.

"Come on, lover. Let me help you get your clothes off. Oh, I wish you had two hands and could help me undress."

Problem was, it was late and both of us were very tired. We hugged a little, but that was it. We fell asleep right away.

Morning came too fast. But morning came with a surprise.

I woke up with a hand on me. Down in the nether regions. It made me forget about my taped up left arm and shoulder wound. Before I knew it, I was looking up at the beautiful face of the woman I'd come to love. She'd crawled over on top of me and leaned down to kiss me and continued to kiss me until we both came at the same time.

She put her arm across my chest and whispered in my ear. "Good morning, lover. Are you awake now? You must be. You were… uh, up early."

We laughed in giddy exhaustion and held on to each other for several more minutes. Then we both got very serious thinking about the gas incident last night.

Carol then looked over at the clock and realized it was getting late. "I'm so sorry, lover. I do have to get up and get ready for work. Before I take a shower, let me give you another of my famous sponge baths. Come. Get up and come sit in the tub. I'll put a little hot water in it."

Over the last week, I'd gotten to love Carol's style of sponge baths. Sometimes she'd get too carried away, and we'd have to change the water to rinse me off again, but this time, since she was late, she didn't get carried away. She dried me off and helped me get dressed, then she went in and took her shower.

Twenty minutes later, she was dried off and dressed for work. Before she left, she made a phone call. She asked for a patrol car to come park in front of her house and report on any odd occurrences. Carol told me Burt suggested it after last night's attempt on my life again.

She came over to kiss me once more before she left.

"Carol, Jimmy's going to drive me to the doctor this morning. I have an appointment at eleven. We might pick up Carla and Dria, if they're up to it, and go out for lunch somewhere. I know they've been uncomfortable in the commune with just Deke there and Zeke always showing up there all day and into the night."

"Lover, be careful out there. Be really aware. Is the doctor going to change your dressing again?"

"I think so. I'll probably be getting another X-ray to check on the bone healing too.

"Again, lover, be careful. I love you, my sweet Robbo."

"I really love you too. Please, please, you be careful out there, too."

Chapter 24

Manic Depression

Robbie

The next week was mostly uneventful except for the wonderful bedtimes with Carol. However, because of the number of leads, she had had to get up earlier. After cleaning up she would run to get a quick breakfast for us from the convenience store a short walk from her house. She'd always bring back coffee for both of us. We'd eat together and talk until she took off to the police station a little before nine in the morning.

Jimmy had driven me to another clinic appointment the previous week, and from the X-ray my doctor told me my bone was healing much better. When he changed my dressing, he also said the bullet wound was healed enough, so he removed the stitches. They'd been in for a while and hurt when he cut and pulled them out. I was wearing the restraining sling until my bone, my clavicle, healed more.

After the gas issue, there was a constant police presence in front of the house. I'm sure that kept both houses safe from break ins and/or more attempts on my life and maybe the lives of those next door.

Carol had been working a lot, putting in eight-to-ten-hour days, six days a week. She was getting very tired all of that time working and not being able to play or sing or be with me. Each day it showed a little more.

It was Friday, and when Carol left for work, she was especially unhappy. She told me about the day before that she and her police buddies again hit a brick wall. They were putting an effort into finding a mob informant who might have info on someone who might be the shooter, but he seemed to have disappeared. They expected the worst, but hoped he was just in hiding.

Jimmy came over by himself at five carrying a bag from a local taqueria. I sat on the bed and let Jimmy sit in the easy chair.

Before we started eating, I asked him, "So, where's Carla and Dria?"

"Oh, Dria is still having a hard time, so Carla's taking care of her."

"I'm sorry to hear that. I hope she'll be okay soon."

"So do I. She was talking suicide."

"Suicide? Jeez. I hope not. I know she's sad a lot, but she's a sweet girl."

We started eating and didn't say much. Jimmy looked deep in thought.

After eating and sipping on our colas, Jimmy dropped the bomb.

"Look, Robbie, Carla and I have to move. Probably a cheap apartment somewhere. We haven't started looking yet. We're going to take Dria with us. With just us in the house along with only Deke there, we can't afford the rent anymore. Deke says he's going to do something to keep the house, but we can't trust him. He doesn't even wash his clothes, and Carla refuses to help him out. She won't even

136

cook dinners for him anymore, and I don't know what he eats. Also, that jerk Zeke is still hanging around. He keeps bringing in new instruments and sound equipment. Expensive stuff. I know he's planning for him and Deke to start playing 'professionally' at some place across from the old El Rancho Drive In movie theater. Deke told me it's called the Tahitian Gardens, and that Zeke's uncle owns it."

"Wow. Hmm. I wonder if Zeke is wealthy. Maybe that's what Deke meant about keeping the house. Zeke might pay the rent. Or even try to buy it."

"Another reason to leave. Zeke and I don't get along. Especially since I broke his nose. If he's going to be paying rent, I'm sure he'd kick us out."

"I hope you and the girls don't move too far away. I'd miss you."

Jimmy wanted to get back next door with Carla to make sure Dria was okay. He gave me a light hug and headed out.

I got up and went to the front window just in time to see the changing of the guard. Another police car drove up and exchanged places with the one just leaving. I also saw Carol's car drive up. Thank the gods she was getting home early.

Within five minutes, she came in and gave me a nice hello kiss.

"Am I glad to see you, sweet Robbo. I'll be back in a few minutes. I need to use the bathroom."

She kissed my cheek then headed into the bathroom.

She was in there for nearly five minutes. When she came out, she had taken off her pants suit and hung up the jacket and pants in the closet. She slipped out of her white turtleneck and dropped it in the hamper.

Even though we've lived together now for several weeks, seeing her standing there in front of her closet in a white bra and panties, which I've seen several times now, still looked exciting to me. More stirrings.

She put on a pair of loose-fitting jeans and slipped on an old tie-dye t-shirt. She then came over and plopped down in her easy chair.

I was concerned. "You look tired, love. Were you able to get some dinner?"

"Yeah, Alan brought in some mac and cheese his wife made. Not bad. And, yeah, I am tired. It was a busy day. We drove all over the county."

"Really? Can you tell me why?"

"Sure. We got leads on where our mafia informer was. Too many leads. We were put on a wild goose chase. We made it all the way south to the back roads behind Morgan Hill. Pretty country, but no luck finding him. So, lover, anything interesting happen to you today?"

"Not really. Jimmy came over after five and brought some food from the taqueria. Carla stayed next door with Dria. Seems her depression got bad, and she was talking suicide."

"Oh, that poor girl. She's been through a lot. A husband who played around then got killed. Now she has to come up with money for a funeral. I'll ask her if I can help. And, then there's Marty dying. Cliff too. It's like that house is cursed."

"And then that Zeke guy showed up. Jimmy told me the guy has been bringing in all brand-new expensive equipment. Deke told Jimmy that he and Zeke are going to be playing at some club on the edge of town. He said it was across the street from the El Rancho Drive-in."

"Tahitian Gardens? That's the only business there. Everything else around there is warehouses and lumber yards."

"Yeah. That's the name Jimmy mentioned."

"That was one of our leads we got from the FBI today. It was late when we got back, and we didn't get over there. Maybe tomorrow."

"Oh, and Deke told Jimmy that Zeke's uncle owned the place."

"Now we'll have to go there tomorrow. That connection is too coincidental. Oh drat, I don't want to think about that now. I'm still a little wired from work. Would you like to take a walk with me?"

"I'd love to. I'd love to get out. Where would you like to go?"

"Let's go downtown. We can come back through the college campus."

I slipped on my loafers and Carol laced up her ankle-high hiking boots. The thick waffle soles added another inch to Carol's six-foot height. That put her a full two inches taller than me. I didn't care. She was a statuesque beauty with whom I loved to be seen with.

We headed out the front door. Carol told me to wait a second. She wanted to let the cop guard know we were going out and to take notice if anyone out of the ordinary went into either of the houses. He said two guys came out of the commune with guitar cases and drove away together. Obviously, Deke and Zeke. He also said only Dennis came out of my house and was walking toward the college.

We then headed down the street to San Fernando, where we turned right and headed off toward First Street.

A few of the stores on First Street were still open, still operating on Summer hours. The sun was out but lowering in the Western sky. We were casually walking along window shopping when we came to Sherman Clay. Since the music store was still open, we went in. The main showroom was large and had a couple of grand pianos: a baby grand and a larger concert grand in the middle. Alongside of those was a row of upright pianos. What interested us, though, were the guitars and amplifiers along one wall in the back of the store. Carol looked at a newer version of her father's J-145 acoustic electric while I was drooling over a nice Fender precision bass with an all-maple neck hanging on the wall, cream colored with a black pickguard.

Carol called me over.

"Take a look at this. It's a three-quarter-sized standup bass. Look here. It has a pickup attached to the bridge. Have you ever thought of playing one of these? Jazz bass?"

"I hadn't thought about that before, but that would be cool to use and accompany an acoustic guitar. Jazz, folk, progressive rock even."

A middle-aged salesman in a dark blue and slightly wrinkled suit came over. I thought he was going to try to talk us into buying something. Instead, he spoke to us rather curtly. "We're closing in five minutes. You have to leave. We open at ten tomorrow." He walked away.

"Well." Carol said. "That was rude. He sure doesn't want our business. There are other music stores around town. Let's get out of here."

A half block later, we were in front of the Woolworths store. It was also still open, and a couple of people sat at the old-style lunch counter. We went in and sat down too. A cheerful older woman in a white outfit and apron came up to us.

"Welcome. Coffee? Or something else to drink? The kitchen is closed, but I have coffee, sodas, and ice cream. I can whip up a milk shake too. We have a half hour before I have to shut down the counter."

Carol ordered. "I'd like a root beer float. That would be nice on this warm evening. Robbo?"

I asked the waitress, "Can you make a chocolate egg cream?"

"Simple. Okay. One root beer float. One chocolate egg cream. Coming up."

"Robbo. What's a chocolate egg cream?"

"I had one when I was back east visiting relatives with my parents. It was tasty. It doesn't have eggs or cream in it. It's just seltzer water, milk, and chocolate syrup. I'll give you a taste."

The waitress served us within five minutes. She did the egg cream well. Cool and refreshing. Carol expressed surprise at how good it was. She gave me a taste of her float. It was also good.

We finished our drinks just as the waitress was starting to close the counter. Carol left her a two-dollar tip, a big tip for a four-dollar tab.

The sun was setting, so we walked south to San Carlos Street and headed to the college. We walked across the campus in front of the old Morris Dailey Auditorium. We were quiet, both thinking about Cliff being found here. I thought I saw Dennis and mentioned it to Carol. When she looked, there was no one there.

A few minutes later, we were on Sixth Street.

Part 2

Bad Company

Chapter 25

You Keep Me Hanging On

Carol

We expected to just go home and cuddle up in bed, but the flashing red lights in front of the commune meant that would have to wait.

Two police cars, a paramedic fire truck, and an ambulance were in front of the commune. A gurney with a body strapped down was being carefully rolled up the driveway by two firemen and two ambulance techs.

"Christ, Carol! It's Jimmy!" Robbie yelled.

I ran up to one of the policemen, who started to shoo me away until I pulled a badge out of my pocket and showed it to him. He pointed up the steps. I bounded up the front steps two at a time.

In the living room were Carla, and Dria. Both girls were crying. Burt was there, but not Alan. A uniformed cop stood by the kitchen door with his arms crossed. I remember him being the one I talked to when we left for our walk. I rushed up to Burt.

"Burt! What the hell happened to Jimmy?"

"He was attacked in the back. He was getting groceries out of his pickup, and someone jumped him. They must have come over the fence from Fifth Street. His wife was just coming out of the house to help with the groceries and saw it happen."

"Did she see the attacker? Did the policeman out front see anything?"

"She saw him, but he had a ski mask covering his face. She said he looked like a big skinny guy and had a metal rod. She thinks she saw a knife too. He was all in black. He ran when Missus Porter came out and screamed. And officer Cruz here only heard the scream and ran up the driveway to find Mister Porter on the ground."

"But how is Jimmy?"

"He'll be okay. He got hit on the head pretty hard, and he might have a broken rib or two."

"Jeez, Burt, why have these guys been targeted? We're not having much luck with our investigations lately. The only ones who haven't been attacked are Deke and the girls." I directed my next question to Robbie. "By the way, where is Deke? I would think he'd be in here with the girls."

I looked around and saw that Deke was a no show. Besides Robbie, Burt, and the uniformed officer, there were just Carla and Dria sitting on the couch.

Robbie asked Burt if it was okay for the two of us to go down to the basement to see if Deke was there. The officer Cruz started to object, but Burt said to go ahead.

I led Robbie down to the basement. Nothing. No Deke. No Zeke. We wondered if they might have gone somewhere together. We went back upstairs, then up to the second floor to see if Deke might be in his room. I knocked at his bedroom door.

No answer. It was unlocked, so I opened the door and looked around.

"Geez! What a mess!" Robbie exclaimed.

Deke never cleaned his room, nor did he ever make his bed, a twin-sized mattress on the floor. His dirty clothes were scattered next to his bed, making the room smell musty as usual. Another smell almost turned my stomach. Something rotting. I cautiously followed the smell hoping it wasn't a dead rat or something else. I was relieved to find it was only containers of food. They were mostly encased in mold.

"What a slob." I was thinking how I was glad I didn't work with him anymore, then felt bad because of the reasons. Dead reasons.

We went back downstairs to the living room and Robbie sat down with Carla and Dria. Dria had her arm around the crying Carla trying to soothe her.

Burt and I went into the kitchen to talk more privately. "Burt, Deke's not here."

Robbie came in. "Listen. Deke and Zeke have been hanging out and practicing at that Tahitian club across from the El Rancho Theater. They might be there now."

"Tahitian Gardens!" Exclaimed Burt. "That place has been on our watch list for years. Alan and I think that some police and FBI palms keep getting greased, so our investigations keep getting stalled."

"Mafia?" I asked.

"Yeah, but Russian. There's also an Italian mafia in town. The two have been at war with each other for control of San José for quite a while."

"Uh…" Robbie cut in. "Remember that tape I recorded of Deke and Zeke's conversation? Zeke said his uncle owns that place."

"Not good. That could explain some of the attacks. You might have gotten in the middle of the mafia war somehow."

Just then the wall phone in the foyer rang. Since Robbie was the only remaining band member… uh, ex-band member around, he answered it.

"Hello?"

"Who is this?" We could hear the caller shouting over the phone from the other room.

"I beg your pardon, first, who are you?" Robbie said, holding the phone a little away from his ear.

The caller still spoke loudly. "I'm mister Sordi, the owner of that building, dammit! Who the hell are you?"

"This is Robbie Jones. Now, what do you want, mister Sordi?" He started shouting like the caller. Burt and I heard Robbie's reply and came in to see what was going on.

"I'm your landlord! Dammit! You and any kids living in that house are in arrears! No rent has been paid for two months. If not paid in full in fifteen days, I will have you evicted. You hear? Fifteen days!"

We heard him slam his phone down. Robbie looked mad and acted like he was ready to slam his phone too but stopped mid slam, took a deep breath, then gently hung up the phone.

Burt asked. "Did I hear that right? Sordi?"

"Yeah. He said he's our landlord. This is the first time he's ever called us. In the past we always got reminder calls from an agency, who would call only if we were a day or two late."

"Which agency?" Burt asked.

"The Dominico Agency. We would send them our rent checks to their address on Almaden."

Burt turned to me. "That's another place on the FBI watch list. This Albert Sordi is a suspected Italian mafia boss. That agency is barely a half mile from the Tahitian Gardens."

I asked, "So, who owns the Tahitian place? You said that Zeke's last name is Kelly, not Mayfield. That doesn't sound Russian."

"Kelly is the name the owner goes by too." Burt replied. In one of the few files we got from the local FBI, the owner's real last name is Kozar. Artim Kozar. He's known as Art Kelly. He's had that club maybe thirty years. It's been closed for the last year. Now we hear it's opening up again as a music venue."

"That's why Deke and Zeke have been rehearsing so much, even through the recent attacks. Probably why Deke never tried to visit Robbie in the hospital or while he's been recuperating. Zeke kept him busy." I surmised.

Robbie looked at me and pointed at Carla.

"Oh, yeah. Let me drive Carla to the hospital? Let's all go. I think we'd all like to see how Jimmy is doing. Okay, Carla?"

"Let me clean up and change." She said through sobs. Dria took Carla upstairs.

A half hour later the four of us were in my car heading to O'Connor Hospital on Stevens Creek Boulevard.

After we parked, we walked in the front door and up to the reception counter. I, taking the lead, very officially asked if we could see Jimmy Porter.

"Jimmy Porter," the receptionist repeated, writing it down on a notepad. "Let me look that up. Uh… no. No Jimmy Porter in the system."

The 'system' was a large, heavy-looking monitor and a keyboard, probably hooked up to some big central computer somewhere in the hospital.

"How about James Porter?" Carla asked. "That's what is on his driver's license."

"James Porter." The receptionist repeated, again writing it down. "Ah. Yes. No, you can't see him yet. He's still in emergency. Maybe when he's assigned a room you could see him. Are you relations?"

"Yes, I'm a relation!" Carla said a little curtly. "I'm his wife! And these are Jimmy's best friends."

"Please take a seat." She calmly said. "It may be a few moments or a few hours. It all depends on how busy the emergency room is."

We sat down in the waiting area doing just that. Waiting. Robbie held my hand and whispered, "Carol, what can we do about the rent that we owe? Cliff was supposed to be paying that. What did he do with the money?"

"Robbie, don't worry about that right now. We'll figure something out." I said softly to him.

Ten minutes later Burt walked in. He didn't come through the front door, but through a door behind the receptionist, who smiled and looked at him with interest.

"Mrs. Porter." Burt said. "Your husband is going to be okay. No broken ribs. Just torn cartilage. It'll be sore like a broken rib for a while. He does have a concussion, but again, no broken bones. He's in a private room now. Let me walk you up to his room. I'm sorry Carol, Robbie, Miss Wenborn, I can only take one visitor up at a time. Maybe later…"

"Don't worry about it Burt," I said. "We'll wait here for Carla."

"You know she'll probably want to stay with mister Porter for a while. I'll give her a ride home. You all might as well go home too. Jimmy will be here for a couple of days because of his head injury. Maybe, hopefully, you can see him tomorrow."

Burt smiled at the receptionist, and she buzzed a side door open for him and Carla to go through to a secure section of the hospital. Robbie, Dria, and I looked at each other, sighed, got up, and left.

Chapter 26

Gimme Shelter

Robbie

Before we got back, I turned to Dria and suggested, "Dria. We shouldn't just drop you off. You would be the only one there. If Zeke's there, I really don't trust him with you. Carol, is there a room in your house she can crash in until Jimmy gets back?"

"Glad you thought of that, Robbo. There is. Dennis told me he can't afford the phone bills anymore. He's shutting down both the drug crisis and suicide hotlines. He also said they've only had one call in two months."

"Uh… that was me," Dria said, looking down at her feet. "Uh… the girl I talked to sounded more stoned and upset than helpful. I felt sorrier for her than for me."

"Odd." Carol said as she pulled in front of her house. "They were supposed to be all well-trained psychology students. Anyway, one of Dennis's volunteers moved out." There's a bedroom you can use, Dria, if you want. When Carla returns, she can stay here too."

"Thank you so much, Carol." Dria said. "Can I go in the house first and get a few things to take over?"

"Sure. I'll go with you. Robbo, I'll be up to our room shortly."

Carol and Dria went into our ex-commune. I went up to Carol's room, the one we so lovingly share now.

Fifteen minutes later I heard them come in and went into the upstairs hallway to great them.

The bedroom Dria was moving into was almost 12-feet square, with a small closet across from a double futon bed, one side pushed against the window wall.

"Dria," Carol said. "That wall's going to be pretty cold this winter. Let's move it over." Carol helped her slide it away from the wall.

In the closet was a two-drawer cabinet. A small side table with a dusty clock radio that the volunteer left behind was on the right side of the bed. No drawer, but two narrow shelves for books. An old scratched-up chair with a worn cane seat was tucked under a small desk in front of the one window. On the wall over the desk was a single bookcase with a clip-on lamp.

Carol had helped Dria bring her bedding over, and the two of them made up her bed. Dria then sat her suitcase on the bed and opened it. It held some clothes and toiletries. Carol showed her where the back bathroom was. She would be sharing it with the remaining student who lived in another bedroom across the hall from the one Dria was now staying in.

"Dria. Make yourself at home. And you can stay as long as you want. Oh, and if we're not back and you notice Burt drop Carla off, let her know she should move here."

Carol closed the door and came back into the hall where I was standing around wishing both of my arms and hands worked so I could have helped. Carol gave me a hug and kiss.

"As soon as Carla comes back, we can help her move her stuff over. For now, Lover, let's go get something to eat for us and the girls."

Carol drove toward the Willow Glen district on Willow Street and parked across the road from Ricardo's Pizzeria. We went in and ordered a large sausage, mushroom, and olive pizza and sat down to wait at the bar where we asked for some wine while we waited.

The pizzeria was busy at five o'clock, and the tables were nearly full of people who looked like students. All of them looked barely old enough to be drinking beer. Several tables had pitchers of the brews at various stages of emptiness and pizzas of all sizes were on table stands. The smells were making me hungry.

Carol and I both noticed the stage at the end of the room. A couple of guys were setting up drums and amplifiers. One guy had long dark hair tied back in a ponytail. The other had a long black beard and short hair, just a little longer than a butch style. I didn't recognize them.

We were just about finished with our wine when the pizza box was handed to us. We paid for that and the wine and headed out.

When we got out the front door, I turned to look at the posters in the window. Tonight's band was a country-rock group. Tomorrow was a blues group. After that was Raven.

Jeez. Look, Carol. They're still around. I thought they would have broken up after Tommy got arrested. They must have hired another guitarist. Seems like they'd be awfully loud for this place."

Carol laughed. "Yeah. We'll probably hear them across town. Let's go home and eat."

Carol asked Dria if she'd like to join us, and we sat on the floor to eat. Carla hadn't returned yet. The pizza was still warm and tasted good. Carol got some sodas and bottled water out of her small fridge. The water was for Dria, who finally told us that carbonated drinks bothered her.

We sat around and talked, mostly small talk, and ate most of the pizza. There were two pieces left that Carol wrapped in waxed paper and put in her fridge for Carla.

We were still sipping our sodas and water when Carol's phone rang. It was Alan.

"Alan. Hi. What's up? A meeting? Uh… yeah. It must be important. I'll be over soon. See you."

She hung up.

"I'm sorry, Robbo, Dria. I have to go in for a meeting. Something has come up. I've got to change. Dria, will you be okay?"

"I'll be fine. Robbie's here, and you told me Dennis lives downstairs. I'll go to my room and settle in. I have a book I to read anyway. I'll help Carla move when she gets here."

Dria left and Carol closed the door to our room. Carol started to undress then looked at me. She came over and gave me a big hug that almost hurt my shoulder, then lightened the hug and gave me a long kiss. "Sorry I hugged too hard that time. I wanted to have a nice evening with you tonight."

"Carol…"

She gave me another kiss then broke away. "I need to change. I'll be back as soon as I can."

When Carol left, it was almost eight. I turned on her little television and switched it to watch an episode of *Mission Impossible*.

The show was barely fifteen minutes in when it was cut away for a special news announcement. A local newscaster came on and reported a shooting at a San José night club. "Multiple deaths and

152

injuries were reported by our man on the scene. Take it, Mitch Bryant.”

He was shouting over the sounds of sirens and yelling. “Two hours ago, several gunmen broke into the Tahitian Gardens night club and began shooting. Shots were returned by those in the club. Seven people are dead. Five wounded, two seriously. Police and FBI are on the scene as well as several ambulances that you can see and hear behind me. We’ll know more later.”

The news announcer thanked Mitch and said, “more news at eleven” then the station said, “we are now returning to our regularly scheduled program.”

Back to Mission Impossible.

I had seen Alan, Burt’s partner, in the scene behind the reporter, talking to someone whose back was facing the camera. I couldn’t tell who it was. Because Deke and Zeke were practicing for their gig there, I was worried Deke might be one of those dead or wounded. If that’s true, then Jimmy and I are the only ones left from the original band and commune. And both Jimmy and I have been attacked. Why? Why all of us?

The shooting had to be the reason for the important meeting at the police station.

Crap. I missed the main thrust of the Mission Impossible episode, so I changed the channel to UHF 54, the local PBS station. It was a weird British show called Monty Python’s Flying Circus. I was about to change the station again when one of their skits made me laugh. The more I watched, the more I got intrigued by their ridiculously insane antics. A parrot sketch had me laughing so much my shoulder hurt. For a few minutes, it made me forget about everything that’s been happening. I was sorry the episode ended, and reality returned.

Chapter 27

Tell Me Why

Robbie

It was after nine when I heard Burt drive up. I looked out the window and saw him drop Carla off next door at the commune. I knocked on Dria's door (*I think I woke her*) and told her Carla was back so we both headed next door to help her move in with Dria and explained why. I think Carla was relieved to get out of that house. Jinxing of the house had been a topic of discussion quite a few times. The house was now empty. No one was there.

By the time ten thirty rolled around, Carla had moved in both hers and Jimmy's belongings. I had left the TV on and was about to get up and change the station to watch the eleven o'clock news when Carol came in. She looked exhausted. She gave me a quick kiss and plopped down on the bed fully clothed.

"Oh, Carol love. You look so tired. I'll turn off the TV and we can go to bed."

"No, Robbo. Please leave it on. Can you change the station to the channel 4 news?"

I did and sat back down in the easy chair. The intro to the eleven o'clock news was just finishing, and the first of two advertisements came on.

Once the ads were over, the lead story started about the shootings in San José. The newscasters cut to a reporter on the scene, this time, a woman. This reporter was very serious, telling the audience about a gun battle between suspected rival gangs that had left ten dead and two wounded. She walked over to Alan, the news camera following her every move. In the background, I could see Carol and Burt talking to two people in white lab coats. I couldn't see their faces, but I could tell from their sizes that it was the forensics guy, Rhys, and the pathologist, Lucy.

The reporter asked, "Tell me, Detective Spencer, what gangs were involved in this tragic massacre? Do you have any names available yet?"

Alan answered, "I'm not at liberty to say until the investigations are over. Our forensics team is currently working through the numerous rooms and the garden area in the back, which will take several hours to complete. Also, names of those dead and wounded will not be available until notifications of kin."

"This establishment, Tahitian Gardens, has been here for over forty years, but was closed last year. Can you tell us if it was to reopen soon and is that why there were so many people here?"

"All I can say at this point is that the club was planning to reopen as a dinner theater and concert venue. Press releases had been sent out and a projected grand opening was reported in the San José Mercury News yesterday morning. A few of the people who were here were workers constructing a new stage and sound booth."

"I want to thank you Detective Spencer. This has been Karen Newsom reporting from the Tahitian Gardens. Now back to you, Brenda." I turned the TV off.

"Ah. Carol, I can see why you're so tired. That must have been a huge crime scene."

Well, I might as well be talking to myself. Carol had dozed off. The lovely lady was plum tuckered out.

I got undressed and did my bathroom duties. Undressing has been hard since being shot, and Carol usually helped, but I was getting a little better at it now that I was healing a little more.

I crawled under the covers next to Carol trying not to bother her. But she stirred and got up to get ready for bed. She took a while, and I began to wonder if she had fallen asleep in the bathroom.

No, she hadn't. She came out of the bathroom in her gorgeous nude self and crawled in bed next to me. She put her arm over my midsection and gave me a nice loving kiss. That was it. She drifted off. I reached over and gave her a light kiss on her cheek. I thought I saw a smile cross her face, but then she was out. I fell asleep a few minutes later.

I slept so soundly that when I awoke, the clock by the bed said 9am. Carol was up already and had showered and dressed in her light tan working woman pants suit and turtleneck this time. She was ready to leave.

"Robbo, lover, I'm glad you're awake. I'm so very sorry I have to leave already. There's a breakfast meeting at the station I must be at. That damn shooting has all the politicians and the police nervous and up in arms. They think there'll be repercussions and more shootings."

"I miss you already, love. Please be careful."

"Do you have any plans for today?"

"Yeah. I'm going with Carla and Dria to the hospital in a while. Dria's driving. We're going to see Jimmy."

"Why don't you take them to the Crystal Creamery for breakfast before you go. Here. My treat."

Carol handed me two twenty-dollar bills.

"Uh, really?"

"Sure, lover. I'm on the police payroll. Well, as a consultant, but they're paying me detective grade. Take it and have a nice breakfast."

She gave me one of her long kisses, then reluctantly broke away. "Oh, Robbo. I wish I could go with you. I have to leave. I love you."

She pulled her hand away from my cheek and went out the door turning one more time to sadly wave to me. I was worried about her. It put a lump in my throat.

I got up and washed the best I could with the cast and got dressed.

Since I can't tie shoelaces with one hand, I slipped on my brown loafers again. They were a little worn, but still comfortable.

I went out into the upstairs hall and could hear Carla and Dria talking. I knocked on their door. Dria answered. Both girls were dressed. She said they had been up a while.

I asked them about going out for breakfast before going to the hospital and they cheered up a little and agreed. They were both hungry.

Before we left, I told the policeman on lookout duty where we were going. We headed to the Creamery, one girl on either side of me, and we each had a good, filling old-fashioned breakfast of bacon and eggs and sourdough toast. After eating, we headed back to Carol's house and got ready to drive to the hospital.

We jumped into Dria's car, a slightly rusty '62 Chevy Nova station wagon in which she and Terry had driven out from Texas, and waved goodbye to the policeman, still sitting out front.

Forty-five minutes later we walked in the front door of the hospital. This time the receptionist handed us passes and directed us to Jimmy's private room. She buzzed us in. Carla knew the way.

We took an elevator to the third floor and went down a hall to the last room. A police officer, reading a newspaper, sat by the door, a paper cup of coffee on a small table beside him. He put the paper down and stood up when we got to the door.

"One visitor at a time please. Passes? Good. Who's first?"

Of course, it's Carla. Dria and I sat in chairs facing the cop. I tried to talk to him, but he didn't act very friendly and clammed up after a couple of yes/no answers. *He probably didn't like being on guard duty.* He picked up the paper and held it at an angle to hide his face.

Dria and I talked, and she opened up more to me about Terry.

"Terry and I got married because I got pregnant. He wanted our child to have a real mother and father. Everything was fine for three months until we were getting ready to drive to California. I got sick. I was so sick Terry took me to the emergency room. I miscarried. I lost our child."

Tears were dripping down her cheeks.

"At first Terry seemed glad I was going to be okay, then he was angry I lost the child. He blamed me, like it was my fault I got sick. When I was better, we still drove out here to San José. But when we got settled in the commune, he began looking elsewhere to use his manhood. He screwed around. He hardly touched me. He did once, and I thought I was pregnant again. I wasn't. That set Terry off to play with his young bimbos even more."

"I'm so sorry, Dria," I said. "Terry was a good keyboardist, but I was annoyed when I found out he was playing around so much. The way he talked at first, we thought he was with you all the time. It's no wonder you never came to our gigs and didn't talk to us for such a long time."

"Robbie, Carol is so lucky to have a wonderful guy like you. I wish I was that lucky."

"Dria, you will be. You're still young and have a good long life ahead of you. You could even go back to school if you wanted."

"I've thought about that, especially when taking walks around the campus and seeing all the students."

158

"So, what would you like to learn? To do?"

"Well, I've always liked to write. Maybe be an English major. Maybe teach."

"That would be cool. What kind of writing?"

"With all that's happened, I could write murder mysteries. Is that too gross?"

"No, Dria, not at all. Mystery novels sell quite well at Books Inc. over at Town and Country Village. I enjoy reading them myself. Especially the Dick Francis and old Agatha Christie mysteries. I'd like to write some like that myself."

Carla came out and noticed Dria with her head on my shoulder, both of us smiling.

"What's up with you two? Hey, Robbie. Jimmy wants to see you."

I opened the door and went in.

Jimmy was propped up and smiled at me. At least he didn't have IVs sticking in him like I had when I was in the hospital.

"Robbie. I'm glad I'm still around to see you again."

Jimmy's eyes gave him away. I could see he was still in pain. One of his eyes was black, and part of his head was partly shaved to stitch a small cut from what ever hit him. His concussion probably kept his headache going.

"Yeah, Robbie, I see you looking at me. And, yes, I hurt. My ribs hurt too. At least the X-rays show no fractures. So. How's Carol?"

"Oh, Carol is fine but overwhelmed right now. I guess you heard about the big shooting at Tahitian Gardens, didn't you?"

"Yeah. And I worry about Deke. I know he and Zeke were going to play there when it reopened. Any word?"

"Not yet. The police are being pretty quiet about it. I think the FBI is involved in the investigation too. But they haven't been too helpful, I've heard. As jerky as Deke has been lately, I still hope he's alright. Zeke's another story. Carol found out that Zeke's uncle owned Tahitian Gardens. They might have both been victims."

"I… I really hope not. Uh, Robbie, when this is over, are we going to work together again?"

"I hope so. I hope so. Carol wants to. Say, Dria's outside too. Would you like to see her?"

"Sure. She's been through so much. Yeah. Send her in."

We said our goodbyes, and I sent Dria in. I sat down with Carla, who had tears in her eyes.

"Are you okay, Carla?"

"Yeah. I'm just thankful Jimmy's going to be okay. I really hope the police catch whoever did this."

"Speaking of which, there's Carol and Burt coming out of the elevator. Hello, Carol, detective."

"Hi, Robbo. You see Jimmy yet?"

"Yeah. Dria is in there with him now. What brings you here?"

"Burt and I also want to see to Jimmy. We want to ask him if he can remember anything about his attacker. Any little thing he can think of might help. Ah, here comes Dria. Hi, girl. Okay, Burt, let's get this over with. I'm sure Carla will want to see Jimmy again."

Carol and Burt said hi to the guard then went in and closed the door. We couldn't hear what was going on in there.

Fifteen minutes later they both came out.

"Any luck?" I asked.

Burt answered. "A little. Detective Legrand and I are heading back to the station to check it out."

Carol came over and put a hand on Carla's shoulder. "Carla, dear, we'll find out who did this to Jimmy and to the others. I promise you."

"Thank you, Carol. And thank you so much for putting Dria and me up in your house."

"You're very welcome. Like I told Dria, stay as long as you like."

Carol and Burt headed down the hall to the elevator bay. Carol looked back at me and waved as they got into the elevator.

"Carla. You want to go in to see Jimmy again?"

"For a few minutes. I'm sure he needs his rest. His head still hurts."

"I know what that feels like. He's strong, though. He'll feel better soon."

Carla was in there barely ten minutes. "Jimmy needs some rest. He's pretty tired after our visits and with the police interviewing him."

"Did he tell you what he said to the detectives?"

"Yeah. He told them the only thing he remembered about his attacker was his smell."

"Smell?" Dria and I said together.

"Jimmy said the guy smelled like patchouli."

Chapter 28

Light My Fire

Robbie

Dria had planned to drive Carla and me straight back to Carol's house, but we decided to get a few groceries to stock Carol's fridge. I pulled into Lucky's supermarket and purchased some cheese, crackers, a package of muffins, four cans of sodas, and a bottle of chardonnay.

Pulling in Carol's driveway, we noticed a police car and a fancy black Rolls parked in front of our old commune. I figured the policeman there was another one guarding the house, even though no one was living there now. No one was in the police car. *I wondered where the cop was.*

After parking behind the house, we walked up the driveway to go in the front door. We didn't want to use the back door because we didn't want to disturb Dennis if he was at his desk working on his newspaper.

As we headed up the front steps, I heard some talking next door. The cop came out of the house with someone whose loud voice sounded familiar. It was same voice who yelled at me on the phone. I was sure it was mister Sordi. *They seemed chummy. Curious.* The cop shook Sordi's hand and got in his cruiser and drove off.

The girls went into Carol's house. I walked back down the steps and went next door to the commune. I wanted to catch Sordi before he left. I caught him as he was opening the door to his black Rolls.

"Excuse me, are you Mister Sordi?"

He turned with a start. His hand was poised under his pin-striped suit coat. He loudly replied, "Yes? Who are you? How do you know me?"

"Sorry to bother you. I'm Robbie Jones. I was one of the band members who use to live here."

"Ah! Well, Robbie Jones, I've posted an eviction notice on the door! You're to be out in two weeks!"

"Everyone <u>is</u> out. Several are dead. Have you not heard?"

"Heard what? What are you talking about?"

"Three members were murdered. I was nearly the fourth. Another is now in the hospital from an attack in the back yard. And yet another guy is missing. You did hear about the shooting at Tahitian Gardens, didn't you?"

Sordi looked away. He scanned the street then turned back to me and said a little quieter, "Uh, yes. I did hear about that. Okay. Look. I'm sorry to hear about your friends. But business is business. I need to rent this house again. It needs to be cleared out."

No, he didn't seem concerned about my friends at all. He just wanted his slum lord money. However, he looked a little nervous when I mentioned the shootings at Tahitian Gardens. He reminded me again about clearing stuff out, then looked up the street both ways and got in his Rolls and sped away. I went back next door.

Carla, still holding the bag of groceries, and Dria were waiting for me at the front door.

"What did that guy say?" Carla asked.

"Eviction. We have two weeks to get all our stuff out of there."

"Dria and I don't have anything left in our rooms, but we would like to save our kitchen stuff."

"I still have a bed and chair and some records that didn't get destroyed," I said. "My stereo was trashed so I threw it away. We should try to get whatever we can from the recording studio. Also, there are power and hand tools in the woodshop. I also have some art stuff still in my little art room that didn't get destroyed. Crud. I won't be able to lift much with one hand. I'll check with Carol. Maybe she can suggest what to do."

As we went up the stairs, Dria said, "We'll help you as much as we can." Carla agreed as she put the grocery bag down. I thanked them, and the two of them went to their room.

I put the purchases away and put the chardonnay in the fridge.

Carol came home at six on a dinner break. She had to head back to the station for a few more hours, so she suggested all four of us go to the Creamery for dinner again. As we opened the front door and began to walk down the steps to the sidewalk, Dennis came up the steps and passed us. Carol said hi. Dennis said nothing. He entered the house and closed the door.

"Boy," I said. "He looked deep in thought."

"No. He looked mad." Carol replied. "I wonder if something is wrong. I'll have to ask him when I see him again. Come on. Let's head to the Creamery."

When we got there, Carol still couldn't discuss much about the cases. She only said that Deke was still missing. So was Zeke. None of the bodies at the Tahitian Gardens shooting were theirs. Carla, Dria, and I let out sighs of relief.

Carol walked back with us but had to leave right away. She apologized to me, gave me a nice kiss, then got in her car and drove away. Again, I hated to see her leave. I've been missing her a lot.

Since I couldn't play guitar, I thought I'd try to write again. I had picked up a 6 x9 wire-bound notebook while at Lucky's to replace my missing one, and I wanted to scribble down some song ideas. I wasn't too inspired. Instead, I decided to start writing a story. An instructor in one English course I took always said to write what you know. Okay. Talking to Dria made me think I should also write a murder mystery. I sure know a lot about that now.

I'd written nearly twenty pages when Carol got home. I looked at the clock and realized I'd been writing for three hours. It was 11:30. *Where did the time go?*

"Robbo. You're still up?"

"Yep. Geez, Carol. I had no idea what time it was. I've been writing."

"Songs?"

"I started to, but I had songwriter's block. No inspiration. I've been writing a story."

"Really? Lover, that's cool. What's it about?"

"A mystery. A murder mystery."

"Writing what you know."

"That's what my old English prof, Miss Brown, used to tell me. Yeah. I already have twenty hand-written pages."

"Before you write anymore words, let me get you something."

Carol opened her closet and reached for something in the back of a shelf. It looked like a small black suitcase. She set it on the bed and opened it.

"A typewriter!" I exclaimed. "Cool. That's a really nice portable Underwood."

"Can you type?"

"Oh yeah. I can. I learned in high school. I finished the course typing 60 words a minute. Of course, that was with two hands."

"Take it. You can use it for your story and, when you're inspired, for new songs. Robbo, I can't wait for this to be over so we can play and sing again… and play."

That last 'play' she said with a wink, then reached down and kissed me.

"Robbo, it's been a long day. Let's get undressed and get into bed."

Twenty minutes later, after we both washed up and brushed our teeth, we were cuddling in bed.

We 'played' with each other a little, then fell asleep with her spooning up behind me.

Our sleep was disturbed by sirens just outside our window, a window with a daytime glow shining through it. We both jumped out of bed and opened the shades.

The commune house was on fire.

Chapter 29

Great Balls of Fire

Robbie

The fire appeared to be on the first floor, but we could see it working quickly up through the old dry redwood flooring to the second floor.

Carol and I dressed quickly and ran downstairs and out to the front porch. Dennis smiled at her and then started taking photos of the activity.

"Dennis. Did you see it start?" He was still dressed in the same clothes he had on when we saw him when we passed him on the front steps.

"Uh… Yeah. I saw it flare up through my window downstairs. I called 911. The trucks arrived quickly."

We were watching how well the firemen knew what to do. One came up to us and said we should go inside and close any open windows. One of the firemen was going to spray the side of Carol's house to make sure no embers could blow over and catch her house on fire. After all, the two tall, old wooden houses were only twelve feet apart.

We were still watching through a window and could see the firemen getting the fire under control. It did look like the flames got upstairs. I was sure all my remaining records were melted. My bass was probably burned up too. And Jimmy had moved his drums upstairs. They're probably gone as well. I wondered if the basement burned. There were still a couple of guitar amps down there as well as all of Cliff's remaining electronics and the power tools.

I was thinking, *gee, mister Sordi, we got everything out in time. We had help. Sorry about the mess. You can keep our cleaning deposit.*

Fifteen minutes later the fire was out. We expected that the firemen would be around for several hours putting out any glowing embers.

Carol had been holding my hand while we watched. "I'm so sorry, Robbie. You've lost everything you had there. First a break in, then a fire. It's got to be linked."

"It has to be. Someone has cursed us and the house and is doing everything in his power to destroy us. But why? Why us?"

"Listen. Let's head back to bed. It may be hard to go back to sleep after all this excitement, but I have to try. God, look at the time. Five am. At least I don't have to be in until ten tomorrow morning… or rather ten this morning."

"We'll try to get a few more hours of sleep anyway. Come on, love, let's go collapse in bed."

The alarm rang at seven. It didn't wake me, but it did wake Carol. She reached over and shut it off and went back to sleep.

I finally woke up and looked at the clock. It was now nine. Carol was still asleep beside me. I reached over and kissed her forehead. Her eyes opened and she smiled. Then she turned to look at the clock and realized what time it was.

"Oh shit. I've got to get going."

She gave me a quick kiss and rushed to the bathroom and turned on the shower. She was out, dried, and dressed in fifteen minutes.

As she tied up her shoes, I told Carol, "We restocked your little fridge. There're some raisin bran muffins in there if you want to take one or two with you for breakfast. There's also some cream cheese."

"Thank you so much, lover. Hey. I never got to ask Jimmy how he's doing."

"He's going to be fine. The concussion bothers him more than his sore ribs. But the doctor says it's temporary. His headaches should end real soon."

"I hate to leave you again this morning. You look so cute just lying down there. By the way, how is your shoulder doing?"

"It must be getting better. I woke up lying on my left side and it didn't bother me."

Carol gave me another long kiss, then pulled away, sighed, said goodbye, and left.

I got up and instead of just washing up at the sink, I decided to try taking a bath. I filled the old clawfoot tub with about six inches of warm water. That way I could keep my cast out of the water.

It worked. For the first time in weeks, I felt a lot cleaner than from sponge baths, as nice as they were, given the case. By ten thirty, I was dressed and out the door. I wanted to walk around the burned-out ex-commune next door mainly to see if any of my stuff survived. I doubted if anything in my room made it through the fire, but I hoped that my bass amplifier in the basement survived.

I came downstairs and noticed Dennis in his room with his head on his desk. The door was open, but I knocked on it anyway.

Dennis looked up. His eyes were red like he hadn't slept. "Oh. It's you, Robbie. Hi." He shuffled some papers around on his desk.

"Hi Dennis. How are you doing?" I noticed he'd been burning incense.

"Well… I'm… I'm okay. But…"

"But?"

"Yeah. Well… uh, my financial backer pulled out. No more support, so I… I had to let my last volunteer go, and she moved out yesterday. I couldn't pay for her rent anymore. I may need to move. I can't pay mine either."

"That's too bad, Dennis, I'm really sorry. Will you be able to still publish your paper?"

"Paper? Oh, that. No, I can't even do that. My press downstairs is broken and can't be fixed. It's too old. I've been using a printing company on the Monterey Highway, but I won't be able to afford that anymore either. The… uh, paper is dead."

"What will you do?"

"That's what I've been running through my head. Uh, I… I used to teach English here at State. I may not look like it now, but I was a professor there. I… I still know the head of the English department. I think I might clean myself up and go back to teaching."

"That would be cool. Why don't you check with Carol when she's available. We're hoping these murder cases she's working on with the police will be solved and soon over. Anyway, talk to her. Maybe you can keep your room here while you get back to teaching, if that's what you think you'll do."

"I'll think about it. Carol… I like her. She's a nice landlady."

"Well, I wish you luck. Anyway, I have to go. I want to see if I can get in the basement next door if it's not also burned out, or too dangerous."

"I don't know, Robbie, that house looks pretty damaged. I'd wait for clearance by the fire marshal… if that will ever happen."

"Yeah. I probably should." Glancing out Dennis's window that faced the commune, I could see the front of the driveway. A red and white pickup truck with the fire department logo on the side was parked there. "Hey. It looks like a fireman is over there right now.

Looks like police are there too. Hey, I know that guy. See you later Dennis." He closed the door behind me.

I went out the front door, down the steps and walked up to the plain clothes cop, Burt, who was leaning against the fire department truck talking to the uniformed cop inside.

"Hello detective."

"Hello Mister Jones."

"Please call me Rob. Is Carol with you?"

"No." Burt answered. "She and Alan went back to the Tahitian Gardens. Forensics found something there that Carol and Alan are checking out. Rhys, our forensic prof is back there too."

"What brings you here?"

"This fire was started by an arsonist. The fire chief went to the back of the house. Seems that was where the fire started. Ah. Here he comes now. So, Barney, it's what we expected, right?"

"Yeah. My men did say there was a strong odor of gasoline in back. Someone might have broken into the house and spread gas all around. That's probably why the fire got so big so fast."

"Did the basement get burned too?" I asked.

"It seems unscathed. The fire burned up, not down. Why?"

"My guitar amplifier, and recording equipment are still down there. Also, there is a woodshop with new tools and an art room with more of my stuff in it. If it's safe, I'd like to salvage what I can."

"You can't carry much with only one hand."

"The two girls next door said they'd help, and I might be able to get Dennis, also next door, to help."

Barney, the fire chief, said, "Let me make sure it's safe enough in there before you can get your stuff."

"Thank you. I'll wait for your word."

Just then another car, a very expensive looking black Rolls Royce, parked across the entrance to the driveway. It was Albert Sordi again. He got out and slammed his car door in anger. He was fuming.

"Those goddam kids burned my house down!" He yelled at no one in particular. He then noticed Burt, the police car, and the fire chief, and me.

"That's one of them!" He pointed at me. "Policeman, arrest that goddam punk! Arrest all those goddam punks!"

Burt crossed his arms. So did the fire chief. I copied them.

Sordi was almost face to face with Burt. "Are you just going to stand there and do nothing? Why don't you do your goddam job!"

Burt didn't flinch. "And you are?"

"What? What? Am I what?"

"Your name. Who are you?"

"You goddam well know who I am! Sordi! Albert Sordi, goddamit. Arrest that goddam kid!"

Kid? Me? An army veteran?

"And why should I arrest Mister Jones here?"

"I goddam told you, goddamit! He burned my house down!"

"And you know that how?"

"What kind of goddam question is that. All those punks couldn't pay rent, so they burned my goddam house down."

"Mister Sordi, no one was living here. Three of them are dead, two attacked, one still in the hospital. Jones here, as you can see, was the other who was attacked."

"I don't goddam care! I want restitution! I want…"

I could see Burt was getting fed up with Sordi's yelling.

"Would you just shut the fuck up!" An uncharacteristic loud response emitted from normally calm Burt, who poked Sordi in the chest. It worked.

Sordi, wide-eyed and speechless stepped back from Burt. He also looked very mad and looked like he was reaching under his pinstriped suit coat again. A gun?

Burt calmed back down. "Mister Sordi. Do you have insurance? Yes? Then if your premium is paid and current, I suggest you notify your broker to start getting your… restitution."

Sordi removed his hand from his coat and crossed his arms. "But… but how did the fire start?"

At least he asked quietly, and he stopped saying goddam.

"It was arson. Be assured that we will be investigating this fully. We might even bring in the FBI. Now, if there is nothing else, Mister Sordi, we have work to do. Goodbye."

"But… but…"

"Goodbye Mister Sordi!"

That goodbye was more pointed. Yes, this question-and-answer period was over.

Sordi turned on the heels of his highly polished Italian shoes and climbed into his Rolls, again slamming the door, and, without looking if any other cars were coming, peeled out, not stopping at the stop sign and turning east on Santa Clara Street.

"He's worried about getting money out of this?" Barney, the fire chief was telling Burt. "If he's driving a Rolls, he's not poor. Probably owns a lot of property here in town."

"Hmm. I think I should do a little more research on that guy. Did you notice the bulge under his blazer? I'm sure he was carrying a gun and started to reach for it. He looks like he could be a volatile character if pushed. I wouldn't be surprised if he had something to do with the Tahitian Gardens shootings."

Barney said to Burt, "Uh-huh. Well, that's your department." He then turned to me. "Now. One of my men should be here shortly. He and I will go down the back steps and see if it's safe in there so you can get your stuff if it's all okay. It may be a while, so you might as well go home for now. I can give you a call. What's your phone number?"

Burt answered for me, almost saying too much. "I have Carol's…
uh, mister Jones phone number. I can give it to you."

With that, I headed back next door to ask Dennis and the girls if
they could help me move some stuff out of the basement and over to
Carol's basement.

Chapter 30

Under the Boardwalk

Robbie

It was after 5pm, and I was getting hungry. I had missed lunch waiting by the phone for the fire chief. It had been six hours, and I hadn't heard from either him or Burt.

I went into the hall and knocked on Dria and Carla's door. No answer. They must have gone out together. Maybe they went back to the hospital.

The bedroom door across from Dria's room was open. The room was empty except for a double mattress on the floor, a three-drawer dresser, and a small desk and chair. Yeah. Dennis told me his last volunteer moved out. Maybe Carla can move in here with Jimmy. I'm sure Carol would approve.

I went downstairs and even Dennis was gone. *Guess I'm home alone. I hoped.*

I'd never been in this house's basement yet because I figured it was off limits with Dennis's printing press down there. Since it didn't work anymore, as he told me, I thought I'd go down and take a look around. I was curious.

I went down the back stairs to the basement and turned the light on. What I saw surprised me. The full basement was larger than the one next door at the commune house, and the ceiling was a full eight feet high, not seven feet like next door in the rehearsal space. Dennis's broken printing press was by one wall with a cabinet next to it containing all the lead upper- and lower-case letters used for printing on the old-fashioned press. There was a plate on the front of the printing press that showed the make and patent year. Chandler Price. Patented 1882. It must have been hell to get that big press down the back stairs from the parking lot. *Maybe it was moved in pieces and assembled down here.*

I tried to turn the wheel on the side, but it was frozen in place. I was sure it could be fixed, but I suspected Dennis was tired of publishing the paper anyway. There were a couple of red ink stains on the surface.

Across from the press was a hall heading back to a small kitchen. By the appliances was a small, oak three-foot-square dining table. At it were two chairs, one a ladder-back chair with a woven seat with part of the weave broken, the other a lower-backed wooden chair with arms. It looked like an old oak library chair.

I looked around more. The back half of the basement had been set up as a two-bedroom apartment. One bedroom was empty. It didn't look like anyone had lived there for ages. In the second bedroom there were quite a few moving boxes stacked there. *Whose were they? Carol's?*

One was open and a photo was exposed on top. It looked like it had been done by a professional studio. I picked it up. The photographer's name and address were stamped on the bottom of the paper frame. Temple Photography, Oklahoma City, Oklahoma. The picture was of two men in matching suits, bolo ties and cowboy hats. One of them sat holding a guitar in front of him, and the other stood beside him holding a standup bass. The guitar was familiar. Carol's guitar. She did say it had belonged to her father.

On the side of the box was a rolled-up piece of paper. I started to slip the rotting rubber band off and it crumbled in my hand. Pieces were stuck to the paper. I carefully unrolled it, as carefully as I could, with one hand.

A poster for RCA Victor recording artists, The Legrand Brothers. Appearing at the New San José Civic Auditorium, Saturday, July 16, 1938. The picture on the poster looked similar to the one I just looked at, but Carol's dad was much younger and had a different guitar. It was a lovely, red sunburst Epiphone archtop with a single floating pickup attached to the pick guard.

I rolled it back up.

I went back into the kitchen. The old Coldspot refrigerator was still plugged in and running. I opened it. Dennis must have been using it, at least for beer. It still had half a six pack of Pabst in it. There was also a quart of whole milk, long expired, and half a loaf of Butternut white bread. Not white anymore. Quite grey. Very moldy.

Across from the refrigerator was a sink and counter. Above the counter were cupboards. Above the sink was a high window facing out on the parking area behind Carol's house.

To complete the kitchen 'triangle' was an old Kitchen Aid gas stove. It must have been turned off because I could not see any pilot lights under the burners.

I opened one cabinet over the counter. The bottom shelf was yellow and blue Fiestaware plates and bowls of different sizes. On the left side of the second shelf were cups and saucers, also Fiestaware, and on the right side were clear glass drinking glasses. The top shelf had pottery serving bowls. Everything looked very dusty.

I opened the cabinet on the other side of the sink. This one was the pantry. The bottom shelf had a covered butter dish, sugar bowl, salt and pepper shakers that looked like they were stolen from the Crystal Creamery, and some old-looking condiments. The second shelf had a couple bags of cereal, Post Raisin Bran, and Kellogg's Corn Flakes, next to boxes of Ritz crackers and saltines. A long trail of ants climbed up and down the Raisin Bran box. The top shelf had two cans of Campbell's soups. Tomato and Chicken Noodle. The cans looked rusty.

At the end of the hall, past the two bedrooms, were two more doors. I opened the first door. Bathroom. I've always been a curious guy, so I went in and opened the medicine cabinet. There was only a can of shaving cream and a safety razor. Both rusty. The bathroom counter and sink were also dusty. Looked unused for quite a while.

I opened the second door. This one opened to the front half of the basement. It was completely bare. The walls and ceiling were bare studs and joists. The floor was a concrete slab and dusty. It hadn't been used.

I could see part of a stairway at the other end, like the one that was next door at the commune, but I was sure the access to it upstairs was blocked off.

Yes, there's a full apartment down here. With a little fixing up, it could be a nice place to live. Maybe for Jimmy and Carla. *I'll have to ask Carol about it.*

Well, that's enough poking around. Kinda spooky down here.

I stopped by the door to the front stairway and looked back. Gee. soundproof that area, recording studio there… Hmm. Maybe Carol and I can start playing and recording here. Maybe Jimmy could play percussion.

Ah. Dreams.

When I got back to the first floor, I heard the phone ringing upstairs. I ran up the stairs and picked up the phone just as I heard a voice say "crud" and hung up. It sounded like Burt.

I immediately called and asked the receptionist for Burt. He picked up.

"Ah. Good, mister Jones. You are there. I got word from the fire chief. You can go in the basement, but not in the rest of the house. Go ahead and see what you can salvage. It appears most of the basement is okay. But be careful. The chief said there is some water damage. Some of the stuff down there might be too wet to salvage."

"Thank you, detective. It's late now. I'll check it out tomorrow. I'll be careful."

As we said our goodbyes, I heard the front door open and close. No one was coming up the stairs, so I suspected it must be Dennis. *I should go down to ask him about the basement.*

Going downstairs, I almost turned back because I heard Dennis talking to someone. Out of curiosity, I stuck my head through the door to see who Dennis was talking to.

Deke!

Part 3

Blood, Sweat & Tears

Chapter 31

Surprise, Surprise

Robbie

Yes, it was Deke. He looked like he had not changed his clothes since I last saw him two weeks ago in the rehearsal space next door. I was sure he hadn't washed either. And his normally bare face had a spotty beard nearly a quarter inch long. Dennis stepped back and leaned against the wall with his arms crossed and watched.

"Deke! Where've you been? We've been worried sick that you were a victim of that shooting at the Tahitian Gardens."

"Oh. Yeah. Hi, Robbie. I almost was. I was in the storage room playing with one of the old illegal slot machines that used to be in the club when I heard yelling and a series of shots. A couple of bullets came through the wall not far from me, so I dived behind a cabinet and hid."

"Did Zeke hide too?"

"I hadn't seen Zeke for a half hour or more. He said he had some business to attend to. I don't think he was there. He may have been hiding somewhere too."

"But where have you been since the shooting?"

"When the shooting was over and I couldn't hear voices anymore, I got out of there before the police came. I had to hurry 'cause I started to hear sirens in the distance. I leapt over several bodies and ran out into the gardens and jumped the fence. I wanted to get away from that bloody mess as fast as I could."

"But where did you stay?"

"I made my way to the Guadalupe River. I've been living rough with a couple of homeless guys. Yeah, I know, I was taking a chance, but they were okay. Just two Mexican laborers down on their luck and trying to find work. I ate a lot of canned beans with them. One even leant me a blanket. Got a few flea bites though." Deke scratched his arm as he said that.

Dennis spoke up. "Yeah. When I got back from the… uh, campus, I saw Deke in the driveway looking up at the fire damage. I… I invited him in."

"I'm glad you did. Deke, you know the police will want to talk to you about that Tahitian shooting. I know you didn't see who it was, but they'll want to know you're okay. Don't worry, Deke. I know the detectives pretty well now. And Carol is part of their team."

"Carol still is?"

"You knew that. Yeah, she still is. She's been putting in a lot of hours as a consulting detective on the murder cases. She's also had to deal with a lot of reporters."

"Robbie, I'm so sorry I've been so thoughtless about all of that. Marty and I had been arguing a lot, and I was ready to quit. When he died, I decided to stay and try to keep the band going. With the other deaths killing the band idea, Zeke showed up and wanted to start our old folk duo up again, I jumped at it. Zeke told me to forget about all the band problems and just keep practicing with him. I only hope he's still alive."

"Deke, the cops said that none of the bodies were Zeke's. Like you said, he probably wasn't there."

"I don't know. I don't know. There was so much blood."

Dennis gave Deke's back a hard slap. Deke grunted. Dennis said, "Why don't you go into my bathroom and take a shower. I'll lend you a robe while I put your clothes in the washer and dryer in back."

"I appreciate that, Dennis. Robbie, what happened next door?"

"Someone doused the house with gasoline and set it on fire. That was the evening after the landlord posted an eviction notice on the door. He was furious about the fire and blamed me and the rest of the band, even those who had already died, for starting the fire. Anyway, the first two floors are wasted. The basement survived, but there's probably a lot of water down there. I got permission from the fire chief to see if anything is salvageable. I'm planning on going over there tomorrow morning. Uh, you want to go, too?"

"Yeah, I do. Maybe my Fender amp, and Marty's amp are still okay." Deke let out a sigh. "Maybe I could also sell Cliff's tools. I might get enough selling them to get me a new guitar."

"No, you know Cliff's tools should go to his family. Perhaps his father, if they can locate him."

Tears were forming in Deke's eyes. He'd been through a lot. Even though we weren't that close, even in Korea, he played music well and was great at creating the harmonies we were known for.

"Deke, when you get cleaned up and dressed, let's go down to the Creamery and have some food. My treat."

"I'd like that. Real food for a change. Thanks, Robbie."

Two hours later, Deke and I sat down in a booth at the restaurant eating lunch. He was now clean shaven and didn't smell like piss and sweat like he had. His dark shoulder-length hair was combed back and tied in a short ponytail.

While eating, we talked a little about our past in Korea and some of the more memorable gigs we had there.

Both of us had cheeseburgers and fries. I had iced tea. Deke got a chocolate milkshake.

When we finished, I paid at the register after leaving a tip.

As we got back to the house, Carol has just gotten out of her car. Burt and Alan stepped out of their police car and headed up the driveway. Carol saw us, came over and gave Deke a hug, which she normally wouldn't do because he often didn't bathe.

"We've been so worried about you. You look good."

"Thanks. It's Robbie and Dennis's fault," he said with a smirk.

I asked, "Uh, Carol, why are Burt and Alan here?"

"Dennis called 911 again. He said he was in the laundry room and saw through the window some guy jump the back fence and break into your old house. It might be the same person who attacked Jimmy. Robbo, I must go to work now. Be back in a bit."

It was a short bit.

As Deke and I sat on the front steps of Carol's house, Dennis had joined us.

Carol walked over from the commune.

"Well, Dennis. Whoever you saw is not there now. We checked the basement and saw footprints from the water on the floor, but they didn't try to go upstairs. The footprints went into every room in the basement. Robbo, Deke, can you go down there in the morning and see if anything is missing?"

Burt came over and whispered something in Carol's ear.

"Deke, the detective would like you to come down to the station. He wants you to give a statement on your close call at the shootout and probably has some other questions about it too. An FBI agent should be there too. I can give you a drive there. Don't worry, I'll be in on the interview too."

"That's okay. Robbie mentioned I might have to do this. I'm ready."

Deke got into Carol's car, and they drove off, following the other cops' unmarked police car.

Dennis and I watched them leave and started to go up the front steps when we were almost knocked down by a concussion from an explosion. It hurt my shoulder. We turned to see the house slowly crumble into the basement.

The explosion was loud enough that the entire neighborhood could hear it. Carol and the police car spun around, and each blocked the street on both sides of the house. All the neighbors on the block came out to see what happened.

It didn't look like the fire started up again. Maybe the collapsed house smothered it. It was a different story with the new van and a couple other cars parked in back. The blast blew out windows and the new van caught fire. The gas tank must have ruptured. Alan had quickly radioed for the firefighters. Within ten minutes, two fire trucks had arrived along with the fire chief's car. They went to work putting out the van fire. The chief came over to Burt and Alan. With all the trucks and their pumps running and my ears still ringing from the explosion, I couldn't hear a thing they were saying. Dennis and I were both rubbing our ears. He went back into the house.

Carol ran over to me and put her arms around me. "Oh, Robbo. When I heard that explosion, I thought the worst. I'm so glad you're okay."

"I am. Except for my ears. They're still ringing. That was loud. Dynamite you think?"

"That's for the fire inspectors to find out." Carol said. "Burt already called them and the FBI. I can tell you, though, someone placed the explosives in all the right places. The house imploded. It fell in on itself. It didn't blow out, it blew in."

"The blast almost knocked us over. It was awfully loud. God. You could have been in the basement when that went off."

"That was too close, Robbo. We saw the footprints, but we only assumed it was just a break-in to steal stuff. If someone hid a bomb, it must have been on a timer. I hope forensics can find something. It'll be hard with most of the house in the basement now."

"Shit. Three murders, Jimmy and me getting attacked, the house on fire, then blown up. It's like someone is trying to erase us and the house from existence."

"Robbo, lover, that may be what is happening. I'm going to ask Burt and Alan if you can come into the station with me tomorrow morning so we can list everyone we know living and dead. I'm getting an idea I want to follow up on when I get back to the station."

Chapter 32

If I Needed Someone

Carol

An hour later, I was thinking about trying to take Deke to the station again. He still had to give a statement about being at Tahitian Gardens during the shootout. But I wanted to stick around with the other cops a while longer while we waited for someone from the FBI to show up. *They were taking their time.*

The fire inspectors, along with the forensics team, wanted to bring in a backhoe to attempt to move splintered and broken wood to find what detonated but had to wait for the FBI's go ahead. I hung around for a while until I got tired of waiting and went up to my room, where Robbie was sitting in the chair watching television.

"My ears are finally getting back to normal," Robbie said. "That tinnitus-type of ringing from the explosion has finally stopped."

Since he wasn't taking pain pills any longer, he pulled a beer out of the fridge. As he tipped the can up to his lips, I noticed his hand was shaking. Some shock must have set in.

Robbie took a deep breath to calm himself. He said it helped a little.

It was too early for the news, and I could see the current television program was pretty bad. Robbie wasn't really watching it, and he asked me to turn it off. He reached over and turned on the clock radio. It was Big Daddy Tom Donahue on KMPX-FM.

I gave Robbie a kiss. "Lover, the FBI still hasn't shown up. So, I must leave. Deke still has to give a statement at the station. I should be back in an hour or so."

When I returned, some beautiful music was playing on the radio, and Robbie's eyes were closed. Trails of tears were on his cheeks. I took one look at him and could see something was wrong. I put my hand on his face.

"Robbo, honey. What's wrong? Are you okay?"

He let out a big sigh. "Th...this is such b... beautiful music. Incredible playing. Incredible lyrics. Incredible harmonies. L...like what our band had done. Could have been doing."

"I know lover. Even though Clive Davis was interested in us, I'm sure he heard about our problems and... and deaths and just went on with his business as usual... elsewhere. We just had too much baggage."

"I... I've been thinking about how it could have been for us. See... seeing the commune next door b...blown up hit me hard. I c...couldn't stop shaking."

"Oh, Robbie, sweetie." I sat on the armrest and put my arm around him. "I know it's hard right now, but we'll get through it.

We're survivors. And we'll get back to making music together again. Maybe here or, who knows, somewhere else."

I think my presence was relaxing him.

"By the way, I just saw Carla in the hall, and she said Jimmy's improving quite well. He should be out of the hospital tomorrow."

He sighed and said, "That's really wonderful. I just want to heal up so I can p… play guitar and bass again. It's so frustrating." Robbie sighed again. "Oh no. I just remembered that I have another doctor's appointment tomorrow afternoon at two. You wanted me to help you at the station in the morning. Is that still on?"

"Yeah, lover. It should only take a couple of hours. Burt told me it's okay for you to come in to help me figure out names and places. Oh, and I think our investigations might be finally generating some results. However, the rumor mill, the newspaper, is reporting that the fire and explosion might be mafia related. I'm not convinced. Bombs are not a mafia modus operandi. Now tell me. What is this wonderful music we're listening to?"

With the remainder of the Crosby, Stills, and Nash album playing quietly in the background, Robbie and I had another very loving night.

We were still exhausted and sleepy when it came time to get up and get ready to go to the police station. We both reluctantly rose. I took a shower, then helped Robbie get cleaned up.

By ten we were at the police station. My fellow detectives, Alan and Burt, had their own large room together. I was next door in my smaller corner office. They were in the "A and B" room, and I was in the "C" room. The ABC joke of the station. I motioned Robbie to sit in the chair by my desk.

"I've already started a list," I said. "Here. Take a look and see if there's anyone else I should include."

"Let's see. Okay. Band members: You and me, Marty Thomas, Deke Kay, Terry Wenborn, and Jimmy Porter. Wives: Dria Wenborn and Carla Porter. Soundman: Reinhold Clifton, aka Cliff. Additional names: Zeke Kelly, and what about Dennis Dean. That's it?"

"Can you think of any others?"

"How about the landlord. Sordi."

"I'll add that. Albert Sordi. His first name is really Alberto. Yeah. I bet he's going to get quite an insurance settlement on the house now that it's totally destroyed."

"Yeah, he probably blew it up himself or hired someone to do it." Rob said sarcastically. "Also, should we include Zeke's uncle?"

"He's dead, but I'll put his name down. Art Kelly. Anyone else?"

"That's all I can think of right now."

"Now. In the second column, we'll put what each person does. Third column, how each person is associated with the commune. Fourth column, living or deceased. Fifth. For those deceased, the order and type of death."

For the next half hour, we filled in the blanks.

"Well, Robbo. The one question mark is Zeke. He's still missing. His body was not at the Tahitian Gardens, so he may be hiding from the rival mafia. Also, the FBI have known for years that Art Kelly was really Artim Kozar."

"Could Zeke also be a Kozar?"

"Good question. If Zeke's uncle is Artim, then he must have a Russian connection. Now, when I got Deke's statement about the shootings, he added that he and Zeke played folk music in high school. Lodi High School in Lodi, New Jersey."

"There's a Lodi in New Jersey too? Besides California's?"

"Yeah. The high school Deke and Zeke went to was built in the early 1900s. Now. Guess what? Lodi, New Jersey, is where quite a few of the New York Italian mob live with their families. Some of those that died in the shootout were from there and known by the FBI and the New York and New Jersey State police as well as the New York City police."

"Coincidences?"

"That and more." Carol answered. "Terry's dad told us that he played piano in New York at a club in Brooklyn. Cliff was there too. Turns out both of them also came from Lodi. We're sure that the money Cliff was hiding, and that Zeke was trying to convince Deke to help him find, which you heard and recorded… anyway, that money was probably stolen from the mob. Probably while Terry was playing piano for some function at one of the mob boss's mansions. I wouldn't be surprised if Cliff came along with Terry and was the one who stole it."

"Poor Dria. She told me she never wanted to leave their home back East to go to Austin, Texas, but Terry forced her. She ended up really liking Austin and wanted to stay there. Terry forced her to leave again to come to California. She said it was a terrible trip sitting in the back seat the whole time and him not saying a thing to her. She said Cliff sat in front with Terry and they alternated driving. She didn't get to sit with her husband once during the trip. Of course, Dria spent several days in the hospital when she miscarried, too."

"I need to talk to Dria again." Carol suggested. "Being in the same car with those two for so many days, she must have heard something from them about what transpired in Brooklyn or Lodi. They couldn't have feigned small talk that whole trip."

"You know, come to think of it, I haven't been told how and when Terry and Dria met. Was Dria also from Lodi? I also have no idea what her maiden name was."

"Well, I could ask her, or I can look it up. There has to be a marriage license on record somewhere."

We were so wrapped up in the case we didn't notice Alan had come in with several containers of Chinese food. He came over to Robbie and me. "You guys want to take a break and have some lunch? Got enough for all of us."

I looked at the clock and noticed it was after 12:30.

"Carol, I am hungry. I scarfed down only a muffin out of your fridge before we left."

We took a much-needed break and pulled our chairs over by Alan's desk. He handed each of us packaged bamboo chopsticks, and we started passing the containers, taking a few bites of each then passing them on. It was good.

"Carol, when we finish lunch, I do have to go to my doctor for another dressing change. I think he's going to give me another X-ray of my shoulder."

"I'll drive you, Robbo... uh Robbie. I could use a short break from the desk." She smiled at me and put her hand on my good shoulder.

Burt and Alan could see the little interplay, looked at each other and smiled rather slyly.

Less than twenty minutes later we had finished eating. Robbie said goodbye to Burt and thanked Alan for the Chinese food. We left.

Chapter 33

Around and Around

Robbie

It was nice spending a little time with Carol, even if I had a doctor's appointment. The doctor's office was in the same area as O'Connor Hospital so we thought after my appointment we could stop in and see Jimmy.

Even though my appointment was at two, I had to wait fifteen minutes. At least Carol was with me. We talked about music and life together. Finally, the doctor's nurse assistant came out and escorted me to an examination room. She helped me get my shirt off so she could undo the restrictive sling to take off my dressing and allow the doctor to inspect the wound before a new dressing was applied.

When the doctor came in and took a good look at it, he told me the skin was healing well, but he did set me up for another X-ray to see if the collar bone looked better.

The nurse assistant walked me downstairs to the radiology lab where I got the X-ray. She then walked me back to the examination room where I had to wait nearly twenty minutes before the doctor returned with the X-ray that he put up on a light board on the wall so we could see it.

He pointed out that the bone was healing fine, and I should be able to use my left arm and hand again in another two to three weeks. *Damn. I wanted to be able to use them now.*

I was finally able to leave. Carol had brought a book that she closed and put it into her purse. She smiled up at me when I came in.

We left the medical building and walked the two blocks to the hospital. We checked in and took the elevator to the third floor.

When we got there, Carol greeted the current police guard, showing her badge to him. The guard then let us both go in. Carla was there sitting next to Jimmy holding his hand. She smiled at us. Jimmy looked up and also smiled. He looked much better.

"Hi guys. I'm so glad to see you. And, Carol, thank you so much for looking out for Carla and Dria."

I asked. "So, are you getting out of here today?"

"Not yet. My doctor did say I can finally go home tomorrow morning. However, I don't know where Carla and I can go."

"My place. Hey Carla, the larger bedroom across from Dria's is now available. Dennis's last volunteer left. You and Jimmy can have it. And you guys don't have to pay rent."

"That's so sweet of you Carol. But once we make some money, please let us pay you something. I've applied for a waitress job at the Crystal Creamery, and it looks like I'll be starting there on Monday."

"You don't have to pay, but if you want to, I won't stop you. We can talk about that later. Robbo, I need to get back to work. Jimmy, the next time I see you, you'll be home."

We said our goodbyes and left. Carol said goodbye to the cop on duty, and he told her good luck on the investigations.

A half hour later, she was ready to drop me off at her house. We had just gotten out of her car and were about to kiss goodbye when we heard a car screeching around the San Fernando and 6th Street corner.

Carol noticed the driver's side window was down, and a pistol was sticking out of it.

Carol pushed me down next to her behind her car just as five rapid shots rang out hitting the side of Carol's car and shattering the windshield and a side window.

"Robbie! Are you okay?"

"I'm fine. Shaken up again, but fine. You?"

"Fine. I saw the driver, but he had a ski mask on. However, the car looked familiar. Quick. Let's get in the house away from this mess."

Carol first opened her car door and turned off the engine. When we turned to go up the front steps, Dria, eyes wide, came running down the steps. When she saw we were both okay, she tearfully gave both of us big hugs. We all went upstairs where Carol called Burt and told him what happened. Burt said he and Alan would be there shortly. They'll notify the forensics team to come and check out the damage and find the bullets to see if they match the ones that were shot before.

Chapter 34

Act Naturally

Robbie

Because of those last gunshots, Carol never made it back to the station. Burt and Alan showed up right away and the forensics team arrived fifteen minutes later.

Getting shot at again was making me more nervous than ever. I started shaking again. I wanted to stay out of the way of the cops and forensic team, so I grabbed a beer from Carol's fridge and sat down in the easy chair trying to calm down. The beer helped a little. Not much, but a little.

The inspection of the bullet holes in Carol's car and locating and removing the bullets from the steps and side of Carol's house went on for hours. Finally, Carol came into our room, followed by Burt and Alan.

Alan asked, "How are you doing mister Jones? Robbie?"

"Still shaky. I might need more than one beer to calm down." I tried to joke, but it didn't come out too funny.

Carol gave me a worried smile.

"Carol thinks she'd seen the shooter's car before. A light blue Nova station wagon." Burt said. "How about you? Did you recognize the car?"

"Now that you mention it, yes. Terry had one just like that. It had been parked in the back of the commune… uh, the burned-out house next door. His car was the one that he, Dria, and Cliff came out here in from Texas. Dria drove it recently. Was it stolen?"

"There hasn't been a report of it being stolen."

"I'll go look out back." Carol suggested. She was gone barely a minute. "It's gone."

"Okay," said Alan. "We'll put an all-points bulletin out for an older light blue Chevy Nova. Keep your fingers crossed we find it so forensics can do their magic with it. How did the shooter get the car keys?"

"Probably broke in." Carol suggested. "Maybe the same one who turned on the gas in my room."

"Whoever it is, they wear gloves." Burt said. "The only fingerprints found around your room were yours and Mister Jones' here. Now, we need to set up an APB for that car."

I said, "Maybe Dria knows its license plate number. Would that help?"

"Yes, it could. Especially if there is more than one Chevy Nova around town in the same color. A license number would show that the shooter is driving mister Wenborn's car."

Carol was already out the door and up the hall to Dria's room. While she was gone, Burt and Alan asked me to recount the drive-by shooting to see if I had noticed anything else about the shooter and car. I didn't. Carol came back a few minutes later.

"Dria said it still has a Texas license plate. Number FLV685. Also, the back bumper is bent in, and one taillight is broken where Terry had backed into a tree when he had been drinking. She also said the top is rusting a lot around the edges."

"Good for her." Alan said. "That's going to help. Drat, it's 5:30 already. It's too late to contact the Texas DMV's office in Austin. We'll get on it first thing in the morning. Burt, let's head back to the station and sign out. See you in the morning, Carol?" He questioned.

"Yeah. I have to go sweep the broken glass out of my car. We've got to catch this murderous perp before he does any more damage."

Burt and Alan said their goodbyes and left.

Carol came over and sat on the armrest of the easy chair and put her arm around me.

"Robbo, lover. You're still shaking."

"Getting shot once was bad enough. Getting shot at several more times and the house blowing up next door is way too much for me to take in. I just want all this to end so I can go back to writing and playing music… and loving you."

"Me too, lover. Me too."

"Carol, I just thought. Dria came running out right away when she heard the shots. Where's Dennis? He didn't run out."

"I don't know. Let's go find out."

We went down the stairs and looked in every room, including his office. Dennis was nowhere to be found. We saw his small used Honda motorcycle was still in the back yard. It was leaking oil.

"Maybe he walked to the college." I suggested. "He is trying to get rehired there."

"Really? He's quitting the newspaper?"

"His old press in the basement is broken, and he can't afford to continue printing it elsewhere. He said his backer stopped backing him. Anyway, he also told me he used to teach at State and wants to start teaching again."

Just then the front door opened, and Dennis walked in.

"Hey, Dennis." I greeted him. "We were just looking for you."

"Uh. Really? I… I got a substitute instructor job. It looks like I'll be back on the regular payroll as a… real instructor soon. Fortunately, the… the English department head still remembered me. Glad I didn't burn any bridges behind me when I left academia."

"That's really great, Dennis."

"By the way. Carol, what happened to your car? Several windows are shattered. Break in?"

She related all that had happened. It made me start to shake again. I began thinking that this must be what happens to some soldiers coming back from Vietnam. I'd read in the Mercury News about something they called post-traumatic stress disorder, or PTSD. *Am I getting it*?

Carol noticed.

"Robbo. You're shaking again. Come. Let's go back upstairs."

When we got back to our room, Carol opened the fridge and took out a bottle of chardonnay that was still half full. She filled two wine glasses and handed me one. She pulled her desk chair over next to me in the easy chair, and we clicked glasses and sipped. And sipped.

"Are you feeling better lover?"

"I think so. I stopped shaking."

"You hungry?

"Yeah. That Chinese food at lunch didn't last. I <u>am</u> hungry."

"I'll call Ricardo's pizza and have a couple of mediums delivered. I'll go see if Carla's back and see if she and Dria want some also. Oh. I might as well check with Dennis too."

Carla was back and she and Dria had moved Carla's things into the other bedroom. Yeah, they were hungry too.

Carol went downstairs. Dennis said he had already eaten, but he'd answer the door when the delivery came and bring it up to us. Carol gave Dennis twenty dollars to pay for it and leave the driver a tip. She came back upstairs and called the restaurant.

Forty minutes later, Dennis came upstairs with the pizzas. He started to give Carol the change, but she told him to keep it.

Carla and Dria came in and the four of us sat around on the floor eating the cheesy slices. Being with Carol and the girls and eating good pizza eased my mind and I had finally stopped shaking.

Chapter 35

Words of Love

Robbie

After Carla and Dria went back to their rooms, Carol pulled her guitar out of its case and began fingerpicking and singing a lovely folk song.

When she finished, I asked, "What song was that? I've never heard that song before. It's beautiful."

"That was one my father wrote and played for me when I was little. He never recorded it."

"Please play it again."

She did, and I added some harmony to the choruses.

"Robbo, honey, that was so nice. Maybe someday we could record that."

"And dedicate it to your father."

Carol smiled and nodded yes with tears forming in her eyes.

We talked about our future in music for several minutes when Carol finally said we should go to bed. We both washed up, brushed our teeth, and got undressed.

Seeing my lovely Carol once more in her gorgeous birthday suit made me start to shake again. Not from the gunshots, but for a completely different reason. We faced each other, and she pulled me to her and pressed her body against mine.

We got into bed and played for over a half hour, bringing both of us so close then holding off.

Finally, it happened. The climax of the Carol and Robbie show.

Yes, I stopped shaking.

Carol lay on top of me kissing me repeatedly.

"Oh, Robbo. I do love you so much."

More kisses.

"Carol, you've become so much a part of my life. I really love you too."

More kisses, but they were getting weak. We were tired. Carol rolled off me but kept her arm over my midsection.

"Lover, we're both awfully tired. It's going to be an early day for me tomorrow. I want this investigation to be over so we can be together all the time."

"Yes, love. I look forward to that."

Within ten minutes, both of us were asleep.

The following morning Carol was up at seven. I woke up too, but she came over to kiss me and told me to go back to sleep a little longer. She would wake me when she left at eight.

I did go back to sleep and didn't even hear her taking her shower.

When she woke me, her hair was dry and tied back and she was dressed in another clean pants suit with a chocolate brown turtleneck. Darn. I missed seeing her get dressed. Oh well.

I got up and kissed her goodbye, some of her lipstick coming off on my lips. She laughed and pulled a hanky out of her pocket and wiped it off.

"I should have left it on. You look cute in red lipstick." She put her hand on my face. "I'm sorry, lover, but I need to go clean out my car some more and head out. I should see about getting a new car. Or maybe another van. It won't look good seeing a detective driving around in a car full of bullet holes and broken windows. Goodbye… lover." Carol looked sad as she removed her hand from my face and left.

I got up a few minutes later and looked out the window to see Carol drive off. I missed her already.

I sighed, then went into the bathroom to take a nice warm bath.

After I got dressed, I looked in the fridge and pulled out a container of leftover shrimp fried rice. It was still half full, so I ate most of it cold for breakfast. After all, it did have egg in it.

It's so easy to get cabin fever. It was barely an hour after I ate the leftovers for breakfast, and I really wanted to go out for a walk downtown on First Street to Sherman Clay to look at the new basses and bass amplifiers. After all, mine all died in the commune when it imploded.

Then I got to thinking that the sales guy at Sherman Clay hadn't been nice to us. I should check out the three pawn shops on Market Street. They often had nice older basses and amps for sale at decent prices. But Carol wanted me to stay inside in case the perp was in the neighborhood again and maybe watching the house. (*Perp. I was already picking up Carol's police language*.) Well, maybe the two of us could soon go guitar hunting together.

Since I shouldn't go out, I went to Carol's bookcase and looked through for another book to read. While recuperating, I'd already read a half dozen of her books, mostly mystery novels. I pulled a thick paperback off the shelf. James Michener's *Hawaii*. Well, that thick book should use up some time.

I sat down in the easy chair and started reading.

I was barely twenty pages into it when Carol returned. I hadn't heard her drive up.

"Robbo. Put your shoes on. I'm taking you with us, especially since Carla and Dennis aren't here. I don't want to leave you in the house alone. I'm taking Dria to check out the car. We found it."

Chapter 36

Drive My Car

Carol

I had been loaned an unmarked police car to drive since my own car was just plain undrivable for a cop, riddled with bullet holes and blown-out windows. Forensics wanted to examine it some more.

Dria climbed in the back seat. Robbie was in front with me.

We didn't go to the police station. We drove toward the airport then up a side street to the police impound lot. The gate was radio controlled. I clicked a device clipped to the car visor, the gate opened, and I drove through. I parked in front of a building that looked like it was a trailer, at least thirty feet long, with the wheels off and leveling jacks on each corner. It looked temporary. Metal steps led to a wide landing and the front door. There were a couple of lawn chairs on the landing, one on each side of the door.

We got out. Robbie and Dria waited outside while I went in to speak to someone inside. I came out following a casually dressed older man wearing a baseball cap with a San José police emblem atop his head, showing about a half inch of grey hair just over his ears. He was wearing a denim shirt and jeans with a badge strapped to his belt on the left side and a holster with a gun on his right side. He was at least six inches shorter than me.

"Robbie, Dria, this is Damian. Officer Damian Ramirez. He'll take us to the car."

He shook Robbie's hand then Dria's.

"Follow me. Carol, you just missed forensics. They left a few minutes before you got here. They did find something I'm sure you'll notice right away. You'll hear more about it back at the station. Oh. You might want to hold your ears."

We heard the sound building up. It started a distance away, but then got very loud. A commercial jet flew in very low overhead.

"The office has been soundproofed inside so the jets don't bother us too much while we're working. The San José airport landing strip is only three miles from us. We're right next to the flight path. Ah. Here we are."

The car, the Chevy Nova Dria had traveled in on the way to San José, was parked by itself twenty feet away from the other impounded vehicles. Robbie and Dria stood behind the car while Damian and I looked around.

I then asked Dria, "To make this official, tell me if this was Terry's car."

"It is. Same license plate there. See all the rusting around the roof edges? There's even a small hole through the rust right there." She pointed.

"Thanks Dria. Damian, do you know where this was found?"

"Alum Rock Park. It was illegally parked. A policeman called in the license number and was told to stay there until backup arrived just in case the perp was around. They scoured the area looking for anyone out of the ordinary but came up blank. If any of the officers had looked inside, they should have seen it was hot-wired, and they should have also seen the blood in the back. Forensics would have gone there. Instead, a tow truck was called, and it was brought here."

"I wondered about that. Is it okay to open the back hatch now?"

"Go ahead. Forensics got all the fingerprints and information they needed."

Dria handed me her keys.

I opened the back and looked in. Robbie looked too.

"Uh. Carol" Robbie said. "That is blood. Isn't it?"

"It sure is. There's a lot of it. Well, we'll know soon, maybe twenty-four hours, whose blood that is. Damian, I'm sure forensics took a lot of photos, didn't they?"

"Yeah. They must have used up a lot of film. One of them was snapping shots while Rhys and two others took samples and dusted for prints. Actually, Rhys supervised while the two others worked." Damian laughed.

"Thanks Damian. We really wanted Dria here to officially identify the car. But yeah. This vehicle is definitely a crime scene."

I shut the hatch, and we all headed back to the office.

In the office was a Hispanic woman who looked about the same age as Damian. Damian introduced her as his wife. She did all the office work. She handed Dria a pretyped form saying the car belonged to her late husband Terry Wenborn. She tearfully read the form and signed it and slid it back across the counter.

I put my arm around Dria. "We can go now. I'll take you and Robbie home."

When we returned to the house and went upstairs, we heard voices.

"Cool! Jimmy's home!" Robbie exclaimed.

Dria ran into the bedroom across from hers and ran up to Jimmy and gave him a hug. Robbie shook his hand. I also hugged him.

"Jimmy," Robbie said. "It's great to see you back. You look good. A little worse for wear, but good."

"You too Robbie." We laughed.

"Jimmy, you, me and Robbo here have a lot to talk about," I said. "Like our futures. By the way, guys, I have a lot of furniture and nice beds in storage. Most of it was my mother's and father's. You're welcome to it, if you want. It will help you furnish your rooms and make them comfortable. You can even paint the rooms whatever colors suit you. I'll buy the paint. Oh. The kitchen is available now that Dennis has quit his business, and all his volunteers have departed. It's going to need fixing up. Dennis isn't too tidy, and his volunteers weren't either. The stove and refrigerator are decent, but probably need a lot of cleaning." I smiled. "But you guys know how to clean a kitchen, huh? Cleaning supplies should be under the kitchen sink. If you need more, we can get some at Lucky's."

Carla and Dria put their arms around each other. "We'd be glad to clean it up. We don't want to just sit around. We need to keep busy."

Jimmy spoke up. "I'll help too."

"I'll supervise." Robbie joked.

Chapter 37

As Tears Go By

Robbie

Carla and Dria went downstairs and started picking up right away. I knew that it was good for Dria to keep busy. It helped keep her mind off depression. I was glad they had become friends.

Jimmy's head still hurt and was lying down on the bed. At least he had a lot less recuperating ahead of him than I still had to do. He will be up and about quite easily in a day or two I figured. I still had at least another two or three weeks to go before I could get out of the cast, then, as the doctor told me, I'll need Physical Therapy for a month or two. Damn.

Carol had gone back to work, but said she'd try to be back by six. She also said she'd bring back takeout for everyone.

Everyone? Wait a minute. Carol let Deke stay in a room downstairs. I just realized he'd not been seen around for a while. Had he gone out? I went downstairs and into the kitchen.

Carla had cleaned out some cupboards of stale soda crackers and moldy bread, by the look of the contents in the trash can they had brought in. There were also two opened jars of Skippy peanut butter, both with rusty lids, and they tossed three different open jars of jams and jellies that were moldy. Dria was in the process of cleaning out the refrigerator, which had several soggy vegetables and open containers of old Chinese food. An open package of bologna had turned green. *What a job to do.*

I asked the girls. "Have either of you seen Deke around? Carol let him have that small bedroom over there behind the kitchen."

"We haven't noticed him around for quite a while." Carla told me. "Have you looked in his room?"

"I'll do that now."

I walked into the laundry room behind the kitchen and went to the door that was probably originally the maid's quarters. I knocked on the door, but it wasn't latched, and it opened. I could see the bed was not made, normal for Deke, but he was not in the room. The one window was open. But even with the open window, I could smell something that didn't seem normal. I figured it was just old food he left around like he often did in the commune.

There was a single empty container of Chinese food in the waste basket by the tiny desk under the window. That wasn't the smell. There was a glass on top of the nightstand next to the bed. It had about a half inch of soda in it. Cola. I opened his closet.

"Deke!" I yelled. He was hanging by his neck from the closet rod. He looked like he'd been dead for days.

Carla and Dria heard me yell Deke's name and came running in. I stopped them at the door.

"Don't come in. You don't want to see this." I shooed them out and closed the door behind me. "I have to call the police."

Carol arrived before Burt and Alan. I showed her Deke. She cupped her hand over her mouth to mute, "Oh shit". We left the room and closed the bedroom door. Carol took a deep breath, "Oh Robbie. This has gone too far. This has to stop <u>now</u>."

I put my good arm around her, and she leaned over onto me.

Sirens.

Within fifteen minutes, Burt, Alan, Lucy, and Rhys and their forensic teams were all in that small bedroom doing the things those people seemed to be doing a lot of lately. The rest of us sat around on the old office chairs in the living room where Carol used to type up stories for Dennis's newspaper.

It was after 5:30pm when we heard angry voices by the front door. I went to see who it was.

Dennis had come home only to find he couldn't get in the house because a policeman stopped him at the door. They were arguing. I glanced at the policeman, and he looked familiar. *Wasn't he the cop I saw with Sordi?*

"Dennis. Cool it. Don't get upset." I told him.

Carol came up beside me and said to the policeman, "Officer, it's okay. He lives here."

The policeman had no idea who Carol was and still blocked the way. "No one goes in or out girlie. You and your John go and sit down."

Oops. Wrong. I could see Carol's anger rising. I expected her to really lay into the cop. Instead, she took a deep breath, let out a sigh, then pulled out her temporary police badge and held it up to his face. "Look here, officer…" she looked at his name plate on his shirt. It said 'Ashton'. "…Asston. This girlie is your fuckin'… your superior. I'm telling you to let this man in. I need to interview him."

The policeman obviously didn't like a woman telling him what to do and didn't like the way she said his name. His anger was handled irrationally, and he pulled his gun out of his holster. "Okay, bitch. You ain't a real cop and crossed the line with me. I'm arresting you on…"

Carol moved so quickly I almost didn't see it. Before the cop could point his gun at her, she did some kind of… I guess… kung fu move. She did a kick, hitting his wrist, the gun flying out of his hand. Carol caught it in the air and pointed it at him.

"I should arrest <u>you</u> for being such a stupid jerk!" Carol yelled at him. She then emptied the clip out of his gun and put it in her suit coat pocket. The cop's eyes were wide, and his mouth was open as if he was going to say something but couldn't get it out. He sputtered and looked scared and angry at the same time. He was rubbing his hand.

Alan walked up behind me. "What's going on here? Ashton?"

"This… this… bitch… attacked me! She took my gun and was going to shoot me!"

"Carol, do you have this officer's gun? Yes? Well hand it to me."

She did. Alan smiled at her. "Good work, Carol. You still remember your jiu jitsu training. You were the best at the academy. Okay, Ashton, don't lie to cover your ass. We all know your… uh, problem with women. You're relieved. Go back to the station and sign out.

"My gun."

"I'll hold on to that. You won't need it anymore. Especially since you'll be reassigned to parking duty tomorrow."

Officer Ashton looked like he was about to hyperventilate. His mouth was closed so tightly I thought he would crack his teeth. He spun around and bounded out the front door and ran down the stairs to his police car. He peeled out laying nearly twenty feet of rubber on the street.

Alan watched and shook his head. Then he looked over at Dennis. "Sorry about that. Come on in. You can join the others in the living room."

212

Nearly two hours later, the house had quieted down. The medical examiner's team had removed Deke's body, and Lucy told Alan and Carol she'd be doing an autopsy to see how Deke died. Since there were no visible wounds on him, Lucy said it looked like suicide. Maybe. With the other band members having been murdered, she'd be taking a very close look for any anomalies. Rhys checked for fingerprints and bagged up the empty container and the glass.

We had each given statements about what we each knew about Deke. Even Carol gave a statement, then left to go back to the police station. She hoped to be home by seven.

After Carol left, I went back into our room, sat down at her desk and opened the typewriter she had pulled out of her closet for me. I couldn't find any typing paper, so I pulled a page out of a notepad. It was barely half the size of typing paper, but it would have to do for now. I wanted to type up notes on all that had happened. Maybe something would stand out.

Let's see. *Damn. Hard to type with one hand. Oh well, I'll try.*

1. Marty, upset, drove off in my VW bus. Drove far into an orchard and wrecked. And why was the VW driven so far into the orchard. Marty couldn't have driven it, he was buried. Also… Marty, having moved to San José from New Jersey over five months ago, would not have known about that orchard, or how to get to that part of the Berryessa district. He wouldn't have driven very far from the commune… like around town or the college somewhere. So… was his body moved from somewhere else and buried in that orchard? Could someone else have driven it?

2. Cliff, also upset, stormed out of the house. He usually walked to the college, where his body was found. However, he was murdered in our driveway and his body was moved to the college.

Shoot. This notepad paper is not big enough. I can't put all my thoughts down in order. Maybe Dennis has some typing paper. I'll go down and ask him.

I went downstairs and into the living room we were in earlier. I noticed Dennis's bedroom door was open. He wasn't there. An old Royal typewriter was sitting on the desk. Dusty, like it hadn't been used for a while. Next to it was a ream of typewriter paper. I figured since the newspaper was now dead, Dennis wouldn't mind if I took a dozen sheets of paper.

I grabbed the paper and went back upstairs to our room. I pulled the small paper out of the typewriter and inserted the real thing.

After repeating what I had previously typed, I continued. *Ah, better.*

3. Terry went missing. We assumed he was with one of Dennis's student volunteers. He was found in the sewage treatment plant where his body was found in a tank. Where he was killed is still not known.

4. Drive by shootings. One near miss of Carol and me, the next hit me in the clavicle. First shooting by Cliff's half-brother from Raven. (Caught.) He used a rifle. The second, the one that hit me, was with a pistol. Could it be Mafia? Someone else? (Who???) Third shooting was again at Carol and me. Blew out Carol's car windows. Pistol again. Same pistol? Dria's Chevy Nova used.

5. Jimmy hit and beaten in our back parking area. Mafia again?

6. Big gun battle at Tahitian Gardens. Any link to us? Deke? His old school chum Zeke? And where is Zeke?

7. Deke hung. Suicide? Or something else? No word from coroner yet on how or when it happened.

8. House burned then blown up. Okay. Who? Again Mafia? Is Sordi involved? Insurance scam?

214

9. Oh, and what about the gas getting turned on in Carol's room while I was sleeping? If the murderer snuck in, they could have easily killed me while sleeping. Why turn on the gas?

Okay. What else? Let's see…. I kept typing.

Are there two or three different things happening here? The first three murders had the same MO. Everything happening after that was different. The first shooting was solved. The other shootings, the beating, and the house fire and explosion are different MOs. The gas in Carol's room was different. And what about Deke. I really doubt he killed himself. He wanted to keep playing and singing with Zeke.

Okay. What else? This might be unrelated, but I'll put it down on paper anyway.

Dennis closed down his three businesses and sent his volunteers packing. Let's see. His printing press froze up, and he said he was using a commercial printer out on the Monterey Highway. He told me he couldn't afford them anymore. He also said he applied at the college to return to teaching and got a substitute position for now. Is that true? We really don't know anything about Dennis's background or where he's from. He's been very hush hush about that.

Hmm. Maybe I should check it out, but I shouldn't leave the house without Carol and her police revolver. There's been too many close calls.

The phone rang. I picked it up. Carol.

"Robbo. I'm still stuck here. Maybe for another hour or more. You doing okay?"

"Yeah. I've been typing up a list of all that's happened. You know what?"

"What?"

"There's too many MO's. After the first three murders, everything was different. I get the feeling there's two or more people involved in this whole mess."

"That's good thinking, and something we've recently been discussing here. I'd like to see what you've come up with that we might have missed."

"By the way. What do you know about Dennis?"

"Really? Well, actually nothing. He was already in the house with his businesses when I bought it. He had been paying rent to the previous owner."

"Carol, who owned the house before you?"

"You know, I really don't know. I purchased the house through a real estate agency. They had signature authority for the owner for some reason. Oh. Yeah. Kind of odd now that I think about it. I was just too excited to get the house at the time. I should look into that. Maybe ask Dennis."

"Please get home soon. I miss you."

"I miss you too. Ah. Alan's calling me in for another meeting. I'll try to be home as soon as I can. Goodbye lover." She whispered.

Chapter 38

It's Not Easy

Robbie

Carol finally got home after nine to find Jimmy and me talking about music and our futures again. I sat on the edge of the bed and Jimmie was in Carol's easy chair. He got up when she came in. We both could see she was really tired.

"Sit down Carol," Jimmie said. "You look beat. Robbie, we'll talk more later. See ya guys."

Jimmie headed back to his and Carla's room. I looked at Carol and could see her eyes closing. I got up and kissed her on top of her head. She opened her eyes and smiled up at me.

"Oh Robbo. I'm sorry I'm so tired. This has been a long, hard day. I have things to tell you, but I can't keep my eyes open. Let's get in bed before I fall asleep in this chair."

I woke up at seven. Carol was still asleep, so I quietly got up to do my bathroom duties. I did a one-handed dressing and was slipping on my loafers when Carol sleepily woke up.

"Hi love," I greeted her. "Were you able to rest up okay?"

"I did. I'm going to hold off going in early today. I want to spend some time with you and tell you what's been going on. I'll get dressed and we can go have breakfast at the Creamery. I need coffee. Lots of coffee."

The Creamery was busy so Carol couldn't tell me anything about the case there. She did have two cups of coffee along with her oatmeal. I barely drank half of my coffee and just had toast and jam. With all that's been going on, I didn't have much appetite.

When we got back to our room, what Carol told me made me think the murders could have been done by the same person. Not two or three different people like I thought.

"Robbo, Deke did not kill himself. Lucy did find an abnormality. She found heroin in his system."

"Really? That's not like Deke. He was afraid of hard drugs. Even LSD. He only smoked pot. Uh... did the heroin make Deke hang himself?"

"Like I said. He didn't kill himself. And he didn't ingest the drug. Lucy found a puncture wound on his neck. The overdose of heroin was injected by someone. Lucy thinks Deke might have still been alive when he was hung. Oh, and also, Rhys found that there were fingerprints on the glass."

"Did he find out whose fingerprints those were?"

"Yes. Zeke's."

"Zeke killed Deke? Damn! I never liked that bastard!" I angrily blurted out.

"Easy Robbo. We don't know that yet. We do know how long Deke was dead. At least three days. Also, Lucy said Deke hadn't eaten anything for six to eight hours before his death. The carton of Chinese food had been in the trash before Deke moved into that room. Probably left by a volunteer. But the glass of cola was recent. Anyway, Alan and Burt have put out an APB to try to apprehend Zeke."

"Sorry I got angry. Yeah, I know better than to jump to conclusions. That's what Marty, Deke, and Terry always did."

The phone rang.

Carol picked it up. Burt.

"Hi Burt. What's up?"

"You should come in. We found Zeke."

When Carol told me why she was going to the precinct, I took a chance and asked if I could go. I already knew the answer.

"Sorry Robbo. I wish you could, but that wouldn't be appropriate. I really wanted to spend more of the morning with you. I don't know how long I'll be. I'll call if I'm going to be late. Yeah, I need to rush."

Carol gave me a quick kiss on the cheek, started to leave, then turned back to me and planted a much better kiss on my lips. *Ah. That's better.*

After she left, I started to sit down in the easy chair then jumped back up realizing I had another doctor's appointment in an hour. I'd forgotten about it while being with Carol and talking about the case. I went into the hall and knocked on Jimmy and Carla's door. Carla answered. She was still in her nightgown. I think I might have interrupted something.

"Hey Carla. Sorry to bother you. Can you or Jimmy drive me to my doctor's appointment?"

Jimmy spoke from behind the door. "Uh… yeah. I'll be glad to. Give me a few minutes to get cleaned up and dressed."

Yeah. I did interrupt something.

I called Carol to let her know I had to go see my doctor, but she wasn't available. I left a message with the receptionist.

Twenty minutes later, the three of us squeezed onto the bench seat in Jimmy's little Datsun pickup and headed down San Carlos then on to Stevens Creek Boulevard. With the lights against us, it took almost a half hour to get to my doctor's office. I made it with a minute to spare.

Instead of another complete dressing change, the doctor said my clavicle had healed enough that I didn't need the restraining cast any longer. I would still need my shoulder taped up and my arm in a sling while awake and moving around, but I could now sleep without it. The doctor told me that the next time I was due to come in might be the last. *Good news! Well, I'll still have to go to Physical Therapy*!

We returned to the house. Then Jimmy and Carla said they were going to McDonald's on Almaden to pick up some Big Macs and fries for all of us for lunch and shouldn't be gone too long.

When I got back to our room, I noticed the answering machine light was blinking. I turned on the tape. Carol.

"Hi Robbo. I'm calling from the police station in Morgan Hill. I may be here a while."

Lots of noise and talking in the background. Sounded like a busy place. Carol was talking loudly. "I got the message you had to go to your doctor. I hope everything is okay. I wish I could say more. We'll talk at home."

Curious. Why is she in Morgan Hill? Ah, yes. Deke said Zeke had come up from Morgan Hill. Maybe that's where he was found. I wonder if he was found dead or alive.

Pondering while I stood at the front window, I glanced down at the street and saw Sordi's black Rolls pull up and park in front of the ruins of our old commune. A new black Cadillac pulled up behind his Rolls. Sordi got out as did a man who looked about the same size and weight as Sordi. Both wore near-identical three-piece pin-stripe suits. They shook hands, said something to each other and started laughing.

Why were they so cheerful? I mean, Sordi's house is destroyed. People have died. The Cadillac guy pulled a camera out of his car. Looked like a 35mm, and he started taking photos of the house. Maybe that's Sordi's insurance agent. *Jeez. He looks like another Mafia type. Yeah. I bet Sordi's going to get quite an insurance payout.*

I turned away from the window and started to sit down on the easy chair when I heard car brakes screeching outside, followed by a series of shots then another screech as the car quickly sped away. I jumped up and carefully peeked out the window. No, the shots weren't directed at Carol's house. Sordi and the other guy were spread out on the gravel at the front of the driveway. Blood pooled around them. Shit. Had to be a real Mafia hit.

I went to the phone and dialed 911.

Fifteen minutes later the street had been blocked off, several police cars were in the middle of the street along with a paramedic van and an ambulance. I also saw another black car with two guys with dark glasses in plain blue suits. They were talking to the police. *FBI?*

I was hoping that Burt, Alan, and Carol would have shown up by now, but they were in Morgan Hill. I hoped they were notified about the shooting and were heading back.

Dria and I were standing on the front porch. Did I need to give a statement? After all, I was the one who saw and reported the shooting. None of the police seemed to even notice me. In fact, I didn't recognize any of them. I stood there for over a half hour. When they all left, I headed back inside and up to our room. I would have thought that the forensics people would have been here checking out the bodies and bullets. I didn't see any of them. Odd. I'll have to ask Carol about that.

Damn. The answering machine light is on again. I pushed the button to play the tape. Jimmy.

"Hey buddy. We couldn't get back with the burgers. The street was blocked. Not another attempt on one of us, was it? I hope not. Carla and I will wait until it's over and try to get back soon."

And I heard them drive up before the message finished. A few minutes later all of us were sitting around the small kitchen table. From Carla and Dria's cleaning, the old oak table was spotless.

"Sorry the burgers and fries are a little cold." Jimmy said. "We had to wait at the end of the street until it was open again. I went to a phone booth at the college to leave you a message."

"I was outside with Dria. I thought the police or FBI would have interviewed me since I saw Sordi and his friend get shot, and I called 911. Nothing."

"Bummer. I'm sure if Carol and her two cop friends came you would have been interviewed."

The phone was ringing again. I ran up the stairs and picked it up before it went to the answering machine. Ah. Carol.

"Robbo, lover. Are you okay?"

"I'm fine. I'm okay." Carol must be on a private phone. No noise in the background this time.

"We're still in Morgan Hill, and we just heard the report of another shooting on Sixth Street. What happened?"

"Sordi and some guy that was with him. It was a drive by shooting. They both looked dead."

"God. After the Tahitian Gardens shooting, we thought the Mafia war would escalate. Sordi must have been involved somehow."

"Carol, I called 911 when I saw what happened. None of the cops interviewed me. I think the FBI was there too. In fact, your forensic people weren't even there."

"You're kidding. Who took the bodies? They should go to the police morgue for Lucy to check over."

"A regular ambulance took them. I thought that was odd, since I remember seeing a police van pick up... uh, bodies... before." I was choking up thinking about whose body I saw them pick up recently. Deke.

"Robbo. I don't like the sound of this. I have to go tell Alan and Burt about this. We should be done here shortly. I love you."

"I love you too." Darn. I could have been talking to myself. Carol had already hung up.

Carol finally got home at six. She looked exhausted again and plopped down on the bed fully clothed. She rubbed her eyes.

"Carol, love. Can I get you anything. Water? Beer?"

"No, lover. Just let me rest a little. In a while we could walk over to the Creamery and have some dinner. Then we need to talk. No. Don't look so worried. Not about us. Lover, I'm happy with us. I just need to talk.

Chapter 39

Stupid Girl

Robbie

Carol told me she was rested enough a half hour later but didn't really look like it. She smiled at me, but it seemed unfocused. We headed over to the Crystal Creamery. She had her arm around my shoulder, and I had the feeling it was for support.

I had only been at the Creamery for breakfasts and lunches. Their dinner menu was quite different. It was Carla's first day, and she waited on us. My appetite was better, so I had their daily special: turkey, mashed potatoes, and dressing with gravy, and string beans. Carol got a slice of pot roast, also with mashed potatoes and string beans.

I was hungry this time and ate all of mine. Carol picked at her food and barely ate any of it. Unusual for my tall lover.

We barely talked. Carol seemed so far away thinking about something. Probably about the case.

Carol paid for dinner and left Carla a ten-dollar tip.

She finally opened up when we got back to our room.

"Oh Robbo, lover. I'm so sorry I'm so tired again. I spent the whole day down in Morgan Hill. Zeke had been hiding at his parent's cabin out by Chesbro Dam. His mother convinced him to turn himself in and tell the police about his movements. He contacted us last night."

"Did Zeke kill Deke?"

"No. Zeke was with Deke a day before he was killed. That's why his fingerprints were on the glass. He told us when he returned later to start practicing with Deke again, he found him dead and hung in the closet. He panicked thinking he could be blamed or also killed and took off to Morgan Hill. He admitted that his father had mafia connections and was in hiding himself."

"So, was it mafia money Zeke used to buy all the expensive equipment and guitars?"

"Yeah. We spent hours interviewing Zeke, then took him to his parent's place and we spent many more hours interviewing Zeke's mother, Mrs. Irene Kozar."

"Kozar? Like the Tahitian Gardens Kozar?"

"Yes. Same family. Anyway, when we drove up to the cabin, she came out pointing a rifle at us. She put it down when she saw her son, Zeke, with us. Turns out she was worried the Italian mafia might show up. She was also very tired of the mafia war in San José and wanted herself and Zeke to have protection. She wanted to tell us <u>everything</u>. First, Zeke was being protected and changed his last name to Mayfield when he was young and in high school with Deke. She then told us that her husband, Mick, was brother to Artim Kozar. And it turns out he was the drive-by shooter who killed Alberto Sordi and his insurance cohort. Mrs. Kozar said her husband has left. She had no idea where he went."

"So does that solve that shooting?"

"Maybe. But, Robbo, there's more. Zeke knew Cliff and Terry back in New Jersey."

"That must be why he was looking for the money Cliff had."

"And Zeke told us where the money came from. It turns out that Terry was playing piano at an Italian mafia wedding reception. Cliff and Zeke were hired by the caterer to help serve. While the festivities were in full swing and the alcohol flowed, Cliff and Zeke wheeled a trolley of hors d'oeuvres into another room and found an open safe full of money and no one around. It was huge Mafia donations for the bride and groom. Zeke said it was Cliff's idea to take it. They hid it all in a caterer's trolley, closed the safe, and rolled it out to their car and left before the festivities ended. To keep the mafia from finding them, they picked up Dria and immediately left for Texas"

"Jeez. They must have taken a fortune. I mean, that bag I found in the studio had a lot in it."

"Yeah. Alan counted it at the station. Over forty thousand dollars. And that was only part of it. Cliff must have spent more than fifteen thousand on electronics and tools. Zeke said he originally had the same and spent around the same. He said the rest of his share was hidden under the floor at his parent's cabin. He pulled it out and gave it to us. Zeke said Terry also had a share."

"Terry? Huh. Cliff's money was found. Zeke told you where the rest of his was. So, where is Terry's. Do you think Dria knows? I mean, Terry and Dria always seemed so poor. Their car was barely running and awfully rusty. An act?"

"You know, Robbo, I don't know. If Dria knows, then she's a really good actress."

"And Terry and Cliff were good actors. If Dria is acting, is there a way to find out what hospital Dria was in when she said she miscarried? If that's what really happened?"

"Robbo. You should have been a detective. Hey, lover, for now, I really need some rest. Tomorrow morning is going to be a roundtable discussion that Burt set up with everyone working on these cases. One item will be about the Sordi shooting and to try to find out who picked up the bodies and where they went. Someone from the FBI is supposed to be there too. After it's over, I'll bring that up about Dria to Burt and Alan."

As Carol got ready for bed, my mind was racing thinking about all she told me. Could all the deaths be mafia related? Stolen money related? Or something else entirely? *No, I can't go to sleep with my mind so active.*

Carol, in her lovely altogether, crawled into bed and was asleep in minutes. I sat in the easy chair and watched her drift off. *God, she was so lovely. So smart. And so talented.*

I turned the overhead light off and turned on a lamp by the chair to read for a while.

Two chapters into my book and my eyes started to close. Then opened wide when I heard a door close in the hall.

I turned out the lamp and crept over to our bedroom door, carefully opened it and peeked out.

I saw the back of Dria heading to the rear stairs carrying a small suitcase.

After I heard her close the back door downstairs, I went down the rear stairway to see if I could find out what she was up to.

When I reached the kitchen all the lights were out, and no one was around. But I did hear the sound of a car driving over the gravel in the driveway. I ran to the front and opened the front door just in time to see Jimmy's Datsun Bluebird pickup leaving.

I leapt upstairs two treads at a time and knocked on Jimmy and Carla's door. Jimmy answered. He and Carla were listening to music on the radio. Jimmy turned it off.

"Hey, buddy, did you lend your pickup to Dria?"

"Hell no. I've never leant my old truck to anyone. Why?"

"Where are your keys?"

"Uh… no. They were on the corner of the dresser. Robbie, Dria was visiting Carla earlier. She must have taken them. But why? Why take my car?"

Carol must have heard us talking. She came out into the hall in her robe. "What's happening out here?"

"Carol, remember what we were talking about and the chance that Dria knew about the money?"

"Well, yes. Of course. Why?"

"I heard Dria close her door and looked out and saw her going down the back stairs. I thought it was odd, since she always went to bed early. I heard a car on the driveway gravel and ran out to the front and saw her drive off just a few minutes ago. Dria stole Jimmy's pickup."

"Damn. I hope Burt is still up. I have to call him. Crap. I wanted to sleep tonight."

Carol went back to our room and phoned Burt. He was still up and said he would call the station to initiate an all-points bulletin for the Bluebird pickup. It's such a unique old truck, it should be easy to spot. Carol sighed with relief.

She took her robe off and crawled back into bed. By the time I finished brushing my teeth and undressing, she was out. I gingerly crawled in with her but felt I couldn't sleep yet. *What was Dria doing?* My mind was racing, but the finish line was within sight. I closed my eyes and finally drifted off after midnight.

Chapter 40

Empty Heart

Carol

When I woke up at six thirty, I felt kind of refreshed. I yawned and stretched, my feet dangling off the end of the bed. I looked over at Robbie and draped my arm over his chest.

He was already awake and turned on his right side to face me and smiled. We kissed.

"Oh Robbo. I'm sorry I was so tired last night. I do so want to spend more time with you and make beautiful music together. Let's rise and get cleaned up so we can get to the Creamery for breakfast early. I need to take a quick shower first."

"Do you mind if I come into the bathroom to wash up at the sink while you shower?"

"Sure. When do you get the big bandage removed?"

"Maybe next week, I hope. I still have to have my arm in a sling while I'm up and around."

I gave my best seductive smile. "And maybe next week we can shower together."

Less than twenty minutes later, we were dressed and headed out the door.

We were early enough that the onrush of students and local senior citizens hadn't filled the place yet, and we found a nice roomy booth away from the windows and close to the kitchen. Today Carla was working the breakfast shift and came over to say hi. She wasn't smiling as she handed us menus.

"Carla, are you okay?" I asked.

"I'm okay. Just really disappointed in Dria. I thought we were good friends. We did so much together. Jimmy and I don't understand why she stole his keys and took his truck."

"The police are looking for it," I said. "They put an APB out. It's a unique looking old truck and should be easy to spot. Yes, we'll find out why she stole the truck."

"Thanks, Carol. Can I get you some coffee?"

We turned our cups over and Carla filled them. We then ordered our breakfasts. By the time Carla served us, the Creamery was full. The two other very young waitresses seemed like they were nervous as they rushed from table to table. One even dropped a full plate of pancakes. I thought she was going to cry. Carla must have waited on tables before. She was very calm and made sure each customer didn't have to wait long for coffee or their food. I was impressed with her efficiency.

When we departed, I again left Carla another ten-dollar tip. Big tip for a fifteen-dollar breakfast.

When we got back to our room, and after we brushed our teeth, I looked at my answering machine and saw the light blinking. I turned it on. Burt.

"Carol. When you get this give me a call. It's important."

I dialed the direct number to Burt and Alan's office. Alan picked up.

"Hi Alan. Carol here. I got a message from Burt to call. What's up?"

"We found that Datsun pickup. It was at the San José airport's short term parking lot. The keys were still in it. We checked and it seems Mrs. Wenborn boarded a flight to Austin, Texas. And get this. She is flying first class."

"She has to be using some of the mafia money. Why is she heading back to Texas?"

"No idea, yet. Anyway, we've notified the Austin police, and they'll be waiting for her when she gets off the plane."

"I'll be there in about a half hour, after I change."

"Instead of coming in, wait until you hear from Burt or me again. They're going to tow mister Porter's pickup to the impound lot. When it's there, you could drive mister Porter over to check it out for damage then, hopefully, pick it up. The paperwork he must sign will be ready by the time you get there. Make sure he has his driver's license with him for identification."

"Thanks Alan. I'll wait for your call."

"Well, Robbo, lover. Looks like we have a little more time together this morning. Uh… well, right after I go tell Jimmy they found his Datsun. And, you know, we should check out Dria's room too."

Jimmy was glad to hear his Datsun was found. I told him I'd drive him to the impound lot later in the morning.

After talking to Jimmy, Robbie and I attempted to go into Dria's room. 'Attempted to' because the door was locked.

"Odd that it's locked," Robbie said. "I didn't think these old doors could lock. I didn't see her locking it when she left."

"They do lock, but easy to unlock. Let me get my skeleton key."

I went into our room and opened the top dresser drawer then came back to Robbie in the hall.

"It's gone. I wonder if Dria snuck in and took that key."

"Crud. Say, do either Jimmy or Dennis have any keys to their rooms?"

"I know Dennis does. He has several. His own and a couple he gave his volunteers who were living here. I'll run downstairs and grab one of them from him."

Five minutes later I was back with a key that I inserted in the keyhole. The door opened.

"I got a key just in time. Dennis says he got a day job substituting at an English class and was just leaving. Okay, I'll check her dresser," I said. "You look in the closet."

Robbie opened the door to the small closet. "Let's see. Carol, there are two coats in here. Both are leather. One black motorcycle jacket, and one brown flight jacket with fleece lining. You know, I think these are both Terry's. Dria must have brought those over from the commune. There's some blouses and jeans. Those are small. Dria's. There are two pairs of tennis shoes."

"She must have packed in a hurry, Robbo. Her dresser is nearly full of her socks, undies, and t-shirts. Maybe that suitcase you saw her carrying had something other than clothes in it."

"Uh… Carol."

"What'd you find?"

"When I moved the flight jacket aside, I felt something. There's a baggie of little pills in the flight jacket's side pocket. Uh… two baggies."

"Let's see. Yeah. These sure aren't vitamins. Definitely suspect. Unmarked. Homemade. Not good. We need to give these to Rhys to find out what they are."

"You think these were Terry's?"

"Could be. If so, Dria probably knew about them."

"Carol. Remember how I kept that tape I recorded of Zeke and Deke under my mattress? You think Dria kept something under hers?" I'll reach down to lift it.

"Robbo, let me lift it. You can't with your one hand."

I lifted it straight up and leaned it against the wall. What was under it surprised me.

"My journal!" Robbie exclaimed. "Dria took my journal! Why the hell…"

"Are all the pages still there?"

He flipped through the pages. "Seems to be. A couple of pages are dog-eared, though. I didn't do that. Wait. There _is_ a page or two torn out. I wonder why."

"Maybe she was looking for something." Carol said. "Did she take those pages with her? We should also check what's on those dog-eared pages. Hey!"

"What?" Robbie questioned.

"Dria's purse!"

On the bottom shelf of the bed's side table was Dria's shoulder bag.

"Dria always carried that purse everywhere she went. Why did she leave it?" I asked. "She must have been in a hurry."

Robbie reached down to open it.

"Wait! Don't!" I cautioned. Remember both girls said they were carrying kitchen knives for protection, and told them that wouldn't be very effective if someone shot at them?"

"Yeah. Is a knife still in her purse?"

"It could be." Robbie started to reach for it again.

"No. Please don't touch it, lover. That's another item for Rhys to check out. Tell you what. I want to call Burt and Alan and have them get Rhys and his team over here."

What is Dria up to?

Chapter 41

I Can See for Miles

Robbie

Burt and Alan arrived first. Carol showed them what we'd found. Ten minutes later, Rhys and one of his assistants arrived and began to turn the room upside down looking for anything else Dria might have been hiding.

I didn't want to get in the way, so I went back into the hall. Jimmy had come out of his room and was leaning against the wall watching the excitement. I joined him.

"You know," Jimmy sighed. "I always thought Dria was a sweet little girl who had a hard life with Terry. She was always helpful around the house and became a good friend for Carla. I thought."

"Yeah. I know what you mean. Looks like there's another side to her we never noticed."

"Remember when she popped Deke's cherry? There was something about the way she looked when she offered herself to him. And it wasn't sweetness."

"Hmm. You're right. Even though Terry suggested it, it was kinda out of character. Dual personality maybe? Or was that her real self and being around us was out of character for her? A big act?"

"Well, stealing my Datsun and flying back to Austin first class may be the type of character she really is. Plus, what about those drugs? Terry's or her's? Or both?"

Carol came out of Dria's room and came up to us.

"Well, guys. Rhys noticed the waste basket by the desk was empty. They went out back and looked through the garbage can to see if it was dumped. It was. They found a couple of envelopes addressed to Dria and some torn up letters. And… they found a syringe. Rhys's assistant bagged everything up to take to their lab."

Burt and Alan came out of the room.

"We're heading back to the station." Alan told Carol. "Rhys just left. You coming too?"

"I'll be there a little later. I promised to drive Jimmy to the impound lot to get his pickup. Jimmy, let's head over there now. Robbo you want to come along?"

"Yeah. I don't want to stay here by myself. Carla's working and Dennis must be at his new job at the college."

After Burt and Alan and the forensics duo left, Jimmy and I got ready and followed Carol down to her unmarked police car.

A little over an hour later we had been to the impound lot where Jimmy checked his pickup for damage (*none*), signed a couple of forms, and he and I drove back to the house in his pickup. That way Carol could head straight back to the police station.

Less than an hour later Carol was back at the house, with Burt in tow. Jimmy and I were in his and Carla's room talking when I heard them arrive and went in our room. I came in to find Carol pulling a banker's box out of her closet and set it on the floor. She sat down on the floor beside it and started thumbing through the papers.

"Uh… what's up?" I asked, wondering what was so important that Burt was watching her.

"Hey Robbo. You reminded me of something the other day. We've been so wrapped up in all that's been happening, I forgot to check this." She held up a thick manila folder wrapped with a large rubber band.

"What is that?"

"All my paperwork for when I bought this house. Remember, I told you I bought it through an agent who said the owner wanted to remain anonymous?"

"Is the agency who we thought it was?" Burt asked Carol as he looked over her shoulder.

"Yes, it is. Dominica Agency."

"Really?" I questioned. "That's the same agency the commune paid rent to."

"Yeah. I remember hearing that. I just didn't put two and two together at the time."

"Okay, Carol," Burt said. "Let's go get a search warrant and head over to that agency and see what we can find."

Burt quickly headed out of our room and down the stairs. Carol put her box of files back on the top shelf in her closet. She started to leave, then turned back to me and planted a lovely, gentle kiss on my lips.

"So sorry, again, that I have to leave you." She sighed. "Soon. I hope soon this will be over." Carol looked sad.

"Before you go. Any news about Dria?"

"Nothing yet. I'm still upset she might have conned us. So hard to believe. She always seemed so nice." Carol sighed again. "I have to go. Burt is waiting for me. We have to pick up Alan. I hope we can get the search warrant right away. Don't worry, Robbo. We should have some backup just in case. No telling who or what we'll find there."

She gave me another kiss and left. With the sad look on her face, I had the terrible feeling I might not see her again. The thought put a lump in my throat.

The sun had set, and I had been trying to keep busy all day. I tried to type more on the story I'd started but gave up after staring at the same words for a half hour. I tried to pencil notes for new songs, but I pressed down too hard in frustration, giving up when my pencil lead broke. I tried to watch television but gave up when I couldn't find anything good. I missed the six o'clock news. Damn! I miss Carol.

I hadn't eaten much all day, just nibbling on corn chips and cheese. I was hoping Carol would get home soon so we could go to the Creamery again for dinner.

I was lonely, so I thought I'd go downstairs and see if Dennis was around. I was curious how his substitute teaching job at the college was going. I'd rather see Jimmy and Carla, but since Jimmy was feeling better, they took a drive after Carla got off work. Hopefully, they'll be back soon.

So, I walked downstairs and knocked on Dennis's bedroom door. Or I should say his office door. The old parlor room was his combination office and bedroom. During the day, when he was working on his paper, he closed up his sofa bed so the sofa could be used by visitors. So he said. I'd never seen or heard anyone except his volunteers in there.

When I knocked, the door swung open. It wasn't latched. Odd, he usually locked it when he wasn't there. Well, Dennis wasn't there, and his sofa bed was still open and unmade.

I figured I'd leave him a message, so I went to his desk and pulled a notepad over to me. No pen or pencil, so I opened his top desk drawer to grab a pencil.

I didn't see a pencil, but I did see the missing pages from my journal. *Why the hell does he have those.*

I pulled the pages out, closed the drawer, left his room, and went back upstairs.

Sitting down in the easy chair, I looked at the pages to see why Dennis had them. My notes described Dennis when I first met him. There was nothing there that I could see that said anything worthy of him stealing the pages. I just described the guy. His greying hair. His eye color (hazel). The scar on his cheek. Well, I did write that I wondered where he got the scar.

Wait a minute. If Dennis had my journal pages, why was my journal under Dria's mattress? Did Dennis put it there? After all, he had several skeleton keys he said he gave his volunteers. Did he use one to get into Dria's room? It was locked, but he could have locked it after going into her room.

God. I wish Carol would get here.

I heard the front door close. I know it was locked, so it's either Carol, I hoped, or Jimmy and Carla, or it could be Dennis coming back from the college. *I'll just wait and see who it could be. If someone comes upstairs, it should be Carol or Jimmy and Carla. Odd, though, I didn't hear Jimmy's car drive in the gravel driveway.*

As I was wondering who it was, I heard the front door close again. I looked out the front window and could see from the porch light Dennis stomping down the wooden front steps. His hands were clenched, and he looked up and saw me staring at him. Damn. I didn't think to turn the light out. He started running back toward the college.

As I was still looking out the window and I saw Jimmy's Datsun Bluebird pickup drive up and pull into the driveway. About the same time, I saw Carol get out of a black police sedan and wave goodbye to

238

either Burt or Alan. I couldn't tell which one was driving. I felt much better with everyone back. Boy. I couldn't wait to tell Carol what I found out.

Chapter 42

(I Can't Get No) Satisfaction

Carol

When I came in the front door, I met Jimmy and Carla who had come in from the back. We went up the stairs, and I opened the door to my room. I invited them in. Robbie greeted us. I greeted him with a quick kiss.

"Hi Robbo. Jimmy, Carla, please sit down. I have a lot to tell you. You all have a right to know what's been going on."

The three of them sat on the edge of the bed. I stood in front of them with my hands in my pockets. I paused, took a deep breath, and began.

"First, it took a while to get the search warrant. While we waited, we heard from the police in Austin. They picked up Dria. She's being held there until we can arrange for her to be transferred back here. The thing is, that syringe Rhys's people found had heroin in it. It also had a fingerprint. It's not Dria's. Rhys is still trying to identify whose print it is. I think I already know. Now, the knife in her purse. It had been cleaned, but the wooden handle still had a few tiny bits of blood still on it. They were a match for both Marty and Cliff.

"Now. When we finally got the search warrant, we made our way to the Dominica Agency along with backup. Turned out we didn't need them. We asked the cops to stick around, just in case. There was only one person there. A Miss Sordi."

"Our late landlord's wife? Robbie asked.

"No. His daughter. Anyway, she freaked out when we told her we had a search warrant and she reached for the phone to, she said, call her lawyer. We started to open one of the filing cabinets and it was locked. She refused to give us a key. Alan went back to our car and came back with a pry bar that made short work of the locked drawers. Miss Sordi screamed and swore at us. Pretty bad language for a thirty-something professional-looking woman.

"Just thumbing through the files, we could see why she was so upset. Turned out Dominica not only acted as a real estate and rental agency, but they also made large loans to some very interesting people. Those loans appeared to be more like gifts. Money out. No money paid back."

"Who was getting these gifts?" Jimmy asked this.

I answered, "Right now, I can't say until an investigation is launched and completed. There's a chance I might have to appear in court.

"One of the other file drawers had names of mafia members, several who were killed at the Tahitian Gardens, and quite a few still alive in the San Francisco Bay area.

"A second file cabinet had all the real estate sales and rental units in it. That's where we found another interesting thing. Burt saw my name on a folder. He opened it up and it was the papers I signed when I bought this house. Here I was thinking Sordi might have owned my house prior to me, because we found out he owned quite a few houses in San José. It wasn't him."

"I'm sitting on pins and needles!" Carla said. "Who?"

"Dennis Dean."

"Our Dennis?" Carla exclaimed.

"Downstairs Dennis?" Jimmy broke in.

"Carol, I have something to add." Robbie said.

"What've you got, Robbo?"

"I think Dennis has been up to something. I was lonely because everyone was gone, so I went down to visit him. He wasn't there, but his door was open. I went in to leave him a note, and when I opened a drawer on his desk to find a pencil, I found the missing pages from my journal."

"Robbo, it might have been a good thing Dennis wasn't there. When Dria was picked up, she was scared about being sent back here. She said she was frightened of Dennis. She saw him coming out of our room carrying your journal. She thought he didn't notice her, but she said that he later slipped a note under her door threatening her. She also said that's the main reason for leaving late at night and in a hurry. In addition, she admitted she knew about the mob money and took Terry's share to pay for the flight. Jimmy, she said she was really sorry for taking your pickup. It was the only way she could think of to get away quickly."

"Carol, you think it was Dennis who turned on the gas in our room?" Robbie asked.

"I'm pretty sure. He's the only one living here who could have known about the faulty heater."

"So, are you and your two police friends going to check out the English department at the college? See if Dennis really got hired there?"

"Yeah, Robbo. We should. And to think, I was working for him on his newspaper. He always seemed so dedicated to that. Hmm."

"What?"

"He told me several times he loved having me around. Now that I think of it, I think he liked me. He was not like that with his volunteers. By the way, Robbo, did you open any more of Dennis's desk drawers?"

"No. When I found my journal pages, I came right back up here. Why?"

"I'm going to go down there to look around more. I was only in his office once when I gave him some news that I had typed up for him. I remember he covered up something on his desk when I came in. When I left, he closed and locked his door. I figured he was hiding something he didn't want me to see, so I didn't think any more about it. Then. Now I want to check it out."

"I want to come too," Robbie said.

"Carol, why don't Carla and I keep a lookout and let you know if Dennis comes back." Jimmy said.

"Thanks guys. Good idea. But before we go downstairs, I need to call Burt and Alan."

Carol went to her phone and dialed Burt's number at the station. No answer. She dialed Alan's number. No answer."

"They're not there. You guys stay here while I go down to my loaner police cruiser and try to radio them."

I was gone for ten minutes. When I returned, I said, "I got Alan. They were back at the Dominica Agency. Another shooting. Sordi's daughter."

"Dead? Another mob hit?" Robbie asked.

"Obviously the mob war. Miss Sordi is badly wounded and was probably left for dead. Alan said he and Burt were just leaving and will be right over. Okay, Robbo, guys, let's go downstairs.

Chapter 43

Paint It, Black

Carol

We went downstairs and walked up to the door of Dennis's room. The door was closed and locked. Dennis must be back or had been back. I knocked.

"Hey, Dennis. It's Carol. You in there? I want to let you know about some work I plan to do on the house." I fibbed, trying to get a response.

No answer.

I went over to Jimmy and Carla and whispered to them. "Go ahead and go out front and let Burt and Alan in when they get here. Leave the front door open and let me know if you see Dennis. If he comes up the front steps, just greet him like a friend. I'll hear you. Don't try to confront him. Just let him come in."

Carla looked nervous. From the look in Jimmy's eyes, I got the idea he would really like to confront Dennis and punch out his lights.

244

I knocked again on Dennis's door. Still no response.

"I don't hear any movement in there," I said as I pulled a key out of my pocket and unlocked the door. "Stand back, Robbo, just in case Dennis is hiding in there."

I think Robbie forgot that I carried a police gun hidden under my suit coat. He looked nervous as I pulled it out. With my left hand I turned the doorknob, stood aside, and pushed the door open with my foot.

Nothing. Dennis wasn't in there, so we both entered. I put my gun away. I reached in my coat pocket and pulled out a pair of latex gloves and put them on.

I started opening desk drawers. The top middle drawer, where Robbie found his journal pages had no more than a couple of rulers, one metal and one wood, two unused spiral notebooks, a box of crayons, a few pencils of various lengths, and a ball point pen.

Each side top drawer had stacks of paper folders. I opened each only to find typed up news items.

"These folders have some of the news items I typed up. Uh… what's this?"

"What?"

"Mixed in with my typing is one of the house sale papers I signed. It has the Dominica Agency logo on it. It shows the sale price, the agency's cut, and what Dennis got. Wow!"

"Wow what?"

"Dennis didn't get much out of it. The agency took over 50% of what I paid. Either they screwed Dennis, or Dennis owed them a lot of money."

"Carol, remember he said that he was closing everything up because his backer backed down? Do you think he ran out of his house sale money?"

"That could very well be. Let's see what's in door number three."

I opened the two bottom drawers. The sound of a ticking started. We both looked to see what was making the sound. A small battery powered alarm clock. An alarm clock attached to some wires.

"Robbo! Get out of here! Run!"

"No! I'm not going to leave you."

"Please leave. I can't try to dismantle this bomb with you here. I don't know if this will go off if I try to… Lover, if it goes off, I want you to…" My voice was cracking, and I felt tears forming.

"I'm not leaving you! Do what you can."

"I… I don't know if I can." I wiped my eyes.

"I know you can. Carol, you are so intelligent. You can figure out anything" He snapped his finger. "Hey. How about the battery?"

"Battery?"

"That alarm clock. Remove the battery."

"But…"

"Try it."

I gingerly lifted the alarm clock, turned it over, and removed the battery cover. A single AA battery was in there.

I hesitated. I hope not too long. I then took a deep breath, reached in and removed the battery.

The ticking stopped.

Once the ticking stopped, Robbie and I collapsed on the floor in shock and giggled insanely. It took a while for us to get our senses back. I finally called it in.

The bomb squad arrived in all their protective gear a half hour later.

"That was a real close call," Alan told us after the bomb squad left. "You guys are lucky you didn't end up in pieces."

"Gee. Thanks, Alan." Carol replied. "For the disturbing image."

Alan chuckled. "No problemo. I'm glad you didn't. Anyway, the bomb squad found out Mister Dean had the whole house booby trapped. We evacuated your neighbors just in case."

"So, what about Dennis?" I asked

"That's what Burt and I are going to check on now. We'll head for the English department and see if Mister Dean really did have a job there. I sincerely doubt it. Carol, stick around in case he comes back. Mister Jones, you and your friends head upstairs out of harm's way. No telling what this Dennis will do if he returns. He could be armed. He could be our shooter."

Chapter 44

Not Fade Away

Robbie

We hung around in Carol's room talking and waiting for Burt and Alan to return. Our street was still blocked off. Probably in case there was any gunplay.

Fifteen minutes later, I looked out the window and saw Burt and Alan's car drive through the barricade and park in front of the house. Jimmie, Carla, and I followed Carol downstairs. She opened the door for her two mates. Burt shook his head as he and Alan walked up to us.

"Just as we thought, Carol," Burt said. "Mister Dean was not rehired by the English department. In fact, the administrator said he disappeared on her three years ago. Left in the middle of term without a word."

"Really?" Carol said. "Dennis never seemed irresponsible when he was working on his newspaper. But…uh."

"But?" Burt, Alan, and I each said, wanting to hear her continue.

"But… he did lock his door all the time. When I was typing up stuff for him and went to hand it in, he'd just open the door enough to grab the papers from me. I couldn't see in. I just figured he needed privacy for his work. Maybe he was doing something else, like taking drugs… or making bombs?" Carol said that as a question.

I had a thought. "Carol, what type of paper was the Cinnabar? I've never seen a copy of it. Did you have any in your room?"

"You know, I never looked at one. I only worked on it for a few weeks, and I have no idea where he distributed it. He never told me. And, Robbo, we didn't see any newspapers in Dennis's room when we were in there. You'd think he would have a record of publications."

Alan asked, "Carol, what were you typing up when you volunteered to help?"

"Pretty standard newsy stuff like you'd see in the San José Mercury-News. However, I now see he didn't use any of it. My typed-up notes were all piled in one of his desk drawers."

"Well, Rhys and his crew will be here shortly," Burt said. "They'll tear his room apart to look for any evidence of Mister Dean's activities."

"There's one more thing we might want to check out," Carol suggested. "That printing company Dennis said he started using when his own printer stopped working. I think he said it was on the Monterey Highway. There can't be that many printing companies in the area."

"There's only one," Alan said. "And it's been on the FBI watch list for a while. That's one of the only things the FBI has been up front with us about. They found poorly copied anarchist anti-government papers and reprints of Nazi and Communist manifestos in their trash. For the general public they'll print business cards and posters. But that's their front."

"Maybe they have some copies of Dennis's paper." I suggested.

"Search warrant?" Carol asked Burt.

"Search warrant." He answered.

Alan tapped Burt on the shoulder. "I'll stay here and wait for Rhys's group to get here. You go apply for the search warrant. When you get it, come back and the three of us will head down to check out that printing company."

I looked at my wristwatch. "Uh… Carol, I'm supposed to be at my doctor in a half hour."

"Oh. Can Jimmy take you?"

Jimmy spoke up. "Come on, Robbie, let's go."

The two of us walked up the driveway. But when we got to Jimmy's Bluebird pickup, he took one look at it and started angrily swearing. All his tires were slashed. Not just punctured, but with large gashes through the sidewalls.

"Jimmy." I tried to get his attention. He had tears in his eyes and was still swearing as he walked around his pickup. "Jimmy."

"Jeezus, Robbie. Why? Dennis again?"

"It could be. But don't touch anything. Maybe some of his fingerprints are on your car. Maybe the forensic guys can get prints off of it. I don't know. Let's head back out front."

Jimmy went to Carla and told her what happened. They tearfully hugged each other. I told Carol the same.

"Rhys is on his way and should be here in a few minutes." Carol said. "I'll send them in back to dust Jimmy's car for prints. Robbo, love, when they get here, I'll drive you to the doctor. My car's parked across the street."

A police panel truck arrived as we were talking. Rhys and three others, two men and one woman, all dressed in one-piece white lab outfits, got out. Alan told them the situation. Rhys walked up the driveway. His crew jogged ahead of him.

"Okay, Robbo," Carol said. "Let's get you to the doctor."

I was a few minutes late but was able to get right in to see the doctor. He had told me before that this would be my last time to see him. He removed the bandage and had me do a couple of arm exercises to make sure I could move it well. Having been trussed up for so long, my arm was weak, but I could move it. He then gave me a referral to a physical therapist who would contact me. Finally, he gave me a clean bill of health. He shook my hand, said goodbye and walked out of the examining room, and I hoped out of my life. I put my shirt back on and returned to Carol in the waiting room.

When I told her I was fine, she gave me a nice hug and kiss. I heard the male receptionist give a wolf whistle.

On the drive back to our home, Carol was talking about remodeling her house. What she had said at Dennis's door got her thinking about it. She wanted to modernize the interior while keeping the exterior original. We also talked about creating a rehearsal and recording space in her basement. We figured we'd move out whenever work started. She was going to ask Burt and Alan if they knew of any rentals.

By the time we arrived back, Rhys and his team were now in Dennis's room. Jimmy and Carla were not there. I asked Alan where they went.

"They said they were going to the Crystal Creamery. Oh, and Burt's on his way. He got the search warrant. We can head over to that printing place as soon as he gets here."

"Carol," I said. "I think I'll head over to the Creamery and meet Jimmy and Carla there. Can I get you anything?"

"No, Robbo. I got a quick snack from a vending machine while you were in with your doctor. We can go there again for dinner this evening. Ah. Here's Burt. Robbo, I love you."

She encircled me with her arms and gave me a long kiss. The look in her sad eyes put another lump in my throat. I felt a tear drip down my cheek. Hers or mine, I couldn't tell.

Once more I felt that might be the last time I would see her. I was wrong before. I hope I'm wrong again.

Chapter 45

Out of Time

Robbie

I joined Jimmy and Carla at the Creamery. Jimmy's hamburger and Carla's BLT were barely touched. They were holding hands and looked quite dejected. I sat down next to Jimmy.

"Did the forensic crew find any of Dennis's prints on my Datson?" Jimmy asked through gritted teeth.

"I don't know. They're probably still there checking it out.

Carla patted Jimmy's hand. "Honey, the police will find him. Besides, you can get new tires for our Datsun."

A waitress Carla knew came over and said hi to her. She took my order. Jimmy's hamburger looked good, so I ordered one.

After we talked a while and finished nibbling our food, we paid our tab and walked out together through the side door and around the block to Carol's house.

Carla went in, but Jimmie wanted to check out his little Datsun again. I went with him.

When we got to his car, I noticed the basement door was open. I pointed it out to Jimmie and said Dennis might have come back. Jimmie's anger made him rush into the basement. I yelled for him to stop then heard him talking more calmly to someone. It wasn't Dennis. The voice sounded British. Rhys?

I was leaning on the back of Jimmie's pickup and was thinking about heading into the basement too. I didn't hear anyone come into the parking area behind me.

I felt the pickup move, and when I turned to see why, I saw Dennis had climbed over the back fence and was trying to squeeze his way around the front of the pickup. I jumped back.

The look in Dennis's eyes made him look insane. He had a gun in one hand and a long carving knife in the other. He was struggling to reach me and finally climbed onto the hood, which couldn't hold his weight. The hood nearly collapsed under him making him lose his balance. He dropped the gun.

He got his balance back, jumped off the side of the hood, picked up his gun, and started coming at me.

As I backed away from him, I yelled for Jimmie. I don't know if he heard me. Then I stepped in a pothole in the gravel driveway and fell backwards. Dennis loomed over me with both his gun and knife raised. I knew this was it. He was going to kill me.

I closed my eyes tight waiting for the sharp pain and darkness that I knew was coming.

Crack!

A gunshot.

Am I dead?

Within seconds I felt a hand on my throat. I opened my eyes to see Carol crouching beside me.

"Are you an angel? Am I dead?"

"Oh, Robbo, my love. I thought I lost you."

"You… you almost did." I leaned up on my elbows and saw Dennis's body lying backward across from me, the gun and knife still in his hands and a bloody hole in the middle of his forehead. I started shaking again.

"Take it easy, Robbo." She put her hand on my head. It felt soothing. "It's over. It's all over, love."

Burt and Alan ran up the driveway, guns drawn. They put them away when they saw the body.

"Whew. Carol, you always were a good marksman… uh, markswoman," Alan said.

Jimmy ran out of the basement along with Rhys and one of his assistants.

"Did I hear a shot?" Rhys said. He then noticed Dennis's body. "Oh. My goodness. I have to call Lucy."

"Why?" Carol questioned. "He doesn't need an autopsy."

"No, but the body we found in the basement does."

"Body?" I questioned. "I was in the basement several weeks ago. I saw no body."

"It was inside the old printing press. We noticed some dried blood on the surface and unscrewed the side panel. It had been in there a long time. Lucy will try to determine how long and who it is."

"I saw that, but I thought it was ink. I also tried turning the platen wheel and it was stuck."

"Stuck because of the body. That press couldn't have been used for a long time," Rhys said.

"Dennis told me he'd been printing his paper on it, and it broke." Carol remembered. "He's been using that printing company we just got back from. They did have copies of his paper. Real anti-government crap. A lot of writing on what he called undesirables: Students, artists, musicians. He wanted to eliminate them all. There were even plans to make bombs."

"And there were some bomb making items in the printing company's storeroom," Burt added. "We started to grab the two owners, who ran out the back right into the arms to the officers we stationed in the alley. The FBI showed up and took the owners in custody. They're also bagging up the evidence."

Alan spoke. "So, Carol, you going to keep working with us? You've done so well; we wouldn't mind working with you permanently. You could be on a regular payroll."

"Thanks, but no thanks, Alan. My heart's in music. I promised Robbo... Robbie, to get back to playing and singing with him and Jimmy over there. I also promised my father before he..." Carol choked up. "...before he passed away."

"We'll miss you. You know, there will always be a place for you at the station if you ever want to come back. So, if you guys play anywhere in San José, let us know."

"I do need to come back shortly and drop off my loaner police car and clear off my desk."

"I'll have finance cut your final check," Burt added.

"Thanks. Also, guys, can you let me know when Lucy finds out whose bones those in the basement belong to?"

"Will do." Burt and Alan said at the same time and laughed that they did.

Carol turn to the others and said, "Robbo, why don't you take Jimmie and Carla back over to the Creamery for coffee or something. I'll meet you there in maybe an hour or so when I get back."

I stood up and Carol helped me dust the driveway dirt off my back. *She seemed to be spending more time dusting my butt than my back.* I turned around, she smiled, put her arms around me, and planted a very long tongue-filled kiss. It relaxed me from my ordeal, but excited me thinking about our lives together.

Alan and Burt both looked at us and chuckled. Alan then tapped Burt on his shoulder and motioned for them to head out.

Chapter 46

Happy Together

Robbie

When Carol finally joined us at the Crystal Creamery, she told us about her plan to remodel her house. We were excited and couldn't wait for work to start. However, it would take a while to get plans and permits.

Three days later Alan stopped by. Carol greeted him at the front door and invited him in.

"Hey there, Carol. You all doing okay?"

"Sad from losing band mates, but we're doing fine, Alan. How's your wife? And Burt."

"My wife is doing great. We just found out we're pregnant."

"That's wonderful."

"Thanks. And Burt's finally taking a week off. He's gone to Yosemite to do some hiking with… uh, his girlfriend."

"Wow. I didn't know he had a girlfriend."

"They've been seeing each other for a while. Uh, they have been living together."

"Wow, again."

"Now, the real reason I stopped by is to let you know who the body was in your basement. Lucy was able to trace it through dental records."

"Don't leave me hanging, Alan."

"Dennis Dean."

"What? You're kidding, aren't you?"

"No. After Lucy found out who it was, she had the body of who we thought was the real Dennis transferred to her from the Funeral home's morgue. It turns out that his fingerprints match up to a schizophrenic guy who got released from a New York prison ten years ago. He was in for a manslaughter charge. Hit and run. Evidently, he ran down a couple of protesters and kept driving. Knowing about him now, it was probably intentional."

"What was his real name?"

"His first name really is Dennis, but his last name is Gallo."

"Italian?" Carol questioned. "Was he with the local mafia?"

"There's no link in his record, and we found no evidence of mafia-related items at the printing shop, or in your home. He seemed to just really hate… well, like we found out at the printers, undesirables."

"Alan, has there been any more news on that mafia war?"

"Some. When Sordi and his insurance guy were killed, their bodies disappeared. Whoever picked them up must have been on mafia payroll. Now, as far as we know, the local Sordi family are reduced to just Alberto's daughter and her husband. The Kozar family are basically gone. That Zeke guy's father, Mick, was found floating in Uvas reservoir. Shot and dumped. Zeke and his mother have disappeared. The FBI found their cabin empty."

"Whew. Sounds like the war has wound down. I hope. Thanks for keeping me up to date, Alan. You going to take some time off too?"

"Yeah. I want to take my wife on a little trip to the mountains before she gets too far along. We have a small camper van. We both like to fish."

Carol said goodbye and came upstairs to tell us what Alan had said. We all sighed in relief. Soon after, we took a short walk to have lunch at the Creamery.

Three months later Carol got her plans and permits. With construction about to start, we moved, temporarily, a few miles away into a small three-bedroom house in the Naglee Park area.

Dria had surrendered Terry's mafia money to the police and returned from Austin to join us. She was in a better mood and much more relaxed now that the evil Dennis was dead and gone. She was even smiling. And she and Carla got back to being good friends. Carol got all her family stuff out of storage, so we now had nice old furnishings. And Carol and I were still so much in love we couldn't keep our hands off each other.

We stayed in that house for almost a year, then moved back to Carol's restored Victorian with its updated interior and with a soundproofed rehearsal space and recording studio in the basement.

We had shopped around the pawn shops and music stores for months. Jimmy finally found a jazz-style drum set similar to the one that was destroyed. Carol still had her father's Gibson J-160e, but she purchased a new Fender Telecaster. I located a 1957 Fender Precision Bass at a pawn shop and picked up an electrified ¾ size standup bass like the one Carol and I saw in Sherman Clay.

We practiced as a trio daily and started playing at clubs and concert venues, including a return to the Fillmore.

One year later, Clive Davis came through and did get us into a Bay Area studio where we recorded our first album, *Survival*.

Authors Notes

There's truth to parts of this story. As I was taught in the Writing of Fiction classes I took in college, and what my protagonist said, "write what you know". I did.

There were junior college classes where I excelled only in art. There was the army entertainment corps in Korea where I played bass in a traveling rock band. I lived and played in a band commune in San José for two years. My band played a concert on a stage in a temporary park (now location of the Center for Performing Arts building). And we played at the Fillmore West. My experiences were fodder for this story.

To summarize: I was drafted in 1966 because I was failing most classes in junior college. I ended up in Korea instead of the quickly escalating "police action" in Vietnam. While in Korea, I auditioned and got into the entertainment corps, living at Recreation Compound #1 a few miles south of the Korean DMZ. (The entire story is covered in my book, *On Guard in the General's Chorus*. Available as softcover, ebook, and audiobook in bookstores and online.)

Yes, two of the members of the rock group I played with in the army asked me to join their band when they got out of the army. And that really happened.

We created a band commune in San José and became very popular, playing colleges, outdoor gigs (like the park gig), and at the Fillmore, where we were approached not by Clive Davis of Columbia, but a representative from Electra records.

Of the two years in the commune, most of the time was spent rehearsing or traveling to and from gigs. There did occur a few communal dramas. There was one guy who we did call the "dictator", because he always tried to run everything. Another guy had a big ego. Another one complained all the time of being a virgin. And another guy was hot headed and caused some problems in the group. (No murders though.) He didn't last and moved out.

The San José Victorian band commune I lived in had quite a history. In the mid-1960s it was known as the High House because some of Ken Kesey's acid tests took place there. In attendance were the Warlocks, who changed their name to the Grateful Dead that week, two of the Rolling Stones (who were in town for a concert), Timothy Leary, and members of the Merry Pranksters. This event is chronicled in Tom Wolfe's book *The Electric Kool-aid Acid Test*.

After the acid tests, the house was rented to the SDS, Students for a Democratic Society. On other campuses, the SDS was quite active and caused some serious trouble around the country. In San José the only thing they were known for, at least by us, was trashing of the Victorian we moved into. When we moved in, there were holes in the plaster walls, broken windows, and gouges in the kitchen counters and cupboards.

262

And, yes, we spent time repairing the house. Downstairs, a lot of the work creating and soundproofing the basement rehearsal space was the result of midnight lumber supply. Our soundman (electronics genius) and a few others would drive the band's van late at night out to new housing tracts and steal… uh, acquire lumber.

There were four of us in our band who wrote songs. And one member was known for creating our unique harmonies. And, yes, we did have a Farisa organ.

Originally, we had three guitarists, a drummer, and me, the bass player. One guitarist occasionally played the organ and vibraharp. Our music was progressive and had both jazz and classical influences. A couple of our songs were in 5/4 time. We did have some hard rock and roll songs too, several that I penned.

Our old San José Victorian survived. It was originally located a half block from San José State College but was relocated when the area became the new City Hall. The house was moved several blocks away and restored by the new owners. They did a beautiful job. I was able to tour the house and let the new owners know about the house's history. They were amazed and excited.

And the beat goes on…

The Song Titles

Under the chapter numbers are song titles from the 1960s up to 1967. Most are from The Beatles and The Rolling Stones, but others are from The Doors, Jimi Hendrix Experience, Jefferson Airplane, Buffalo Springfield, Mamas and the Papas, The Byrds, Spencer Davis Group, Turtles, Moby Grape, and even from my own songs that I wrote while in my own band commune in San José.